1.

They had made the cubicle of an easy to wipe clean board. The walls and doors sealed to the floor, and that was easy to scrub down. It begged the question in her mind, what did the people who designed the ladies' toilets in which Verity was sitting expect to happen in there?

Of course, that was not why she was in the toilet. She had made her excuses and escaped; to hide from the people who were currently sipping overpriced drinks and bitching with each other about the other people in the room. There was no need to be in the room to know what they were saying. The same conversations had been happening forever.

Truthfully, the last thing she needed was to be at a party. The month she had just lived through screamed and demanded a Friday night spent on the sofa wearing something soft and forgiving. She should be watching something that required no thinking, perhaps under a blanket, sharing the sofa with her sisters. Instead, her feet were pushed into red killer heels, and her body was squeezed into a skirt, which was making it hard for her to bend in the middle.

It had started with work problems. She had spent most of her adult life building a career, and a reputation which brought clients to her offices. She had represented some very high-profile people through some extremely difficult divorces. More than represented. She had negotiated some of the largest settlements achieved over the recent years. Other lawyers, she knew, described her as 'the rottweiler.' Life had been good.

At the start of the month, the client who occupied the chair on the opposite side of her desk had seemed very like many of the women who had been there before. She was sleek, groomed and polished, but about to be replaced in her husband's life. The humiliation of being the last to know, imagining people she called friends laughing behind her back. It hurt all the way to her heart that she had been pushed aside; despite how hard she worked at the gym, or how many procedures she had put herself through to delay the aging process. The bitter taste of defeat. The knowledge that her children would see their father every other weekend. Added to that, her income would be determined entirely by the settlement her lawyer was able to obtain.

The first questions were always the same, and the answers hardly changed. The woman herself, though, was different in that she was Verity's aunt. Which made the straying husband Verity's uncle. "I know this is going to be difficult for you, Verity, but your mum is my sister, and I need you to help me. I have tried so hard. You know how he is." She pulled a breath in. Her silicon enhanced breasts lifting towards her chin, which shook with emotion. "I want you to do your best. Get me the most you can. Squeeze him until he squeaks." She signed the paperwork before she picked up her bag and coat. "He has no right to have treated me like this." The control over her emotions faltered, and a tear escaped. She ran a finger under her eye before it smudged her make up.

"I know." Verity slipped her arm around her aunt's shoulders. "They will serve the papers on him by the end of the day. I'm sorry Aunt Jess, that he hurt you. I'll do my best. Are you OK, the diabetes and everything?" Her perfectly maintained aunt had nodded and gathered her dignity along with her possessions.

"I am better, healthier, and happier than I have any reason to be. Don't waste your time feeling sorry for me, just do the legal stuff, and get me a good settlement." Jess smiled, and for a moment, she was back to being the aunt Verity had adored as a child. "I'm taking the pills and being good about my diet. I think we have both had enough of each other. Let's try to sort this out with a little dignity?" Jess's smile might have been tinged with some sadness, but she was keeping it pinned on. She knew better than to let the mask slip. Perhaps she had been holding everything in for such a long time; letting it go was not an option.

Verity sent an email to the process server she always used and prepared the papers. It would be an expensive divorce, and there would be damage that would spill out into the rest of her family. Aspects of her aunt and uncle's lives would be open to discussion and argument. A divorce lawyer is more involved in the financial, emotional and sexual lives of their clients that any other branch of law. It was not something that she relished, but it was necessary to get the very best deal she could.

The afternoon brought the expected reply from lawyers acting for her uncle. The dance had begun. His lawyers would match her steps and, with luck and experience, she could bring them all out to the other side with as few scars as possible.

She worked late that day, preparing for the day to follow. She was sitting at her desk in a pool of light, while the darkness gathered, her shoes pushed away and lying sideways on the carpet.

It was time to go; she pulled her jacket on and pushed her feet into her shoes. The little Italian restaurant around the corner was her favourite.

There she knew she could eat in peace before she went home, where she knew there was nothing at all to eat. She ordered her favourite, and while she waited for it to arrive, drank a glass of rich Italian red wine. The stresses of the day eased away; a little further with every sip. The tables around her were full; people chatted, and the sound was soothing after the silence and concentration of her office.

"May I join you?" She looked up to find a man around her age. He wore a suit, but his shirt was open at the neck. His face was handsome in a boy band sort of way. His dark, wavy hair was a little out of place. "The rest of the tables are full, and I have eaten nothing since lunchtime. I love the aubergine thing here." He raised his eyebrow. She looked around the restaurant. What he said was true.

"Yes, that's fine." She looked up at the man and watched him pull out the chair opposite her.

"Thank you. I'm Basti." He held out his hand. His eyes stayed focused on her face. She studied the outstretched hand in front of her. It had been a long day, and she had planned not to have a conversation, but perhaps she had been avoiding socialising too much lately. She took the offered hand and shook.

"Basti? Short for?" Her eyebrows pushed together.

"Sebastian. My brother shortened it for me when he was very young. It stuck." The waiter took his order, and brought two more glasses of wine, both rich ruby red. The food arrived, and they laughed to see that they had both ordered the same dish. He watched the people at the next table for a moment. They were clearly a couple. He smiled to himself, savouring the taste of the food, before he turned back to his fellow diner.

"My sister still calls me Etty sometimes. Very annoying. Verity." She sunk her fork through the parmesan and the rich tomato sauce. The aubergine was soft and the flavour delicate on her tongue, and tasted even better when it was washed down with the wine. It was her favourite meal. In her first-choice restaurant. Despite her initial resentment at his disturbance of her peace, she was enjoying eating with someone else. It had been a long time.

There was no talking while they ate. The rich flavours and the smooth sauce leaving no room for chatting. When both dishes were empty, they ordered a coffee. She watched him over the rim of her cup and listened to him. His accent suggested a good private school, his conversation told her he had received a good education. She was listening to the rise and fall, the inflection of his voice, and missed the question.

"Sorry, I drifted for a moment. It's been a long day." She shrugged. "You asked a question?"

"Yes. I wondered what you do for a living?" His smile was genuine, his elbows on the table, leaning in to hear her answer. He watched her eyes, noticing how dark they were.

"I'm a lawyer. You?" She waited, sipping her coffee to cover how interested she was in finding out.

"Snap. Me too." He laughed. Nice teeth, she noticed. "Look, would it be weird if I asked to see you again?" He folded the napkin and placed it next to his cup. "I've enjoyed chatting to you. I have to go; early start, but may I call you?" She met his eyes and chewed her lower lip. It had been a long time since she had been out with anyone. He had been interested, and interesting. Maybe it was time. She slipped a business card across the table. He whistled low. "Nice firm. Big bucks!" She smiled but made no comment. It was true she had been lucky to get the place at the firm, and she had worked hard to keep it. She would be a partner in the next five years, but he was right. They paid well. He tapped the card on the table and slipped it into his pocket, nodding his head and raising his hand in a small wave. "I will speak to you tomorrow." He was gone, and she still had said nothing.

She checked her watch. It was time to go home. She paid her bill and asked the waiter to call her a cab. It was a ten-minute walk, but she was in no mood for anything but a quick ride in a cab and sleep. The city that she loved danced past the window of the cab. Bright lights reflected in the wet pavements. Her thoughts were full of her aunt and uncle, leaving only small spaces for thinking about the man who shared her love for Italian food.

Basti walked home through the back streets. She was not his usual type; he had not expected to like her. His phone rang. He ignored it. There were things he needed to sort out in his head before he answered any more questions.

2.

"Verity? Auntie Jess says you were so wonderful to her, she was nervous about coming to see you in your office yesterday. You're such a kind girl, always were. Ring me when you get a chance, darling. Your sisters will be coming home for dinner tonight if you felt like coming over? Let me know, darling. Love you." She closed her eyes. Messages from her mum had changed little in the last fifteen years. The compliments which felt like accusations, and the invitations that held a challenge. She would call, but not immediately. First, she needed to work her way through her emails and a pile of papers.

Her head ached. Too much coffee, and the guilt trip she had been on for years. Huffing out a breath, she closed her eyes, gave into the guilt, and scrolled through the numbers on her phone. "Hi. Mum? You phoned?"

"Hello love. Yes. Lola and Mim will be here for seven. I hoped we could all be together." She set down a coffee cup and clicked on the kettle. Serena knew that her daughter would be able to hear what she was doing. Such familiar sounds.

A place they all knew so well. The oven glove hanging on a hook by the cooker. The sign they had bought her saying 'Serena's sick of cooking.' The kitchen where they had laughed and fought through her children growing up. Verity was avoiding her, she knew that. Her oldest daughter, and she was hedging on the phone.

"I'm working like crazy at the moment. I will try, but getting to yours at seven is a long shot." She had agreed, but given herself a way out. Her fingers worried at the cuff on her sleeve. Perhaps it would be alright if her sisters were there.

"I'll keep you something warm in the oven if you're late. Get here when you can. I'm looking forward to having all my girls together." The kettle bubbled and spat; she had put too much water in again. "I know you're busy. We'll chat then."

"Bye." She kept her tone light, hitting the red icon to end the call a little too definitely. She slumped into the chair and closed her eyes. Her family were too much. But they were the only people in the world who shared her DNA, except for her father, and that was a whole different genetic kettle of fish.

The rest of the day was busy, but by six o'clock she was finished. She wanted to stay in the office and find something else to do. Of course, she could prepare for something else, but that was unfair. There was time. She could make it, almost on time, if she left immediately. Each moment she waited, every step, pushing papers together, looking for her bag, she took her time, putting her phone into her bag, putting her coat on. She was, she was entirely aware, being ridiculous.

Her phone rang, and she pounced on it, grateful for the distraction of an unrecognised number.

"Hello." She waited for the familiar click and delay of the call centre, but nothing happened.

"Verity?" There was a moment; a heart-beat when she wondered who it was on the other end of the line. But the voice was so engrained, etched into her, that it resonated and pulled up feelings that she had locked away for so long. It hurt to bring them to the surface.

"Dad?" She was six. On her favourite step at the top of the stairs, listening to them shouting, not the words, the feelings. The tears and anger. He had a bag packed, slung over his shoulder, but he had turned to see her on the stairs, and had smiled, blown her a kiss, and pulled open the front door. That had been the last time she had seen him. There had been no birthday cards, no phone calls. He had stayed away.

"Verity. I wondered if you might have time to meet me, perhaps? It has been such a long time. What do you think?" His flat was high up, the city sprawled beneath him. He imagined her, not too far away from where he stood. Her life experience and his were a million miles apart.

The warmth of his voice found a cold place in her that had craved the comfort for years. She was, however, no longer six.

"It has been a long time. What has changed?" She wanted to believe that he had missed her, and maybe her sisters, too. That he had stayed away for the last twenty-six years, and now he was coming back, just as she had dreamed when she was growing up. She shook her head at her own stupid childishness.

"I have. Time has taught me a thing or two, and one of them was that I was stupid to walk away. I missed my girls growing up. My fault. I am asking for the chance to put it right." The silence between them grew and stretched until she could bear it no longer.

"I have wanted to hear you say that since you left, but now that you have, it feels strange." She breathed. "Alright, I will meet you. On the weekend. Where?"

"You decide. I will meet you anywhere. Thank you." He took a breath, letting it go slowly.

"OK, there's a coffee shop, Gail's Bakery, on the High Street in Highgate. I'll meet you there, on Saturday morning, ten-thirty?" Suddenly, in a hurry, she pulled her coat together and gathered up her bag.

"That's great. I'll see you then. Thank you. Really."
He ended the call.

She stared at the phone. It was time to go. Her
mother would call to hurry her up. Guilt, guilt.

The evening was warm, and the traffic was light.
She parked the car and pulled a bottle of wine out
of the back seat. The house where she had grown
up was a little further down the street, but she
enjoyed walking down the street she knew so
well.

Mim opened the door. "Hi! We haven't eaten yet.
Mum will be so happy. She's on a bit of a downer.
I think she's worried about Jess and everything.
She didn't say so, but you know." Mim turned
away, leaving her older sister to close the door.

Verity walked into the house, and the smell of
dinner filled the air. She dumped her coat on the
bottom of the bannisters and carried the bottle
of wine and her bag through to the kitchen.

"Verity, you made it!" She was wrapped in a hug,
and relieved of the wine bottle. The smells and
sounds of her family surrounded her. Had she
betrayed them, been disloyal by agreeing to meet
him? Should she tell them about it?

They sat at the table in the seats they had
occupied growing up. The conversation with her
father rumbled around in her head, but stayed
locked in. She would meet him and see what he
had to say. The talking washed around her, while

she dropped a smile and nodded at the right times.

"You're very quiet." Mim was leaning on one elbow, her hair hung down like a curtain. A heavy one.

"Your hair looks nice, Mim. How do you get it like that?" Lola wrapped the pasta around her fork. "I had a call from Marcus, by the way. He says Jem's furious."

"Bound to be. He was always closer to Jess. Marcus was always stronger." Mim pushed her hair back and dipped a piece of garlic bread into the sauce on her plate. "This is very good."

"We aren't going to gossip about this. Jess is my sister, and she is in a very bad place at the moment. We are going to support her and your cousins. That's it." The three of them were quiet while she cleared the table. "I made pudding." She carried the cake to the table. The knife shook a little, but she took a breath and steadied herself. The whole thing had her a little rattled.

Big slices landed on their plates. It was sweet and light, like they had all known it would be. Their mother had baked all their lives, and it was a treat. Cake always came with coffee, and that night was no exception. For Verity, it came with extra guilt. Her father had come back. She owed her loyalty to her mother, the one who had stayed, but she had to know. She had missed him too much not to find out.

"I have news. Big news." Everyone turned to look at Mim. "I have put down the deposit on a salon. It has a flat above it, so I can live there. I have two stylists who want to rent a chair, and a woman who will rent a space to do nails. I get the keys in two weeks!" Her face was wrapped in smiles. She was so excited. This was the announcement she had dreamed of making since her first day at college. Everyone hugged her, and they were genuinely pleased. One thing that being a single parent family had given them was the close bond, the feeling of being part of the team. They had fights, like every family, but the bigger enemy was the world outside. They fought that one together.

Verity watched her sister with her sleek, beautiful hair. She had come a long way. She was too young when he left to remember their dad. This was the only family she had ever known. Lola was the baby of the family. She was fiery, likely to fly off the handle at the least provocation. Mim was the opposite, so open to the world and trusting.

"Can I book an appointment? On your first day?" Verity had her arm around Mim's waist. "For all of us." Mim smiled back at her, and nodded. There were tears in her eyes, and her face was shining.

3.

The meeting was arranged. It was often a worthwhile exercise. Sometimes it could avoid taking a divorce before the courts. Negotiation was always a better option, and considerably cheaper than the cost of appearing before a court.

However, with the two parties being her aunt and uncle, she approached the meeting room with her jaw set against the grim hour which stretched ahead.

"Verity?" Her aunt walked towards her, stopping to wait for her outside the meeting room. The room was walled in glass, and the heavy door of thick glass, with a long chrome handle, waited for them. "I'm nervous. Crazy, right?" She rested her hand against the shiny handle. Her niece, professional and confident, covered the hand with her own and together they pushed the door open. It felt a little safer that doing it alone.

Simon and his lawyer sat at the table. Of course, they could only see their backs, but both recognised Simon's broad back.

Verity met her aunt's eyes, noticing the nervous flicker around them. "Let's see if we can come to an agreement. It will be better for both of you." She gestured with her hand, and her Aunt Jess let go of the handle and held her head up high so that they both walked into the room with confidence.

"Good morning. Thank you for coming in today." She smiled at her uncle, his expression closed and hard to read. She sat at the table and looked across at his lawyer. "Basti?" She kept her voice and expression as level as she could, took a deep breath and let it go slowly. His eyes met hers and then focused entirely on the papers in front of him. There were so many questions racing around her mind, but this was not the time for them. "Right. Before we start. Is there any way back from the brink? I have known you both all my life, and though nobody else has any idea what goes on between two people, I wonder if you can find a way to make this work again?"

The silence in the room was heavy. She could feel the tension in Jess sitting next to her. Across the table, her uncle ran his finger around the inside of his collar. His lawyer remained entirely silent and still.

"We have decided. That is, I have. I have moved on. Jess, I'm sorry, but there is nothing I can do." His eyes closed and his chin tucked into his chest.

"In that case, I have drawn up some suggestions." Verity pushed a folder across the table and put a copy in front of Jess. "It is an approximate division of the matrimonial property. Of course, your children are no longer living at home. Although this means that custody or maintenance is not an issue, a quiet separation would be easier for them, as well as for both of you."

"This is outrageous! Verity, I will not give up my house and every bloody penny. I will be destitute. Is this what you want, Jess?" His colour was high, and his nostrils flared.

"It is half, and you are, after all, the one who wishes to leave. If this is the price of your ticket, is it too expensive?" Verity met his eyes. They were hard and focused.

"You always were an evil little cow." His words spat with such vehemence across the table.

"Perhaps you should think about the proposals, and your solicitor can come back to me with some suggestions of your own if you are unhappy with my ideas." Verity smiled her tight professional smile, straightened the papers and nodded. "Unless there is anything else you wish to discuss? Perhaps it would be sensible to arrange a further meeting once you have had a chance to discuss it, or it can be dealt with between myself and your solicitor."

"No. I told you Jess. You'll keep the house, and I'll pay the bills, that's it. I told you how it's going to be." He slapped his hand hard on the table. He had always made the decisions, made the money. He would not be told by his wife and her snippy little niece what to do.

"The point of a settlement is to draw a line under this part of both of your lives, not to have you carry on controlling the money which belongs to both of you. My client may wish to move from the house, or move on, and meet someone else. Your control of her finances would be something I could not advise her to agree to." Verity tapped the pile of papers with her pen.

"I will not agree to this nonsense." He puffed his chest. His swagger and bluster had always been part of who he was. He was not foolish enough to think that she would entirely go along with what he had wanted originally, but that did not mean that he would enjoy it.

"If we cannot find an agreement, this will go to court, and a fifty-fifty split is standard. The court costs, and the legal fees would climb, obviously. I am just trying to find a way to make this easier for you both." She raised an eyebrow at her uncle. He had nothing to say to her, it appeared. She waited,

"I suggest we take a few days and discuss the proposal. I will come back to you with my client's thoughts." Basti's first comment in the meeting. He raised his eyes and met hers across the table. She was angry. He had expected that, and it was fair. No point pushing his luck. He dropped his eyes to the documents in front of him.

"Thank you, Mr..." She checked the paperwork. "Culpepper." Verity smiled, gratified that he had at least the decency to keep his eyes on the paperwork, rather than meet her glare.

She guided her aunt to the door and through to her office, signalling to her secretary to bring tea.

"It's a hard meeting, I know that. If I could have, I would have done it without you there. From now on, I will do that if it's possible. Thank you, Maisie." She straightened her skirt and placed the cup on a coaster on the desk.

"He's being so unfair. Has he always been like that? Was it just I looked the other way?" She wiped a tear that slipped from her eye, pulling herself back under control. It was easy to watch her niece take control, but this was not going to last forever, and she would have to go home and deal with the consequences of the past hour.

"His lawyer will talk some sense into him. Next time, we will have a more sensible discussion. Otherwise, I will talk to his solicitor, and we can discuss it calmly, without either of you being present." Verity pointed at the tea. "Best thing for washing away the nasty taste."

"How could he do this to me?" Jess grabbed a tissue from her bag. This was harder than she had imagined. "I knew he saw other women. I always knew that. Perhaps I should have done something about it years ago, but when the kids were young, I wanted them to have a proper family life. We used to fight about it. Then we stopped fighting." She wiped her nose. "I knew this was different, though. He was different." She took a breath. "Sorry Verity. I know this is difficult for you."

"How did Marcus and Jem take it?" Verity sat down next to her.

"They were angry, sad, all of that and more." She huffed out a sigh. "I tried to tell them it would be OK. The truth is, I don't know how to help them through this. I feel that I've let them down, Verity." She shredded the tissue between her fingers. "I remember how it was when your dad left. Your Mum and I used to sit and cry with each other over a bottle of wine. I helped her out with paying a few bills when it got difficult for her, then I went home to my shiny house and kept my mouth shut, because I didn't want that for my kids. I know that makes me a bitch. Perhaps I deserve what is happening now, but it's the truth." She looked around her, at the shiny office where so many women like her had spilled their darkest secrets, and faced their deepest fears. None of that made it any easier.

"Jess. Look at me." Verity rested her hand on her aunt's arm. "You made a life, for you, for your kids, and for your husband; you deserve them to have had that life and enjoyed it. Your hard work made that happen. Don't let this make you feel like it was a waste. Your sons are wonderful people, and that is your doing. You should be proud of what you did." Verity had said most of those things to other women in the same position before. They had never meant more to her, or been more completely true.

4.

She was ready to go by eight and cursed herself for arranging to meet her father at ten-thirty. Her decision made, she had to go out. She could not bear to wait another minute in her house, which felt too small to contain her energy. Once she had checked her handbag, for the hundredth time, and slipped her feet into comfortable trainers. She pulled a jacket on and locked up the house. It would take her half an hour to walk to the café where she had arranged to meet him, but she could take a slower route, have a look in the shops, before that. She had plenty of time.

The first hour was fine, spent walking up the hill, smiling to herself at her attempts not to huff and puff at the steepness. She strolled through the park, and even sat on a bench for a little while, enjoying the spring sunshine. She checked her watch every two minutes and found that only two minutes had passed each time.

The shops would be open at nine. She made her way to the high street and looked in the windows. Not much grabbed her attention, but she made herself go in and look at the clothes on the racks. She tried on a dress, which would be nice for the summer, covered in flowers and bright colours. When she was out of the office, she made a deliberate decision to look different. Her work clothes were muted greys and browns, sedate suits and soft shirts. Decision made, she bought the dress, and paid, checking her watch again. She still had ten minutes to go, but she could not wait anymore.

The café was at the other end of the High Street, so she walked towards it, slowly, and found that there was a table near the back wall, where a man sat alone. He had been early too. His face lit up when he saw her. He had aged, of course he had, but she would have known him anywhere. He jumped to his feet while she worked her way between the crowded tables.

"Hello. I was early, couldn't wait to see you." His face creased into a smile. His salt and pepper hair flopping over his forehead. She had forgotten how floppy his hair was. They were strangers. He was awkward around her, but clearly pleased to be there. They were saved from not knowing what to do next by a waitress who wanted to take their order. "I wanted to contact you before, but I had agreed to stay away. It was what was decided. I had no choice but to get in touch now." He took a breath. It seemed to steady him a little. Along with the breath he took in the way she looked, how poised she was. He had never imagined that she would be so amazing, and it surprised him.

"I'm glad you contacted me. I really am. All this time, I never really understood what had happened, why you had to go away, why we couldn't see you now and then." The waitress brought their coffees and a slice of cake, which was nowhere near as good as her mother's.

"I know. It was what had to be. You'll understand a little more in a minute, but please, you need to know, I have missed you every day since I walked out of the door. I have followed your career. I was so proud when you qualified. So proud." He took a bite of the cake and washed it down with coffee. "The thing is, I couldn't explain to you why I had to leave when you were so little, but it was the safest thing for everyone." Her eyebrows pushed together, and he held his hands up. "No, no. I know it sounds really over dramatic. But this is why I needed to talk to you today. Why I had to contact you after all these years."

"Look, hang on a minute." She closed her eyes and took a breath. "Before you left, there was fighting, shouting all the time. You and Mum were screaming all the time." She shook her head. "What was the fighting about?"

"It was about Simon, mostly. Serena, sorry, Mum, brought him into everything. I could barely turn around without finding him there. Everything he said was gospel with her. I knew nothing. I had behaved like an idiot too often. Of course, I see that now." He breathed carefully. The memories of that time, and his own stupidity when he was younger, tasted bitter.

"I remember Simon and Jess being around all the time, and all of us, the cousins, were at the house. We all grew up together." She cast her mind back. "We loved it. Loads of kids around to play with."

"I wanted to warn you to be careful around Simon. He's dangerous. I know you will represent Jess the best way you can, but try to keep out of his way if you can." His eyes were so familiar, deep brown and wide set. She saw them every day when she looked in the mirror. This was exactly what she had hoped for every single day since he had left.

"I know he's been mean to Jess, but I think dangerous might be pushing it." She smiled, trying to lighten the moment. Jess had been at the house often when they were kids. Perhaps she and Simon had been having troubles in their relationship for a long time.

He bowed his head. "Your Mum and Jess were really not very close. We had a happy marriage. We struggled with the bills, just like everyone else. Then Jess married Simon. He was an arse, a bully. Jess came round to see us, flashing jewellery and her new boobs around. She wanted to make your mum feel small, and she succeeded. To be honest, I felt I had let Serena down as a husband. Simon would come to the house and look down his nose at everything. The big problem happened when he told Lola to be quiet, not in a nice way. I told him to leave. He told me that until I paid him back the money I owed, he could do as he pleased. Your Mum had borrowed from Jess. I had no idea." He linked his hands behind his neck. "They added interest, a great deal of interest." He chewed his lower lip. "I couldn't afford the repayments, obviously. He said I could do some running around for him to pay it off. I tried. I really did, but I was rubbish at it." He smiled, and it was as familiar as a sip of water. She smiled too, and he watched her smile reflect back at him. He had missed this. His girl, the only one who had ever looked at him with those wide eyes, wanting him to tell her what was happening, to take care of her. She was the best thing he had ever walked away from, and he was fully aware of what he had lost.

"I thought Uncle Simon had a car showroom back then?" Verity picked up her coffee, but it was getting cold. She put it back in the saucer.

"He did. He sold cars and finance. Among other things. I was rubbish at the things he asked me to do. Perhaps I wanted to be bad at it. I don't know." He took a deep breath. "It was a very bad time for your mum and me. Jess too. She was caught in the middle to a very large extent." He met her eyes, then looked the other way. "I did something idiotic. Really bad. OK, time for complete honesty. I was behaving like an idiot. It was my fault. In the end, Simon gave me a choice, or no choice, whatever. I had to leave and stay away. That was the only way to keep you all safe."

"What? How on earth could he do that? Why would you let him?" Tears filled her eyes. Whatever had happened between them, Simon's behaviour had been unreasonable.

"OK, so there was more to it than that. I left out the part that explains why." He dropped his head into his hands.

"You slept with Jess?" It was a whisper.

"No. I didn't." His eyes opened wide in horror at the suggestion. "Simon hit her. She turned up at the house with a black eye. It was insane. I could not believe that even Simon would stoop so low. I made her tea. She was crying, sobbing. All I did was put my arm around her. That was it." His shoulders sagged. "I had left the front door open. I was so shocked to see her like that. Simon came in, and whether he truly thought I had slept with her or not, He used what he saw. He called your mum, she was at work, and told her he had found us in bed. Whatever I said made me look more and more guilty. My beautiful Serena shouted with hate in her eyes, and in the end, I gave up trying to convince her I had only ever loved her." His voice broke with emotion. He shook his head and swallowed hard.

"Why did Simon want you gone?" She leaned her elbows on the table.

"I knew things about his business. Maybe not everything, but enough perhaps. He's an opportunist. When he saw a way to get me out of the way, and I think he just took it." He shrugged. "All of that is ancient history. I contacted you because I had to warn you, what he is capable of, and the danger you are in." He reached across the table. "Please let me be your dad, just this one time?"

She rested her hand in his, felt the warmth of his skin on hers. "I've missed you." She wiped a tear as it tumbled down her cheek and took a deep breath. "Now, let's get another coffee, and you can tell me everything."

5.

"There's a Mr Culpepper in reception. He has an appointment." The receptionist's flat West Midlands accent tipped slowly down the phone.

She opened the door to her office and waited for him to walk down the hallway towards her. He was a good-looking man. Taller than... Why was she still comparing everyone to the last one? He was carrying two coffees in take-away cups. His smile covered the nervousness around his eyes.

"I came to apologise. I was a little intimidated. You have a reputation. I will admit that I was curious. I should not have tried to have a meal with you." Verity took a breath in and out. "I therefore brought you a coffee and a pastry, by way of conciliation." She moved out of the way so that he could carry the drinks inside. "Thank you. I also brought paperwork." He pulled a paper bag out of his pocket and pushed it across the desk. While she thought about it, he deposited the cup holder on the desk and waited for her to react. The tension that had been building in his shoulders on the journey over from his office hitched a notch.

Verity sat behind her desk. The coffee was from the shop around the corner. She recognized the logo on the cup. It smelled really wonderful, and she knew that if the pastries were from the same shop, they would be crisp and light and sweet. She opened the bag. She was right; they were.

"This does not in any way form part of a negotiation." She held the pastry between her fingers. Her eyebrow raised, she waited for him to accept her terms.

"Agreed. However, they may create a better climate in which to negotiate?" Basti picked up one of the cups and held it out, as though he would clink with her. She shook her head and sat down. The coffee was a generous but also a smart move. She respected smart. She always had.

"Show me your proposals. Let's see what we have in the way of common ground as a starting point." Dusting the sugar from her fingers, she held out her hand for the papers.

"Honestly, not much. My client is digging in his heels. He will agree to your client living in the property. If your client wishes to sell, he wants a half share of the house." He shrugged and sipped from the cup.

"Unreasonable. There are two ways forward. Either they sell everything. That includes the matrimonial home, the holiday home in Spain, the boat, both cars, and the flat in London;

and then divide everything, including the rental portfolio, stocks, shares and savings between the two of them. Or, we have to look a little more closely at the things my client has already agreed to take off the table. She said at the start that she would leave his business alone and would not require maintenance. This is a one-off settlement deal. If your client is not prepared to discuss it in a reasonable way, I will recommend that we go to court. I know your client will be overjoyed to have a court assessment of his holdings and his business. They will not be as generous as my client, as you know." She lifted the ends of her mouth, but there was no smile. Careful to watch his reaction, she waited to see if he would fight her, or cave in. She was unsure which way she hoped he would go. He had surprised her before.

"Are we just doing the standard dance here? I had hoped that we could sort this out." He sipped some coffee.

"I am happy to dance, Basti, but you have to get your client to at least put the music on." She shook her head, quirking a sad clown face. "Damn, though, these pastries are good." She delved into the bag and fished out another one. It melted on her tongue.

"So, are you maybe free for dinner one night? I know you like Italian food, but how are you on Indian? I have been craving a curry for the last week." He rested his chin on his hand. "I'd rather have company than get a sad take-away for one, and stuff my face alone." He smiled across at her.

"I haven't had a curry in the longest time." She chewed her lip. "Not a date, just friends."

"I usually want to be friends with people I date. No point going out with someone who doesn't like me." He cupped his hand against his mouth and whispered the last part. She laughed. It was a little cheesy, but he was nice. She liked him, and that hardly ever happened. In fact, it had last happened with the last one. No point in thinking about it.

"Right. Wednesday is the only evening I'm free this week." She met his look with one of her own.

"I will book a table." He collected his papers together. "I will also speak to my client about the musical possibilities." He nodded to her. "Keep the pastries."

"I have every intention of doing so." She watched him leave. How much did he know about his client's business? Or had her father's opinions made her question things that perhaps needed to be left alone? She slipped another pastry into her mouth. Her family were complicated before the ground shifted beneath her. Work and family had always been kept separate in her life, for good reason. It would have been unkind to refuse to take on Jess's divorce, though. Once again, she questioned herself over the timing of her father's reappearance and Jess and Simon's divorce. Coincidence was not something that she was comfortable with.

6.

The car park was in darkness. She had worked later than she intended, wrapped up in the work, putting together arguments and counterarguments. Her schedule meant that she would not be in the office in the morning, but she was now ahead. She held out the key fob and pressed the button. The indicators flashed. She opened the passenger door and threw in her handbag and her briefcase.

The hand that grabbed her from behind was large and smelled bad. She knew it was a man when he covered her mouth and nose. Panic ripped through her. Her lungs fought against the lack of air. Her arms and legs flailed wildly. This was her nightmare, the one that woke her soaked in sweat, always the panic of not being able to pull a breath in. The terror of anything around her mouth and nose. The tightness of her lungs, the restriction of her breath. She felt his mouth against her ear, and a sense of the size of him behind her.

"Stop fighting. I need you to hear what I am going to say." His other hand wrapped into her hair and pulled. "Behave. I know you met your father on the weekend. Be careful not to piss off the wrong people. Find out where your sister borrowed the money to open her salon. Ask your mother how she stays up to date with the bills. Find out first, before you break everything." His hand in her hair released, and the one around her mouth was gone, leaving her holding the side of her car. She was heaving breaths into her lungs and appreciating the wonderfulness and joy of oxygen. Her fingers gripped the top of the door while she hacked and gasped, digging into the cold metal.

Slowly, she sank into the soft driver's seat, tears dripping off her face. Fear had pushed her back into her childhood, back to when everyone around her was powerful, and she was nothing. Before she went to law school to learn how to be the strong person, the one who protected other people. All of it had been taken away, in one moment, by someone who could do that because they were bigger, stronger. "Fuck, fuck fuck." She punctuated her words with her fists on the steering wheel. "Bastard bullying fuck." Her eyes burned with the tears. Her heart burned with the injustice. She sobbed her heart out, resting her head down onto the steering wheel, and letting go of the hurt that lived between her lungs and her ribs. She searched her bag for a tissue, wiping the tears and snot. Finally, she took a breath. A proper one that gathered from her toes upwards.

Her fingers dipped back into her bag, pulling her phone out. She scrolled through the numbers and selected the one she wanted. "Mim. I have to know. Don't ask why, please. Did you borrow money from Uncle Simon?"

"Yes, to start the salon." On the other end of the phone, her beautiful, talented, younger sister with the fabulous hair saw nothing wrong with what she had done.

"How much?" Verity wiped her finger under her eyes, where the tears threatened to spill again. "How much do you owe him, Mim?"

"Twenty-five." The little girl Verity remembered creeping into her bed at night. Frightened of the monsters who chased her, who hid under her bed, knew her big sister would protect her. Verity ran her hand over her hair. She had frightened her younger sister. That was against the rules. Little Mim. Her feelings back under control, she pushed herself to keep her voice level.

"I will give you the money. You pay him back. I will get it for you. Please, promise me, you won't borrow money from him ever again. Mim. Promise me." Verity gripped the phone hard. The air was still sweet in her lungs.

"OK. Sorry Etty. I didn't mean to upset you." There was a shake in her voice. Mim knew that she had upset her big sister and it rattled her.

"No. It's OK. Just transfer the money back to him. I will send it over tomorrow. OK?" She sucked a breath in. "Sorry, don't be upset. I just want the best for you. I love you. Still my lovely sister, right?"

"OK. Yes. We're OK. You sound like something bad happened." The last thing she wanted was for Mim to be worried.

"Nothing happened. Just, if you need to borrow, come to me or go to your bank. Nobody else. Please?" Verity leaned into the steering wheel and took a breath. Her forehead against the wheel, summoning the strength to make her voice normal, inject some humour. "Jemima? Are our bookings in for the first day? Mum and Lola and me? We had better be. Don't be double booking us!" She bit her knuckle.

"You will be the first customers. All booked. Thanks Etty. Love you." She sniffed a little down the line.

"Love you too, Mim." She did, she truly did. "I'll always be here for you. That's the deal."

They said goodbye and Verity sat in her car. Letting the reality of the world sink in. Every penny in her savings, and then some, was going to disappear from her account once she got home. It would buy her sister's loan.

The next call was going to be harder, and she pushed herself back into the seat before she phoned, keeping her breathing slow and steady. "Mum?"

"Hi Verity. This is a nice surprise." The familiar sounds in the background again.

"Mum. I have to ask some things. About Simon." There was a beat, a moment, where there was silence, then she heard the kettle boil.

"What do you want to ask me?" She could hear the water pouring into a cup.

"Does Simon help you with the bills?" She pulled in a breath. "It's OK if he does. I just want to help if you need help."

"He has done, over the years. I was on my own after your dad left. Sometimes it was hard to make ends meet." Verity could picture her moving around the kitchen, wiping with a cloth, adding milk to her tea.

"OK. Please, from now on. If you need help, ask me. I can afford it. You don't have to rely on him. OK?" Her hands shook, but she fought to keep her voice steady.

"OK love, but you really don't have to worry. Even with Jess and Simon splitting up, he has been so supportive. I'm fine. It's all OK." Another sound in the background caught her attention.

"Are you alone there?" There was a pause. She felt it, and she knew he was there. "Is Simon there with you?"

"Yes. Simon's here, just popped in for a coffee, to make sure I'm OK." Cold settled into Verity's gut.

"OK. Just from now on, please come to me, not him. Agreed?" Verity consciously uncurled her fingers, smoothing out her fists into flat palms.

"Has something happened? Is this because of Jess? Verity, tell me what this is about. Simon has been a very helpful brother-in-law for years, and a part of this family. You know how it was when you were growing up. I would have been on my own, had it not been for Simon and Jess, of course." He was there. She bit down on her lip.

"I just think that you should rely on me, rather than him. It's not fair. OK? Your choice, obviously, but I think we can be more self-reliant as a family." She leaned her head back against the seat and looked at the roof of her car. Her eyes fluttered closed while she tried to get the message across to her mother. "Listen, we'll talk again when you don't have visitors. No problem. See you soon."

She slumped against the seat. It was true, her family was tied to Simon financially. How could she have had no idea? She ran her fingers over her forehead. Too busy? Too self-absorbed? Trying to distance herself from her mother, from the too tight, too much, too needy bond? Absolutely. All of those.

7.

"Mr Culpepper on line 4 for you." She thanked the girl and hit the button.

"Hello?" She reached across her desk and pulled out the folder for Jess's divorce.

"Good morning. I have some news. I wanted to tell you this morning, so that we could relax and enjoy our curry later." He was smiling. She thought she could hear the smile in his words.

"OK, what's the news?" She opened the folder, but the details were pretty much in her head, anyway. Her fingers rested on the papers.

"My client has agreed to have everything valued, all the properties, cars, and so on, in order that we can then discuss the division on a more up-to-date valuation. He says that the family home has gone up considerably in value. Therefore, if your client takes the house, she should receive a smaller percentage of everything else." The suggestion was not out of the ordinary at all, except that Verity knew from Jess that the property had been valued only a few weeks before.

"This sounds like a delaying tactic to me. The family home was valued only... hold on." She checked the date on the file. "Four weeks ago. I know house prices are on the rise, but I think we can say that is recent enough." She smiled to herself. Her uncle was playing a game. "As far as the other properties are concerned, if you would like to send me a list and values, I will have them checked. A day or so at the most, I imagine. Is this the only stumbling block to an equal division?" This was standard divorce procedure, but it felt different. She trapped her lower lip between her teeth. This was her family that she was pulling apart.

"I have sent over a full list of all the properties and their most recent valuations. Let me know what you have as far as an updated value once you have looked at them. I will do the same, then there can be no argument about it. At the moment, I think we are travelling smoothly towards a settlement." He paused. "I'm looking forward to curry."

"I will see you then." She hung up the phone and looked at the screen on her desk, clicking on his email. The list was comprehensive, as he had promised. It included the seven properties that they let out, the family home, the London flat, and the holiday home. It was all there. One address jumped out at her. Her breath caught in her throat. How did Jess and Simon own the house she had grown up in? How was that on the list?

She pulled her phone out of her handbag and dialled the number. "Jess? Hi, it's Verity. I have a question. When did you and Simon buy my mum's house?" There was silence at the other end of the phone.

"Ah, yes. She was in trouble after your dad left. It had been difficult, and she owed money all over the place. She was talking about selling up and moving into a rented place. It seemed daft. When we were buying rental places, it helped all of us. Her rent is lower than it should be, but it still gave us a good return. I thought she would have told you by now. Honestly, I did not know that it would be a surprise. I'm sorry Verity, that must be hard for you." Jess sounded so reasonable, so like the aunt who had been there when she was growing up. It made sense. Her mum had worked, but she had made very little money. Three children and a small income. It all made sense, yet it screamed wrong, wrong, wrong at her.

"Right, I see." She shook her head. In truth, she saw nothing. There was no reason why it would have been a secret. "So, I have a list of properties and investments. I will have them independently valued, and then we can go through them. OK with you?" It was, and Verity was pleased to put the phone down. She felt as though she had been lied to, or at the very least, kept in the dark. She went into the Land Registry website. Serena had transferred the house to Simon when Verity was ten years old. Before that, it had been in her mum's name. No mention of her dad. Why was his name not on the deeds? She had no clue and no way to ask anyone who might tell her the truth.

This was fast becoming the worst week of her life, and yet she had no way of finding the route out of it. Her fingers burned on her coffee cup. She sipped. Her mouth burned too.

"Fuck, fuck, fuck." The only word that worked for her. The only word that worked in the whole ridiculous world. None of the world made sense. She was locked in. Locked out. Lost and found.

8.

The restaurant was warm and welcoming, with a fug of onions and garlic hanging heavily in the air. They ordered, ate the poppadoms and talked about nothing. She crossed her feet under the table. She felt wrapped around herself, tied in to so many secrets and lies.

"Sorry, I was miles away. Say it again?" She was drifting, not paying attention.

"I said, you're distracted. Was this a bad idea? I mean, I know we're in the middle of a divorce. Was it wrong to invite you to eat with me?" Basti leaned forwards, closer to her. He looked good. The open-necked shirt made him look more relaxed. His smile made her feel more comfortable with him.

"No. If it felt wrong, I would have said no! I just have some complicated family stuff going on at the moment, quite apart from acting for my aunt in her divorce, I mean." She shrugged it off and took another piece of deliciously crisp poppadom.

"OK. I have a similar issue." His face, pulled long

and sad, despite the cheekbones and eyebrows she would have arm wrestled him for. "My mother keeps on phoning me, once, sometimes twice a week. She is driving me insane." A smile split his face.

"Families!" She chuckled, despite herself. "So, you said you had a brother who changed your name for you. Just the two of you against the parental barrage of calls?" She propped her chin on her hand and watched him.

"Yes, just the two of us. He's called Per. For years, he used to tell people it was short for Perseus. It's short for Jasper and revenge for me being called Basti. My mother, apart from her phone addiction, is also very much into poncey names for her sons." He laughed, and it changed his face. His eyes crinkled and sparkled. She laughed too. "You said you had a sister?"

"I have two. Mim, short for Jemima, and Lola. She's the youngest, so I think my mum just looked for a name it would be really hard to shorten. We used to call her La, just to make her feel like she wasn't left out. But she used to just sing la la la, and we would fall over laughing." She sipped her wine. He concentrated hard on her. She felt as though she was being studied. She was grateful that he had not asked about her parents. That was somewhere she was not ready to go. Her dad was worrying at the edge of her thoughts, and her mum brought her own challenges.

"Did you always want to do family law? Personally, I mix and match, with criminal law, I quite like the variety, sticking to one thing too much starts to feel stale." He held his palms up and shrugged his shoulders. "Also, not all of us have the luxury of working for a swanky pants firm!" He had seen the relief in her eyes when he only asked about her sisters. He knew more about her family than he was comfortable sharing.

"Swanky pants?" He nodded. "Family law being a roller-coaster of laughter and joy?" She shook her head. "Yes, I always wanted to do family law. I still volunteer twice a month at a women's refuge, free legal advice, and trying to get some legal framework of protection for the women and their childrcn." She chewed her lower lip.

"Really? That's such a nice thing to do. You're not what I expected." His brows pulled together.

"Ah, let me guess. You thought I would be snapping at your ankles, teeth bared, snarling and shouting? You just haven't annoyed me yet!" Their food arrived, and they tucked in. It was spicy and delicious and totally what she had hoped for. They talked about the food and avoided the subject of their respective clients. It seemed the decent thing to do.

After dinner, finding that the shared bottle of

wine was empty, they had a small brandy each and called a taxi. His flat was on the way, and he asked if she might like to come in for a coffee before she made her way home. She thought about it. For a moment, she imagined being the sort of spontaneous person who would throw caution to the wind and say yes. She was not, however, that person.

"I have to work in the morning. Another time though?" She creased her brow a little. "If there is another time?" He reached across the back of the taxi seat and took her face in his hands. The kiss he gave her was gentler than she had expected, and it shook her resolution.

"There will be another time." He whispered it against her mouth. He tasted of brandy and garlic, and she felt him smile. Then he was gone, and she wished she had gone in with him. Sensible might be a good way to live, but it was less fun than other options.

9.

"Twice in a week?" Verity's mum held the door open and stepped back. "Is it my birthday?"

"No. I wanted to talk about some things, just the two of us. Is that OK with you?" Verity followed her to the kitchen and sat down.

"Of course, it's always good to see you." She fluttered around the kitchen, her fingers touching and cleaning and moving things, but not settling to anything.

"Why didn't you tell me that you sold the house?" Verity watched her mother's fingers stop moving.

"I thought you knew about that." She kept her back to Verity. Her back was ramrod straight.

"How? How would I know about it when you didn't tell me?" Verity kept her voice low.

"Verity, you were a little girl. We needed the money, and Simon and Jess needed an investment. It worked out for all of us. We kept our home." Her fingers were on the move again, worrying the neck of her top. "It wasn't charity, if that's what you're thinking. I pay rent."

"OK. You are entitled to keep your secrets, but you knew I was acting for Jess. You knew I would find out. Why would you not tell me?" She tipped her head and leaned it against her hand.

"It was such a long time ago." She put the kettle on. The noise it made filled the space between them. A space that was tense and angry.

"What are you saying? You forgot that you sold the house?" Verity shook her head, her smooth, straightened, professionally highlighted hair shook with it. Her face pulled tight with anger.

"No. I just, well, I'm not good at these things, you know that." The kettle popped, and she poured the boiling, steaming water into cups.

"That is about the most enormous pile of bollocks I have ever heard." Verity accepted the cup of tea and took a biscuit from the open packet on the table.

"Please don't." Serena crumpled into a chair and grabbed a biscuit, dipping it into her tea. "It's complicated."

"Tell me, then. Explain." Verity laid her hands flat on the table. She watched her mother's eyes flutter closed. "Let me in. Let me help you." She sipped the tea, giving her mother time to pull herself together. "What is it that is so bad that you can't tell me?"

The doorbell rang, and she ran to answer it, as

though her feet were off the floor, flying.

"Oh! My goodness, two visitors in a day. I have won the lottery." Her voice was too loud, pitched too high. She was telling the person on the doorstep that she had company. Perhaps she was warning them? Verity sat forward, intrigued to find out who the other visitor could be. When Simon walked into the kitchen, she was shocked.

"Hello Simon. How are you?" Verity sipped her tea. She sat still and waited.

"Verity. Nice to see you, not in the office." He sat in the chair at the end of the table, like it was his table. There was something so proprietary about the way he did it. Verity sat up straighter, her hackles raised.

"I'm the same person, Simon. Whether I'm in the office, or here, or in, maybe, a car park." She huffed a breath. "Still the same person."

"OK." His brows knitted, a picture of confusion. "I suppose you are. Just so you know, Jess is not the saint you imagine. We have been unhappy for a long time. I just want to get out and get on with my life."

"Good. I believe your solicitor has some papers for you to look at." She stood. "I have to go. I have an appointment in a quarter of an hour." She squeezed her mum's arm and nodded a smile at her. "Love you, Mum. Bye Simon." Outside, the air felt fresher, cleaner.

She walked, striding through the streets she had known her whole life. Questions and possibilities fizzed through her brain. She hoped, really, truly hoped, that she was wrong.

She stopped and took some deep breaths. Her mum was going to tell her nothing. She was no further forward than she had been that morning. Her phone rang. "Hello?"

"Verity. I wanted to check when you are free for dinner. Now that we have shared Italian and Indian food, I thought we might try Indonesian or Inuit?" He was laughing, and she was grateful for the distraction. She stood still, listening to his laugh, and to the possibility of another meal with him.

"Is there an Inuit restaurant locally?" She felt her face crease into a smile.

"I will find out. So, in theory, if there was a cuisine that we could agree on, Inuit or whatever, you would be prepared to spend another evening in my company?" There was laughter bubbling down the phone line to her.

"Yes. I would share an evening." She started to walk again. "How about next week? Maybe Friday, if you're free?"

"Nice thinking. That would be great. OK. I'll research restaurants." She turned the corner, she could see the refuge from where she was, and the man across the road who was watching it. She said goodbye and straight away phoned the local police, who knew her well.

"Hello. I have a man watching the women's refuge on Percival Street. Can you spare someone to have a look?" She had learned over the years that a visit from the police could stop something before it started. "Might be nothing, but I would be grateful." The officer agreed, and she waited for the next few minutes, fiddling with her phone, even taking a quick photo of the man who was intent on the building across the road. When the police car pulled up, she walked straight past them. She blocked the view from the road, while she entered the security code and let herself in through the gates, and then the door of the refuge.

"Verity? I didn't think you would be here until later on. So glad you are, though." Helen's accent was as strong as it had been the day that she had stepped off the train from Glasgow.

"I thought my earlier appointment would take a little longer. Anything I can do?" Helen pointed to the room where the women congregated next to the kitchen, but with comfortable chairs. Inside, she found four women, two of them she had met before, the other two were new to her. "Hi. I'm Verity. I'm a solicitor, specialising in family law. Here to help if you need it, or to just chat if not."

"The injunction you got me? Is it going to run out? Do I have to renew it?" She pulled out the document and held it out to Verity. The afternoon fell into a normal pattern, dealing with the worries that they had, and making notes to follow up whatever was needed. In between, they drank cups of tea and chatted. They were nice people, a little frightened by their experiences, and worried for their safety, but just people who had chosen the wrong partner.

Back when she was studying, she had volunteered at the refuge. She had imagined that her family had been through some terrible hardships. Nothing she had seen growing up had prepared her for the brutality the refuge women had been through. It had been a sobering experience, which had taught her so much about resilience and survival. At the end of her studies, she had carried on visiting and helping where she could.

Helen was waiting for her when she pulled her jacket on to leave. "Thanks a million Verity." She raised her eyebrows and checked over her shoulder before she carried on. "Just thought you'd want to know. Cassie?" Verity nodded. She remembered the woman. "She died on Monday. He found her, and beat the living crap out of her." Helen ran a finger under her eye. "It never gets easier."

Verity wrapped her arms around her. "You gave

her the chance to get away from him. You were here for her when she needed you. What a bastard. Cassie was a sweetheart."

"I just thought you should know." She shook her head, wiping away the tears.

"Thanks Helen." Verity squeezed her arm and let herself out of the door. Across the road, the man was gone. She checked again before she opened the gate and pulled it locked behind her.

10.

The valuations were waiting on her desk when she arrived at work. The figures were large, but not much more than she expected. She hit the button to call her aunt.

"Jess? Hi. Can you talk, or would another time be better for you?" She ruffled through the rest of her mail with the phone between her neck and shoulder.

"Yes OK. Go ahead." Verity read out the valuations and the bank balances.

"So now we have a valuation. I will ask Simon's lawyers to agree them. You will then have to decide if you would rather sell everything and split the money or decide between you who gets what to make an approximate split. OK?" There was a pause at the other end.

"I've decided I don't want the house. From the first day, I never liked it. I have been unhappy here for years. Once it's over, I want to move away, somewhere he's never been. I don't want any of the houses. I want to start fresh." She sounded decisive, braver.

"Great, that makes it much simpler. I will go ahead and tell Simon's solicitor. All we need now is Simon's agreement, and we can sort all this out without needing to go to court. Thanks Jess." They said goodbye and Verity sat looking at the phone for a while, thinking about Cassie. She had made some bad choices, but so had Jess. It had ended so differently. Shaking her head, she tapped out an email to Basti, confirming the valuations, and that Jess would not want to live in any of the houses.

Her reverie on relationship failure was cut short. One of the receptionists, who was on maternity leave, popped in to show off her new baby. Verity smiled and made the right noises, but excused herself before too long. Babies made her uncomfortable. The years of care, and worry, the cost and the heartache. The terrible vulnerability. It was all too evident to her. Back in the safety of her office, she thought about the way her own mother had struggled for years to support Verity and her sisters, living half a life. Motherhood certainly held no allure for Verity.

The day was long, and she had forgotten to eat lunch, but she knew that there was a ready meal in her freezer. It was not ideal, but it would have to do. She pushed the plastic container into the microwave and hit the buttons.

Her phone rang, Mim's name came up on the screen. "Mim? You ok?"

"Can I come round, Etty? I need to talk to you." Verity stood still. This was out of the ordinary.

"Of course. Did you eat? I'm making chicken ding."

"I already ate. Go ahead and eat. I'll be there in half an hour." She hung up. Her phone rang again, and it was Basti.

"Hi, how are you Verity?" His voice filled the half-light of her kitchen.

"Fine, thanks, just making dinner. You?" She peered through the door of the microwave and watched the meal turning through a circle.

"You cook?" He sounded genuinely surprised.

"My one and only specialty. Chicken ding." She pushed her hair back out of her face.

"What's that?" His voice held his confusion.

"When the microwave goes ding, it's ready!" She smiled at her reflection in the kitchen window and listened to him laugh down the phone.

"I have found a restaurant which apparently serves very good food. Not far from where we work and live. I wondered if I should book a table for Friday?" She was still looking at her reflection in the kitchen window, and found that she was still smiling.

"I think you probably should. I like very good food. Particularly if it's located not far from my home and work." She laughed. The microwave beeped.

"Is that your ding? Perhaps I should leave you to your culinary delights." She agreed he should.

She ate half of the meal, but it was not appealing. The doorbell saved her from pushing it around anymore.

"Mim, come in." She held the door open.

"I have to ask something." She threw her coat on the sofa and pulled her shoes off. "Why are Simon and Jess getting a divorce? Does it have something to do with mum?"

"First of all, I don't know. Except that both of them are unhappy. Why would it have anything to do with mum?" Verity sat at the other end of the sofa.

"I told him I would pay him back, like you said, and next thing mum was on the phone shouting at me, saying I was being ungrateful." She pulled the cushion on to her lap and wrapped her arms around it. "It just seemed really strange, like she was taking his side against me, and it wasn't even an argument." Her bottom lip stuck out a little. A small but indignant fire had sparked in Verity's belly. Nobody made her little sister feel bad about doing the right thing. Not her fat, arrogant uncle or her flaky mother. She doused the flames back to a glow, needing to think clearly.

"I truly don't know. All I know is what I told you. Simon has been seeing someone else, and he wants out. Just like a zillion other middle-aged guys, looking to recapture their youth, which, they believe, is hiding in another woman's knickers." They laughed. Verity poured two glasses of wine.

"It's unlucky, both sisters picking guys who want to run. You and I are going to make better choices, Verity. We have to make better lives than mum and aunt Jess did." She sipped from the glass of wine.

"We already have. Mim, you are about to open the first of many salons. I should make partner in a few years. We are independent and strong women. Mum never was either. She tried hard, but she wasn't. Lola is headed the right way, too. She's working hard, she'll be a good psychologist. Just like you're a good hairdresser, and I do divorce. We will be three very capable people. If nothing else, mum did that." She reached across to the other side of the sofa.

"My clever sister, you always know the right thing to say." Mim closed her eyes. "Do they teach you that at big sister school?"

"First day." Verity lifted her glass in a toast. "To being independent, to being better." They clinked together. "Oh, I have news. Don't make a big deal out of it. I've been seeing someone, just a couple of times, but I like him."

"Really? Oh my, the ice maiden is melting." Mim laughed, deep and low.

"The ice maiden? Are you serious? I am so not." Verity picked up a cushion and hit her sister's knee.

Mim went home feeling better. She left Verity feeling uncomfortable, with ideas racing around her head, and angry thoughts banging on the lid of the box she kept them in.

11.

Jess opened the door. Her hair was perfect, her makeup flawless. Everything she wore was designer, expensive.

"Verity, we need to discuss some things." She turned away and walked back into the house. Her heels clicked across the hardwood flooring. In the kitchen, surrounded by granite and shiny cupboards, Jess looked completely at home. She was the perfect well-groomed match for the house.

"Are you sure you want to move from here? I've always thought that this was so you." Verity turned and looked out at the manicured gardens.

"You think I'm spoiled? A rich man's wife. New boobs, a restructured nose, gym membership, to keep me looking tip top. Dental work. Did I miss anything on the list? It's OK. All those things are true. There are lots of other things that are true too." She opened a cupboard and pulled out a pad and some cleanser, and slowly cleaned the make-up from her face. The bruises were faded, but they were there. Yellow and purple across her face and neck. She unbuttoned her blouse, the bruises marched across her body. "I'm covered with them. Big and small."

"Who did this?" Verity crossed the space between them. "Who hurt you? Was this Simon?" Jess laughed. It was a hollow, humourless sound.

"I am not one of your battered women at the refuge. You can stop making judgements. Stop. I want this divorce dealt with. Get me as close to half as you can. Then get me out. That is why I am paying you a huge amount of money, after all." She pushed her face into a smile. Her emotions were tightly packed and tied together with fear and years of unhappiness. Verity could see it hurt. "The answers aren't mine to give. I just want to get out."

"Jess. Please tell me what is going on. Let me help you?" Verity reached out.

"I can't. Please, just accept the way it is. Keep your nose out of things that don't concern you. Do the job you are being paid for and let us all get out of this in one piece." Her voice was harsh, fuelled by frustration. "Please." A tear ran down her cheek.

"Can you at least tell me who hurt you? Why we can't phone the police?" Verity ran a hand through her hair.

"No. I will deny anything and everything. You have no clue who is involved and what would happen. Just for once in your life, do as you are fucking told. Despite what you think, you do not know everything. You are being told this as my lawyer, so you can't repeat it without my permission." Jess buttoned up her blouse. "Please speak to my soon to be ex-husband and sort this out so that we can all get on with our lives." Carefully, Jess steered Verity back to the front door and out of the house. Closing the front door behind her with a soft click.

Verity hailed a cab and slid into the back seat. Her breathing was a little ragged, and she felt sick. Had Simon done that to his wife? It had to be that he was more dangerous than she had thought. She leaned forward and changed her journey. There was no point going to her mother's home.

Back at the office. She started an email to Basti, then decided that it was not immediate enough. She dialled his number.

"Basti. My client has instructed me that she wishes to wrap this matter up. Can you tell me why I have not had a response from you on the valuations and division of assets?" She concentrated hard on releasing her grip on the phone.

"Hello to you too. I have sent the list to my client and I am awaiting instructions." She could hear that he was smiling. She imagined his eyes and the skin at the sides that crinkled.

"I am instructed to move this matter to a conclusion today. I need an agreement. There has been enough time spent on this. By close of business today, or I file the matter with the court and let them make the decision." She checked her watch. He had a busy afternoon ahead. "Call me when you have an answer." She hung up.

The rest of the afternoon she dealt with other clients, worked her way through the day, gritted her teeth every time she checked her emails to find no message. She drank a cup of tea, as she usually did at three in the afternoon. She took five minutes and resisted the urge to phone Basti again. Each breath was hard to take. She had been here before, pushing the boundaries and riding the deal to the brink, but not with so much personal involvement. Her family was involved in something, but nobody would tell her what it was. She was, however, at least sure of what she was doing. This was her thing. Her confident place.

At five minutes to five, her phone rang. "Basti. Hi."

"I take it back. Your reputation is fully deserved. My client is crazy go nuts angry, but he has agreed to the sale of all assets and an equal division. I have emailed you the signed agreement, and you will have the original on your desk within the next half an hour." His voice was clipped, and she knew he was angry.

"Thank you, Mr Culpepper. It has been a pleasure.

Please extend my congratulations to your client. This can all be dealt with quickly now. He will be a free man shortly." She took a deep breath. "If you felt that I put you under undue pressure, I apologise."

"Ends justify the means? I didn't enjoy having my hand forced, but perhaps you know both parties better than I do, and it achieved a fair and equitable result." He huffed out a breath. "Doesn't mean I like it."

"Fair enough." Verity pulled her coat on and slipped her handbag over her shoulder. "I suppose I owe you dinner tonight. By way of compensation. Are you thinking French, Italian, Indian?" He was laughing, and part of her was very grateful.

"OK. French would be nice. I'll book a table. It has to be better than chicken ding." She pictured his face and hoped that she was right to feel that life was on the edge of something good.

When she hung up the phone, it rang straight away. She had been expecting the call, the conversation, but not quite this fast.

"Hello Mum." She pushed open the door to the reception area. "How are you?"

"I want to know why you have upset your sister. She phoned Simon and told him that she had made other arrangements to borrow the money. I asked her about it and she was very upset. Very aggressive." Her voice was high and angry.

"I want to know why you are on Simon's side rather than your sister's. Can you tell me that?" She stood in the reception area. Two desks stood empty where there were usually people.

"Now you're being ridiculous. First your sister and now you. What is happening to everyone?" There was a sound in the background. Something, someone else, was there with her mother.

"Fine." She threw up her hands. "What I am doing is not upsetting my sister. I offered to loan her the money, rather than let her borrow from Simon. What I am doing is what I have always done. I am looking after my sisters, taking care of them. What I am doing for Jess is my job. Speak to you another time, when we are alone."

She pushed the door into the hallway, dialling Jess on the way.

"Hi Jess. All done. You have an agreement for half." She made a noise that was a little like a sob or a laugh. It was hard to tell on the phone.

"Thank you, Verity." Her voice was quiet, but there was determination there, too.

"I'll offer Simon the option to keep any of the properties. It will be easier than selling them on the open market, and other than that, you can get the estate agents in." Her phone buzzed in her hand, and she knew another call was coming in. "OK, I'll send a copy of the agreement over in the morning. Have a good evening, Jess."

"You too. Night Verity." She hung up and checked who the missed call was from. It rang again almost straight away. "Hello Basti."

"The table's booked. I'll text you the details. I'm very hungry." She smiled to herself, and took the stairs down to the street, where she hailed a cab and went home. She had stopped bringing her car to work since she stopped feeling safe in the car park.

This felt like more of a date. She needed to have a shower and change, and she just about had time before she had to be at the restaurant. She felt better, with fresh make-up and wearing a soft dress that flattered her figure rather than her usual formal suit. The cab dropped her outside the restaurant only a few minutes late, and she took a deep breath before walking in.

He sat at the table, with his cheekbones and his smile. He looked good. When she arrived at the table, she realized he smelt better than good. He stood up, and reached across to kiss her cheek, the firmness of his hand on her arm and the softness of the kiss starting thoughts of possibilities. "You look very lovely."

"Thank you. You look very lovely too." She was flirting, she knew it, and so did he. A smile spread wider across his face.

The food was fantastic, but she could have told no one what she ate. The wine was smooth and delicious, and they sat together, sparkling at each other, which was better than the food or the wine.

Later, after the food and the wine, they walked a little way. His hand wrapped around hers, the smooth warmth of the touch feeling good. They came to the river, wide and inky dark under the night sky, lights strung above the balustrade that led up to the bridge. He leaned down to kiss her. His lips soft and gentle on hers, his arms wrapped around her body, and for a fraction of a second, she imagined it was too much, claustrophobic. Then she felt his lips on hers, and the warmth of his body through his shirt, and she relaxed, giving herself up to the feelings and the heat of his kiss.

He hailed a taxi, his arm still around her, and opened the back door. His kisses deeper as the cab pulled away. His hands on her waist, pulling her towards him. This time, there was no question or offer. He paid the taxi and unlocked the door to his house. There was no offer of coffee or a brandy. There was only, in the entire world, it seemed to her, his body and hers.

12.

Rushing home to have a shower and change into something office appropriate meant that she sat down at her desk at eight thirty, a little later than usual. Armed with a coffee, she forced herself to concentrate, and ignore the fact that her body was buzzing. No sleep, too much caffeine and sex were a heady mixture.

The original, signed document arrived from Basti as promised. She made the application to the court straight away; including the agreement, signed by both parties to show that they had come to a settlement they were both prepared to accept. The rest was a rubber stamp, effectively.

She made a copy of the agreement and dropped it into an envelope for Jess. Drawing a breath and fetching another coffee, she pushed herself to concentrate. Now that Jess and Simon were on the way to a divorce, she could concentrate on other clients. For the rest of the morning, she worked through the folders on her desk. She pushed for settlements, arguing for contact with children, and bringing everything up to date. By four, she was struggling, her eyes were heavy from lack of sleep, and there was nothing useful that could be achieved that way. She pulled her coat on and left the office, taking a cab home, and sliding into a hot bath, and then soft pyjamas. Her phone buzzed while she was climbing under the quilt.

A text from Basti. 'I have been trying to play it cool and not text you until tomorrow. Don't tell anyone xx.'

She pushed her hair out of her face and plumped up the pillow behind her. 'Your secret is safe with me x.' The smile on her face was for nobody else but her.

She snuggled down under the quilt. It was warm and soft and she needed to sleep, but whether it was the coffee that she had drunk or the thoughts of the night before, sleep seemed a long way away.

After an hour of reading a novel, forgetting what had happened and having to re-read the pages, over and over, she closed her eyes and drifted off. She woke to another text from Basti. She shook her head. It was like being a teenager again. 'Do we still have a dinner date for tonight? It's Friday.'

'Yes, we do. Did you book somewhere?'

'Not yet. Unless you fancy a take-away? Feet up in front of the telly? Your choice.'

'OK. Take-away sounds great.' She smiled to herself, looking forward to seeing him.

'Your place?'

That made her think. Did she want him in her home? It seemed such a big step, but maybe she was overthinking it. She sent him a text with her address and they agreed on a time.

She cast an eye over her house before she left for work. It was tidy and clean. Nothing to be worried about, except the pyjamas she had worn the night before, left on the bed. With a smile to herself, she pushed them into a drawer.

The rush hour had yet to start, and a cab was easy to find. The office was quiet, and she found that almost every email that she had sent the day before had received an answer. She worked through until the rest of the offices around her began to fill up and then took a break to make a cup of tea. She had decided to stay away from coffee for the day.

A text from Mim confirmed that the bank loan she had applied for had been approved and deposited in her bank account. Verity replied that this was so much better, standing on her own two feet. She was proud of Mim. The salon would be going ahead without their uncle having a finger in the pie.

Her phone rang, and she squeezed her eyes closed. "Hello Mum."

"Verity. I hate it when you and I fall out. I have invited the girls for dinner on Sunday. Can you come too? I think we should talk." There was a silence.

"What time are you thinking?" Verity grabbed a pen and wrote down the time her mother suggested. "Ok, thank you for the invitation. See you on Sunday afternoon." She took a breath. "I don't want to argue either."

She sat back in her chair, running over the previous day in her head. The fact that Jess had been beaten so badly, and nobody, including Jess, was prepared to stand up and say it was wrong, worried her. Simon could have been hurting her for years. Although she had the information, there was nothing she could do. She was bound by the rules to keep her client's secrets.

Years of practice had taught her to push things into compartments in her brain to be dealt with later, although she kept coming back to the bruises she had seen between each phone call and email. She had one last meeting to go to before the end of the day. Reception let her know that both sides had arrived and were waiting for her in the boardroom. Lifting the folders from her desk, she straightened her skirt and ran her fingers through her hair. The meeting was over in less than half an hour. No agreement could be reached, and both sides had shrugged at the thought of going to court.

She filed the application with the court before wishing everyone she passed in the office a good weekend, and taking the stairs down to find a cab. In the back of the cab, she checked her watch. She would have time to soak in the bath before he arrived. The butterflies in her stomach pulled their boots on and jumped up and down.

He arrived with a kiss and a smile. They ordered Thai food, walked around the corner to collect it, and ate. They were sitting at her kitchen table, sharing a bottle of wine, and listening to each other's stories. He leaned across the table and held her hand. It felt warm and comfortable. His thumb rubbed the back of her hand.

She had a bottle of brandy in the cupboard and poured them a generous measure each. They took them through to sit on the sofa.

Basti ran his fingers up the side of her face. He smiled, and she could feel the palm of his hand on her face. He kissed her, his lips gently grazing hers, moving closer to her, fingers slipping through her hair. They pulled closer, drawn together like magnets.

Up the stairs, tumbling, fingers fumbling, laughing and breathless. They both were there in the moment. Just as they were, no thoughts of anyone else, of anything outside that room, outside their own bodies and space.

She fell asleep in his arms, and woke wrapped

around him, and smiling. They had coffee and croissants for breakfast, then wandered through the market and stopped for lunch in a small restaurant. It was a perfect Friday night and Saturday. By late afternoon, she was tired, and he needed to go home to get some clean clothes. He kissed her tenderly on the doorstep and walked up to the main road to find a cab.

Left alone, she put on the dishwasher and soaked in the bath, catching up on sleep and enjoying the smell of him on her sheets. The morning would bring whatever it brought, and she would deal with it all then. He texted her in the evening to ask if she was free on Wednesday evening. She thought about it for a few seconds and replied that she was.

13.

Sunday had always been a strange day for her. As a child, she had dreaded the return to school that Monday would bring. She would question whether she had done the right homework, if she had the answers right. What her mother would be doing while she was not there to make sure.

She collected clothes that needed washing. Tidiness and control of her life made her feel safe. She paused, stopping on the stairs to remember a time in her life when she had given up control, perhaps the only time, and allowed Lola to decorate her house. Back then, she had been happy to live with the beige and white scheme the previous owners had adopted, on which Lola had poured scorn and heavy sarcasm. Whilst she had spent a very nervous week on holiday; her younger sister had transformed the space, using colours Verity had not known she loved, until she found that she did. Soft sage greens and dove greys contrasted with the blue kitchen. The deeper tones that ran through her bedroom and bathroom made it feel luxurious and opulent rather than claustrophobic. Lola had dotted the walls with her own artwork, and the whole thing worked. Verity had not changed a thing. It had been an experience for both of them and had made them closer.

She had not seen Lola often in the last few years while she was studying away, but that would come to an end soon, and perhaps she would move back. Verity found that she was hoping Lola would.

Outside her mother's house, she pulled out the flowers and wine she had picked up on the way from the passenger seat. She closed her eyes for just a moment, willing herself to stay calm. Her eyes closed, she whispered a reminder not to lose her temper, to take the flowers and wine into the house and give them in the spirit of reconciliation. If she wanted answers, she would need to have her mother on her side.

Inside, she handed over the flowers and wine, careful to keep her eyes level. Her mother pulled her in for a hug and poured her a glass of wine. She was the first to arrive, so they had a little time to talk.

"Before the others get here, I wanted to ask you how Jess is, really. I mean, I think she doesn't seem too good, and I'm a little worried." She sipped the wine and watched her mother.

"I haven't seen her, to be honest. I spoke to her on the phone last week, no, the week before that.

We don't have much in common anymore." Her mother was busying herself around the kitchen, fussing when nothing was needed.

"That's a shame. How are you?" Verity forced her tone to be light and easy.

"Alright, thanks, I've had a busy week. I had a few days at work, and then everything else in between. You know how it is?" Verity nodded, letting her mum's chatter flow over her. Watching her move around the kitchen. Were her steps a little lighter, was her voice trilling and high, or was Verity reading too much into it? She could feel her daughter's eyes on her every movement. It made her more nervous.

"I've been trying to remember what happened when I was little. Before Dad left. I know I heard shouting, and the house was full up of people. Can you fill in the blanks for me? I want to remember." She watched her mother's hands still.

"It was between me and your dad. It was nothing to do with you girls. He could have come back to see you, but he chose to stay away." She folded up a cloth twice more than it needed. "I have invited Simon for dinner. He's on his own now. It seemed the kind thing to do."

"Is Jess not on her own too?" Verity smiled, to cover the biting edge to the words.

"I'm just telling you, so you know." Her mother

slipped into the walk-in cupboard where she had a small mirror on the back of the door and came out with lipstick on. That was new.

"OK. I know now." The doorbell rang, and Verity watched her mother rush to open it. Before the kitchen door was filled with his bulky frame, she knew it would be Simon. "Hello Simon. I was just asking my mum about what happened just before my dad left. There are gaps in my recollection. Perhaps you can help." His eyes darted to catch her mum's, and he cleared his throat.

"All a long time ago now, Verity." He stretched his face into a smile that was pretended. His eyes were wary, guarded.

"Yes. But you were here a lot at the time, weren't you? Jess and you, and the boys. Perhaps you can tell me what you remember." She watched him squirm and redden. He had no wish to have this conversation at all.

"I was here now and then, more Jess and your mum getting together. I was working hard, long hours, setting up the business." He fiddled with the cuff on his shirt. "Jess was lonely with the boys and me out so often. She used to come over here three or four times a week in those days. She loved you girls." His eyes met Verity's and his smile made it nowhere near them. He was pushing her questions away.

"I remember that. Were you not happy that she spent so much time here? Was that why there was all the shouting before my dad left?" Verity's voice was clear. From years of court appearances, she had tried to make the question sound innocent, while leading her uncle into a corner.

"I was away a lot, and, if I'm honest, I was no angel. Probably not great fun to live with. I tried, but we were too different. She found me annoying. I found her and the kids a bit boring. We had drifted apart." He looked down at the table.

"Did she find out that you were having an affair with my mum?" Verity rested her chin on her hand. He jumped up as though he had been scalded.

"No. That was not what happened. She was the one. I caught her with your dad. To be honest, I was all set to walk away when I realized that what I wanted was to see the boys every night, not every other weekend. I couldn't believe how stupid I had been not seeing it first, that they were the only thing that mattered." He ran his hand over his face.

"You caught her with my dad?" Verity popped her eyes wide. "Where? Here? In this house?"

"In this room." She could see he felt the solid ground beneath his feet.

"They were having sex in this room?" Verity

looked around, as though they might still be at it, and she had missed it before.

"Yes, they were. I walked out, got as far as the front door, and realized my boys needed both parents. We would just have to find a way. We did. I moved into the spare room. We told the boys I had hurt my back, and they had no reason to question it. We put our lives on hold until they were grown up and settled." He shook his head. "We were good parents. They were happy kids. We were a good family. It worked. Now that they have their own lives, it's time for us to have our own. Jess agreed. We discussed it." His head slumped down.

"Why did you fight so hard then, if you had agreed to it all ahead of time?" He met her eyes.

"Had to keep up the show, right? It would be expected." He smiled, aiming for boyish and missing it by a considerable distance. Verity watched her mother rest a hand on his shoulder. He reached to cover it with his.

"You're together now?" She left the question hanging in the air.

"Yes, we hope you can be pleased for us." They watched her expression.

"Apart from the feeling that I'm taking part in a sad daytime television programme, 'my mother is sleeping with her sister's husband." She raised her fingers to make quote marks. "Who is Jess with?" She locked eyes with her mother.

"I have no idea that she's with anyone." Verity watched her mother's fingers grip tightly on to his shoulder.

"Oh, she's with someone. I aim to find out who." She stared down Simon. The doorbell stopped the conversation.

Mim and Lola arrived together. They chatted enough not to notice that the other three people around the table were quiet. Later, when she arrived home, Verity would wonder what it was that they ate for dinner. She had no idea.

14.

"Right! Now that we have had pudding and made polite conversation, can we please all be in on the secret?" Mim pushed back her perfectly shiny hair. There were blank faces around the table. "Verity, please tell us." Anger simmered just below the surface. "Now, please."

"It's really not my story to tell. However, it appears that our mother and our Uncle Simon are now an item. Uncle Simon, brave soul that he is, stayed with his wife, until his sons were grown up, and now that the little fledglings have flown the nest, he feels free to tell the world about his relationship with his sister-in-law. Is that about right? Did I miss anything?" She had been careful not to finish her first glass of wine, afraid that it would let loose her temper, which was on a short leash. She was annoyed to hear a tremor in her voice.

"What? Mum, tell me that it's not true?" Lola looked left and right, as though she was searching for a way out. "No. This can't be right."

"When did you find out?" Mim's sharp eyes cut slices through Verity.

"Today. Just before you arrived. Honestly, I think they planned to tell us all together, but I was early and nosy." Both her sisters swivelled to look at her. "I was waiting until after dinner. I would have told you."

"I am so tired of being treated like a child. This family is so full of shit." Lola picked up her coat and scarf from the bottom of the stairs. The front door bounced on its hinges and her handbag flew behind her.

"I suspect dinner is over. The good news is that your divorce will be through soon, and then at least you will be legally free to make different choices. Thanks for dinner, mum. Glad you liked the flowers." Verity pulled her jacket back on and picked up her bag. "I'll call you later Mim." She ran her hand along her sister's shoulders, and felt, rather than saw, the nod.

"Please, don't go, Verity." Her mother was holding a tea towel in her hands, wringing it, her knuckles strained white against the cloth. "I never wanted to hurt any of you." Verity wrapped her in a hug.

"It's a shock. Perhaps we all need a little time for it to sink in?" Verity tapped gently on her arm. It was a lie, and they both knew it, but a kind one. Her mother felt less solid than she had.

Driving home, she turned on the radio, turned the volume up high and listened to the music, trying to drown out her thoughts. Logically, she knew that her mother was a human being, who had as much right to find happiness as anyone else. Even if happiness looked like bloody Simon.

While she was thinking, she drove, and when she pulled over, she was outside the house that Jess and Simon had shared. If he was to be believed, they had led separate lives except when it came to the children. If that was true, then what was the motivation for him to beat her into next week? None of it made sense.

Her finger hovered over the doorbell. Was she overstepping the bounds, coming here without a phone call first? She shook her head. She had known Jess all her life. The bell rang from somewhere inside the house. The sound muted, Verity waited, but nobody answered the door. Shrugging, she climbed back into her car. There had been nothing in her head that she wanted to talk to Jess about, but it had felt like it was the right place to be. Jess was on the other side of Simon's relationship with her mother, whether it had been going on for years and now was out in the open, or if it was, in fact, new. That must feel like betrayal from both her sister and her husband. It did not explain why Jess was covered in bruises, or tell Verity whether her mother was at risk of the same. The house was a blank, no movement at the windows and no answer at the door.

She drummed her fingers on the steering wheel. Her brain was usually good at puzzles, but this was tying her in knots. Everything she learned made less sense than before.

Driving home, she tried to put it out of her mind, concentrating on the week ahead, on the work she had to get through, even on the music that was playing on the radio, but she was distracted. For once, she found a parking place near her house and walked back. The pavement had been damp from the early rain when she left, but the sun had dried the slabs. The three steps up to her door were dry, too.

She climbed the stairs and stood next to her bed. She knew what she needed to see. Under her bed, in an old shoebox, tucked into the toe of a pair of shoes she never wore anymore. She pulled out the tiny bag. The tiny pendant necklace her father had given her. It was still there, and safe. She had kept it safe for so long; it seemed like a treasure to her. He had told her not to show it to the others, or talk about it. To always hide it. She had done. As always, she had kept her word and her necklace. She leaned back against the side of the bed, tipping the contents of the bag into her hand. The smooth black glass of the pendant was cold against her skin. It was a strange thing to give a child, she supposed, but he had made it seem like a treasure, and it still held that quality for her. It was the symbol of her loyalty to him.

Reassured that it was safe, she dangled it over the bag and dropped it in. Her fingers pushed against the bag, to make sure it was all the way into the toe of the shoe. She slid the shoes into the box, and pushed the box back under the bed, followed by all the other shoe boxes until they were all safely back where they should be.

Lying awake through the small hours between her clean, fresh sheets, knowing that she had more questions than answers, did not bring calm or relaxation.

15.

For no reason that she could explain, even to herself, she kept her worries about her aunt tucked away. The day brought a meeting, a negotiation, and two new clients. She should be filled with confidence and positivity, but her cab ride home was filled with dread.

Perhaps, she considered, her dad turning up had stirred up memories that had been buried a long time, and that was making her feel uncomfortable.

"Hi, Jess. How are you?" Even to her own ears, the strain in her voice was apparent.

"Verity. I just heard from my sister about what happened yesterday. Look, I am so sorry. I wanted to keep all of you away from this. Can we meet? I know you must be very upset, but please let me talk to you." Verity opened her mouth to reply, but before she could, Jess raced on. "I can come to your house. Get the kettle on, darling girl. We need to talk about this." The phone went down. It had been a long time since Jess had talked to her like that.

It was warm outside, unseasonably warm, but Verity was cold. She pulled a cardigan around her shoulders and tucked her hands under her arms. Standing back from the window meant that she saw Jess arrive and walk to the house. Without thinking about it, she crossed to the front door and opened it before Jess could ring the bell. Jess opened her arms wide and engulfed Verity with a hug that made her feel like a little girl again, back in a world where the grown-ups could make everything better.

"Come in, come in. Sorry, it's been a difficult time." Verity swiped the tears from her cheeks.

"Verity, your mum and Simon, they've been a thing for a long time. Simon and I, we should never have married. I knew it was a mistake, almost straight away. I was pregnant. It's not such a big deal now, but back in the day, I was frightened." She held Verity's hands. "If I had been braver, perhaps, but I wasn't." Verity turned away to put the kettle on. "Your dad was kind. He was my friend. Marcus was little, and Jem was a baby. I had no other grown-up friends. Simon was never at home. I knew there were other women. There always had been. I was less upset about it than I might have been. The kids kept me busy all day and most of the night. Your dad was there, happy to escape what was happening with your mum. We were there for each other." Verity passed a cup of tea to her aunt and they sat on the sofa together.

"But if all you were doing was supporting each other, why was Simon so angry? Why would he split up with you, except as far as the boys were concerned, if you were only friends with my dad?" She sipped from the cup, the hot liquid as soothing as her aunt's visit.

"It didn't stop at friendship." She held up her hands when she saw the change in Verity's face. "No! We weren't sleeping together. Not when he made the big deal out of it all. Nothing happened. He followed me to the house. We'd had a row. He'd pushed me against the kitchen cabinets. I was bruised and angry. Your dad had his hand on my shoulder. That was it. He went ballistic. Screaming and shouting. He told your mum we were having sex. The more we denied it, the more she thought we were lying. It was the excuse Simon wanted. I have no way of knowing if he was already with your mum or if he was just looking for a way in, but either way, that's what happened."

"OK. Why would he beat you up, then?" Verity reached across to Jess. "You're covered in bruises. Who did that?"

"Sorry, I shouldn't have shown you that, but I was trying to push you to sort out the divorce. I needed it done, so I can get out. It worked too, didn't it?" She smiled to soften the words.

"You said you weren't sleeping with my dad at that point, but you were later?" Verity kept her eyes level.

"Yes. I was hurt by Simon's lies and by my sister. There was an element of revenge, and we were both lonely. He had been thrown out. Your mum wouldn't let him see you. It was brutal." She took a breath. "He was broken. Not being able to see you was so painful for him. He missed your mum, and Simon had been his friend. They used to go to the football every other weekend together." She sipped her tea. Jess looked at her niece over the rim of her cup. She looked so like Adam. They had always been alike, those big wide eyes staring out so like her father.

"You haven't told me who is hurting you." Verity

"No. I haven't. Look, you're a good girl, you always were. Your dad loves you, and so does your mum. We've all behaved pretty badly to each other. I want out. It's toxic, living the way we have for so long. My sons are independent and safe. As soon as the divorce is settled, I'm moving. Fresh start, that's what I need." She held Verity's hand in hers, her voice dropping. "Parents don't always know the right way to do things. Having a baby isn't a magic thing that teaches you everything. Truthfully, a two-minute fumble can produce a baby just the same as years of love and devotion. You learn on the job, with no sleep and a guess and a prayer. We messed up, all four of us, except, look at the kids we produced, you are so smart, Mim is on the way to owning her own business, and Lola, so creative. My two are no slouches either. We made huge mistakes, but you were all given what you needed." She ran her hand down the side of Verity's face.

"I suppose I just thought you knew what you were doing." Verity laughed.

Jess's phone rang. She turned the screen to show her it was her cousin. "Hello Jem. How are you, darling?" She listened, the lines around her eyes squeezing her eyes shut. "Jem, I'm on the way to see you now. Hold on, I'm getting in the car now. OK?" She listened a little more. "I am going to grab my keys, and I'll phone you when I get in the car. Don't worry, everything is going to be fine." She ended the call. "I have to go. Sorry, Jem's taking this very hard." She kissed Verity's cheek and grabbed her handbag and keys. "Take care, sweetie." She was gone.

Verity leaned against the front door, double locked, checked the lock. Why did everything feel so completely wrong? The garden, though small, was basically a tiny patio with a table and two chairs. It caught the sun in the summer and even now, in the evening sunshine in late spring, the wide kitchen windows spilled light from the garden across the worktops and onto the floor. Verity pulled her cardigan a little more tightly around her body, and crossed the living room, into the kitchen, and all the way to the back door. Her hand stopped on the handle. She took a breath and pushed down. Outside, the noise of the traffic was loud. The air was heavy with traffic fumes. She could hear the kids playing three houses along the terrace, and the couple two further on than that, having an argument. She sat on the little chair, rested her elbows on the little table, and listened to the life all around her. Perhaps Jess was right. They had all just tried to protect their kids the best they could. She had avoided the question about her bruises, though. Honestly, was it any of her business, what her parents had got up to all those years ago?

This was what she tried to avoid every day, trying to find an amicable route out of the angry, hurt feelings that a break up brought with it. The problem was that if people liked each other and wanted to be friendly, they would not, she imagined, get divorced.

16.

The doorbell rang. Basti was outside with flowers.

"Hello." He handed her the flowers. "I need to talk to you. To tell you something." She opened the door wide enough for him to go inside. The flowers smelled lovely, the heavy oily scent of lilies in amongst them. She found a vase from the back of the cupboard and put them in water, and suggested that they sit out in the garden. It felt more comfortable that way. Men bringing flowers always worried her. "I need to tell you this. Because it's no longer true, but it was to start with."

"OK." Her brows came together in confusion. He was making her uncomfortable.

"When I met you, I was representing Simon, your uncle." She nodded. She knew this. "I should have told you, though, full disclosure, that I was also acting for your father on another matter. That is no longer the case. I do not act for your father anymore." He held his hands out in front of him, as though he needed to ward off her blows.

"You should have. Yes, perhaps before we slept together would have been polite. It might have been ethical, too." Her words were clipped and sharp. Just as she was starting to think that she might like him, that they might have something together, it was infuriating.

"I know. I should have. But I was an idiot. I regret it." He held his hands out in front of him. She knew that he was telling the truth, but the betrayal, the way that she had allowed herself to feel about him, made his actions too hurtful. Tears threatened, and that made her angrier still. She resorted to her most professional voice, slipping it on like a suit of armour. Her words sharper than any sword.

"Happy though I am, Basti, to discuss your client list, I really have no idea how this affects me. I have only seen my father once in the last twenty-plus years." She picked at an imaginary piece of fluff on her cardigan, fury boiling in her brain, and threatening to spill.

"No. Please listen. I very rarely do matrimonial work. My practice is almost entirely in criminal law. I am treading carefully here, not to tell you about my client's business. However, I can tell you that one of the reasons you did not see your father was that he was not available to be seen." He raised his eyebrows at her, trying to convey the message without words.

"My father was in prison?" His nod was almost not a movement at all. He was trying to tell her, without telling her. He was caught in the middle. Seeing his discomfort made her no less angry.

"I can in no way discuss that with you. However. I can tell you that I am no longer employed by your father, and that I hope that you and I can carry on seeing each other. Hence the flowers." He sparkled a smile at her, his eyes pleading with her, filled with hope that he had said enough to convince her.

"Hence." She chewed the inside of her lip. He nodded. "So, are you saying that our previous time together has been on the instructions of your former client?"

"No. Yes. Initially. The meeting in the restaurant. The first time, that was him. After that, it was all me." He took a breath. "I know it was wrong. I knew it as soon as I sat across the table from you, and I told him immediately that I could no longer work for him."

"Oh, I have been so stupid. I was grateful that you didn't ask about my parents. Of course, you didn't need to. You probably know more about my father than I do." She leaned her hands onto the back of a chair, trying to steady herself.

"No. Verity, please. You know the rules. I couldn't tell you until I was discharged as his solicitor." His words were genuine. His feelings for her were just as complicated as hers for him.

"My mother is with your client, my uncle." She chewed gently on her lower lip, watching his eyebrows lift towards his hairline. "I only just found out that this has been happening for a while. I don't know if my father is aware, or maybe has been for a while."

"I have no way of knowing." He held his hands out to his sides.

"Thank you for telling me about my father and his instructions. I suspect it was difficult to do." He nodded. "It will take me a while to think about it. Life has recently become considerably more complicated for me; what with my father and my uncle playing silly buggers, and my mother looking for a role in daytime television." Her voice was angry. "You have, however, simplified one element of my life. I can't trust you. Not after that. So, thank you for the flowers, Basti, and goodbye." She held her hand out, and shepherded him into the house, and to the front door.

"Verity. I know you're angry, and with every good reason, but if you would let me say something in my defence?" She pursed her lips and bunched up her eyebrows, but there was also a small nod. "I met you under the wrong circumstances. However, there are two things that are perfect about this. Firstly, you and I have had fun together. I know we did, and secondly, I may be able to help you with your father and uncle. I know them both. Perhaps I could be useful." He tipped his head on one side.

"I will think about it, but Basti, I need to have some time and space to think, and right now, my initial feelings are that you should go away and not come back. Ever." She opened the front door, held it open while he stepped through, and she closed it behind him.

The smell of the flowers followed her around the house. It was lovely, but annoying because he had tricked her with his pretty face and his lovely cheekbones. She had liked him, and now she felt that someone was pulling strings that were out of her sight.

Perhaps that was the thing, to bring everything out into the open. If she had her sisters and their father in the same room, maybe they could sort out whatever the problems were, talk about it like sensible people. Of course, she had no way of contacting her father; and it was likely that Mim and Lola would be furious once they found out that she had met up with him and not told them about it. She swiped her hand across her face and took a cup of tea through to the garden, where she could sit and think again. To keep her mind from going over thoughts of Basti was a challenge.

Picking up her phone, she dialled Mim before she

could think any more. "Hello? Mim?"

"Hi. That was a weird lunch, wasn't it? They tried to tell me all about how happy they are. I had to leave before I threw up. Lola phoned me. She's in a total strop." In the background, Verity could hear the chink of a bottle on a glass.

"Right, well, here's something else for everyone to get cross about. Our father contacted me. I met up with him. There's something strange going on, Mim. Two people have just told me very different versions of why he couldn't come to see us when we were kids. I might be able to contact him. If I could, would you meet him with me? You and Lola?" There was a cough down the line, as though she had choked on her wine.

"Fuck. Lola is going to go totally nuts about this. Actually, you should have told me about it. I am not happy." She sipped and swallowed. It was loud down the line.

"OK. That's fair. If I can contact him, and he agrees, would you go?" Verity waited through the silence while her sister considered it.

"If Lola goes too. I'll go." Mim was curious, although she had no memories of her father. She had listened for her whole life to her big sister telling her about their dad. Verity closed her eyes and thanked the universe.

"Do you fancy giving her a ring and asking her?" The noise that came back down the line was a definite no. "OK, that's me ringing the totally furious sister then. I'll let you know what happens."

Lola's phone went to voicemail. Verity left a long and detailed message about her meeting with their father, a grovelling apology and the hope that she might ring back.

She texted Basti and asked if he had contact details for her father that he would be prepared to share. She had done everything that she could. It was up to them now.

17.

Verity opened her laptop. She ran a search on her father's name, and there it was, all the press coverage of the trial, the sentencing, and the term he had been given.

He had been tried for the murder of Gerry Mulhern. The details were thin, but it seemed that he had died from a heavy blow to the back of the head. A hammer with Mulhern's blood on it had been found in the back of her father's car, and he had no alibi. The evidence had been enough, and he had been convicted. Sentenced to life imprisonment. It gave no release date, but she knew life was generally twelve to fourteen years.

Why would her mother not have told her about this? Perhaps not as a child, she could see that, but later, when she was older. When *they* were older. She could have told them then. It was one of a list of questions she would need to ask.

Her phone beeped. Basti would ask her father if he would consent to his contact details being shared. It was polite. Something about that hurt her more than she wanted to admit to herself.

There was nothing about him more recently, nothing since the trial. Perhaps he had changed his name. Why had he not told her, either? Maybe it had been what they agreed between them, in which case, Jess was lying about it, too. Her head was hurting, and as the afternoon turned into evening, it was becoming cooler. She closed the back door and grabbed her phone on the way upstairs to the bath. Hot water and bubbles would give her some thinking time, and if Lola did phone back, she would hear it.

Her phone rang before she reached the bathroom, but it was a private number, not Lola.

"Basti says you are trying to reach me." She sat on the stairs, just as she had the night he left.

"Yes. I just found out that you went to prison. Why didn't you tell us?" Her voice sounded loud in the quiet of her house.

"I was gone from your mum's by then. I knew that there was going to be a trial, and that if it went against me, then I would go to prison. The man was a scumbag. He owed me money, and he laughed in my face when I asked him for it. I was already angry. Things were bad at home, but that was no excuse. I hit him really hard. I didn't mean to kill him. But that's no excuse. It's just a fact." His voice was quiet. Confessional, maybe. Intentionally?

"With a hammer." She wiped a tear away, trying

to keep her voice from shaking.

"Yes, I should have mentioned that. I hit him with a hammer. I don't remember it, but I must have, because it had his blood on it. It was in my car, and it was my hammer."

"You could have written to us, even from prison." There she was, back at the top of the stairs at her mum's house. She was six again. She was afraid that her daddy was going to let her down again, that she had believed in him for such a long time, and that he was going to make her regret it.

"It was complicated. We made, I made, mistakes. I'm sorry Verity." She could hear the tremor in his voice. She wanted to believe him so much. Each breath in and out was hard for both of them.

"I want to see if I can get Mim and Lola to meet you and me together. Maybe we can work out where to go with this. Or maybe we can't. Either way, this has to be the best chance we have." She swallowed with difficulty. "I don't know if they will agree. This is why I was trying to contact you, to find out if you were up for it."

"I'd love to see them. Of course, I would. Just let Basti know when and where." He sounded pleased, like all his dreams had come true at once.

"You won't trust me with your phone number?" She slapped her palm to her forehead. "You have been missing for years, and I'm offering you a chance to meet your daughters."

"I know, and I'm grateful. Very grateful." There was silence on both sides while they thought about it.

"How did you know I was qualified? Who told you?" There was silence on the other end. "You said that you were so proud when you heard I qualified. Who told you?"

"I stayed in touch with Jess." It was a whisper.

"But not with your daughters." She closed her eyes and watched from the top of her mother's stairs as he walked away. Powerless to stop him, still completely powerless to understand what had happened. "I am trying to work out what happened to my family. My sisters and my cousins have grown up surrounded by lies. Maybe they were well meant, but they have made a nonsense of the whole family. Please, can you just me tell the truth?"

"I am trying, but I have forgotten so much from back then. I blocked out a lot. Prison life is like that. You shut out the memories that hurt, and get your head down, do the day, and the next, and then the next one, until someone tells you to go home. Except there is no home to go to. Everyone has grown up and moved on. I know the guy died, and I totally accept that I had to pay for it. I'm not complaining, just trying to explain how it is." He was trying to explain it. She knew that. "Prison is like one big grey nothing, day after day, interspersed with occasional violence. Each day is the same, from the moment you wake up onwards. It's boring. The only way to get through it is to turn your brain off."

"So, how did you keep in touch with Jess?" It made no sense, but it mattered to her.

"We wrote letters. She wrote every two weeks, told me what was happening with you, and Mim and Lola, and with her boys. I held my breath for the two weeks between each letter. I read each page until the paper was worn through. She sent pictures too, sometimes." She imagined what it would be like if that was all she had in the world. It was bleak.

"Why couldn't you write to me? To us?" She sniffed, fishing for a tissue in her pocket.

"I promised your mum that I would stay away."

18.

The table was booked, the three of them were finally in the cab, and the atmosphere was tense. Verity had explained the conversation with their father, and had left out the connection with Basti, and the dates she had been on with him. She was trying to put the way he had made her feel out of her own thoughts. Discussing it with her sisters would not help. That she thought of him often was something she was trying to keep secret from herself.

They were angry that she had spoken to their father without them. They had missed him too, even though Lola was too young to remember him properly. There was enough nervous energy in the cab to get them to the restaurant without the engine. When the driver pulled into the curb, they piled out onto the pavement, a cloud of expensive perfume on heels.

The restaurant was well lit. They could see him as soon as they opened the door and stepped in.

"Is that him?" Mim's hand snaked through Verity's elbow.

"Wait for me." Lola pushed her hand through Verity's other elbow. The three of them together, they were strong. Were they enough? She did not know.

"Come on. Let's at least have a conversation." She felt Mim's warmth on her arm. It made her a little braver to feel that her sister was relying on her. Lola squeezed her other arm. They were doing this together.

"Thank you so much for coming tonight. I have been so looking forward to this." He stood up as they reached the table. They sat down together and he suggested they order a drink. Verity watched the expressions on her sister's faces. Rabbits caught in the headlights. Their eyes were wide and glassy. She knew they were feeling entirely lost. "I know it's been a long time, but I would really like to get to know you, if you'll let me. It has to be your choice." He smiled across the table at them, a politician's smile. Cracked for the camera. "You all grew up so beautiful." His smile was too practiced.

"Verity says you've been in prison. That you killed someone. That's very scary. I mean, did you just lose it? Are you likely to do it again?" Mim's voice shook a little. She was chewing at her lower lip.

"I hit out because I was having a bad time, not an excuse, but the truth, your mum and me, we were fighting, arguing all the time. The guy owed me money. I went to collect, and he laughed in my face. It was stupid., I just punched out. It wasn't about him, and I was already angry. I wouldn't have reacted that way normally." He took a breath. "That piece of stupidness cost me years of my life, and meant I lost out on any chance of seeing you three grow up. I paid for my mistake." His expression was so genuine, but Verity knew good liars, and she knew she was watching a very good one at work now. Stitch in enough truth to make it believable and sell the lie. She wanted to call him out on the lies, but she was frozen by her hope that he was back, and her loyalty to the man she had loved as a child.

"I don't remember you at all. Verity used to show us photos." Lola turned to look at both her sisters. "Remember, you had them in an old shoe box." Verity nodded. She had wanted them to love him too, and to understand why she missed him so much.

"They were all we had." Verity felt Mim lean into her. Giving support? Taking it? Both maybe. "How long since you came out of prison?"

"It's taken me a little while to get back on my feet. I didn't come to find you straight away. I had to get myself together. It takes a while to get used to being able to decide what to do." He rested his elbows on the table. "I'm back, and I am asking for a chance to get to know you. I hope you will let me." He reached his hands across the table, palm up on the soft table cloth. Verity looked at her sisters. They all three reached across to rest their hands in his. They had missed out on having a father. What did they have to lose by trying?

"We know next to nothing about you. The things that make a family. Like what you like to eat, what you hate. I know more about friends than I do about you." Mim watched him carefully.

"We have to start somewhere, I suppose. Let's order some food, and find out a little more about each other. Is that OK with you?" His smile was warm and his eyes crinkled at the sides. He held on to their hands.

"I could eat." Lola nodded.

"You could always eat." Mim laughed. "It's not fair! If I ate like you, I wouldn't get through the door. You eat like a sumo wrestler and you're thin as a rail." They all smiled. "At least it's not someone's birthday cake."

"Oh my God, I can't believe you said that!" Lola swatted Mim's arm.

"What happened to the birthday cake?" He looked from one daughter to the others.

"It was a long time ago. How old were you, Etty? Nine, maybe?" Verity nodded. "So, the day before the birthday party, the food was all made, the cake was iced. Except I got up early and ate most of the cake. I didn't mean to be unkind. I just like cake." She quirked a smile. They all laughed together.

"Well, we had better order some food quickly, in that case." He held up his finger to attract the attention of the waiter and they all ordered. He looked up to find Verity watching him over the top of her menu. "All ok?" She nodded, but he knew she was still weighing him up. They all were. It was fair. He had been missing for most of their lives. Inevitably, they would not welcome him immediately. He would have to work at it.

Lola ordered a bottle of wine. He spotted a look which passed between her sisters. Perhaps they thought she was drinking too much or had in the past. They were quick to hide it, but he was used to watching people's reactions.

In his head, he pictured Verity as a cat, sleek and very alert to everything around her. He tried to decide whether he was a mouse. Was he waiting for her to pounce? Or was he a worthy adversary prowling around her, weighing up each other's weaknesses and strengths? Mim was instinctive. She was as wary as Verity, but where Verity searched for evidence, Mim felt, she absorbed empathically and reflected the feelings back. Lola was somewhere between. Her temperament was fiery, he felt. She wanted him to prove that he was genuine; she was challenging him.

The food arrived, and it was good. The conversation was stilted, careful; they spoke to him as the stranger that he was. He accepted it would be a slow process.

They ordered pudding after the table was cleared. Verity pushed her nearly full glass of wine away from her. "Are you going to tell us what you have been doing since you left prison?"

"I have been rebuilding myself, my life. I wanted to come back to my family strong, not as a needy, broken ex-convict. It is a cliché, but I am in a good place now. I can be useful to you." He leaned his elbows on the table and leaned towards her. "I want to be able to help you all."

"In what way?" Verity held his stare while she breathed in and out. It was a challenge, as sure as if she had raised a knife above her head and driven it into the table.

"Verity?" Mim's eyes drew together.

She shrugged. "OK. We'll talk about it another day. Let's enjoy the pudding."

"If you have something you want to say, Verity, I would rather you said it, and we can deal with any problems." He spread his hands wide, and she looked at her sisters. They watched her. They looked the way they did when she used to tell them stories as children. She knew they wanted the happy ending. It was too unkind to steal the possibility from them.

"It'll keep." The waitress arrived with plates. "Oh, look, here's the pudding." She directed her attention to the smiling waitress and tried to ignore that her father had no more answered the question she had asked than she had answered his.

19.

"Basti?" She gripped the phone in her hand. "I want to ask you for a little more information. About my father." It felt strange calling him. She had reminded herself to keep it professional.

"You know I can't tell you anything he told me while I was his lawyer." His voice was warm. She closed her eyes, remembering moments and kisses which caught her breath. She stood up abruptly, walking across the living room to the window at the front of the house.

"What about the time when he was asking you to check in on me? What did he want?" Her eyes, reflected in the darkness of the window glass, glared back at her.

"He wanted to know about you, your family, your mother. That was all. The rest was me. I told him nothing about us. Everything I told him was on your LinkedIn profile." He sounded good, and she wanted to trust him.

"OK. So right now, I want you to tell me what he wants from us. He isn't back for a big tearful reunion. He is looking for something. I want to know what it is." She turned away from the window, where the glass reflected her face creased with concern back at her. "Basti. What did he come back for?"

"Verity, he didn't tell me. I know Simon was involved in some way. There was something between them, from years ago. They're both angry about it, and blaming the other for everything. Something went wrong. I don't know any more than that." He huffed out a breath. "That's all I know. The flow of information was mostly one way."

"OK. Thank you, I appreciate your telling me." She closed her eyes. "I am grateful."

"So, are we friends again?" She could hear that he was smiling.

"I am more open to the idea of us being friends than I was." She was smiling too. "I'll be in touch, Basti. Give me a little while to work out what is happening in my family."

"That's fair enough. I'll wait to hear from you." There was a pause while he thought about it. "Look, Verity. If you need to talk or whatever. I'm here. No strings."

"Thank you, I appreciate it." She hit the icon to end the call. The house was so quiet. All she could hear were her own thoughts running around her head.

Her phone rang, snapping her attention back. It was a private number. "Hello?"

"Verity? I need to know when Simon's divorce will be final." She recognized her father's voice.

"When the court issues the paperwork. Not in my hands, I'm afraid." She spread her fingers and raked them through her hair. "Why are you interested?"

"Curious about my friend. That's all. I thought we might have a party to celebrate for them." If he was aiming at relaxed and jovial, he missed.

"Well, unfortunately, I can't help you. The courts are busy. They process at the rate that they work, and Simon's divorce will come through when his application gets to the top of the pile. Why the rush? Simon and Jess don't seem to be jumping up and down about it." She curled her feet up underneath her. Not entirely true, Jess was in a rush.

"You are very like your Mum." She imagined his face, his mouth curling into a smile. As he was when she was little, and as he was now.

"Thank you." She smiled to herself.

"I really didn't mean it as a compliment." He laughed. She heard it huff down the phone.

"I know. Thank you, though." She laughed, despite herself. "Look. Whatever is going on, I am fairly sure that it's not a happy-clappy family reunion that you're after. I will work out what it is that you want. Unless you want to tell me now and save us both some work?"

"I want to be a part of the family, that's all." She could hear him pouring something, maybe a coffee, she thought. "Perhaps I'm wrong, but I thought the meal the other night went well. It's clear that I am a lucky guy. I have three beautiful daughters. It will take time for you to learn to trust me. I understand that, Verity."

"Right, that's very true. Let's see how it goes." She shook her head a little. There was clearly something that she was missing. "OK, well, it's been fun to chat. I have to go." She hung up. He made her feel jumpy, nervous. That in itself was unusual.

Later that night, her mother sent a text to tell her that they were going on holiday. It was a last-minute deal. They would be away for two weeks and hoped to see her when they came home.

She sent a text wishing them a safe journey, asking where they would be going; and when they would leave. It seemed from the reply that it had been a cheap deal, through a friend of Simon's, who had an apartment in Portugal. She closed her eyes and wondered if Simon actually had any friends at all.

The next day was a Saturday, and Verity had planned to walk through the market. Maybe she would meet up with Lola. She liked to shop there too.

She spotted her sister negotiating with a stall holder who sold fabric. Verity weaved through the crowd. She arrived as her sister paid cash for the orange silk.

"Oh my, that is gorgeous. What are you going to do with that?" Verity wrapped an arm around her sister's waist.

"Etty!" Lola ran the silk through her hand. "It's beautiful, isn't it? I don't know, but I couldn't resist it. Are you ready for a little lunch, big sister?" Lola was taller by a few inches. They had always laughed about it.

"Did Mum tell you they are going on holiday tomorrow?" They found a table at the back of the café. The waiter brought menus.

"She said Simon's friend has a place in Portugal. it surprised me we hadn't heard about it before, but maybe it was a last-minute thing." Lola chose a salad, and Verity nodded. She would have the same.

"What did you think of our father the other night?" Verity leaned her elbows on the table. She knew Lola would have an insight to share, one that she could trust.

"He's trying too hard. He has an agenda of his own, I'm sure of that. The whole 'wanting to be in our lives' thing doesn't ring true. Otherwise, why not contact us before? If he was so keen to be our father." She rested her hands on the table in front of her.

"You think he's lying?" Verity raised her eyebrows.

"I think he's telling us what we want to hear. Or what he thinks we want to hear, maybe?" She sat back from the table, taking a breath and considering what she had said. "Some people, who spend a good deal of their time lying, or trying to manipulate other people, tell themselves the story. They start to believe their own bullshit. It's a marker for how far their mental illness has gone. It means they are, for all reasonable purposes, living in la la land. Where they are the mayor, and in charge of traffic control. Our father, as far as I can see, is not only the mayor, but he is building a big house, where we all can live. He is not living in the real world. He is constructing an alternate universe, where he is the good guy, and we are a happy family." The waiter brought their plates, and she smiled, picking up the knife and fork. "Our father is a crazy human. Honestly, he fits right in with the rest of the family." She speared a slice of tomato and popped it into her mouth. "It's a shame. I'm already close to qualifying. He would have made an interesting study case."

Verity nodded and dipped her celery into the

hummus on the side of the plate. Her jaw worked, chewing the crunchy mouthful. "You're right, Lola. There is a lot of crazy in our family." For a moment, tears threatened. It was a strange reaction, and one that surprised her. The image in her head of her dad, her hero, was not as sharp as it had been.

20.

"Mim? Do you still have the key to Mum's house? I left my scarf there the other day, and I wanted to pick it up." Verity scrunched her eyes closed, hoping her sister didn't ask too many questions.

"Yes, I have. You'll have to pick it up from me, though. I am up to my knees in plumbing problems. For some reason it is impossible for me to have hot and cold water at the same time. The backwashes are in. I just need to find a way to not scald or freeze my clients." In the background, there were clanging noises, and someone was swearing.

"OK, sounds like you have things to do. I will pop in on the way home from work. I'd like to see the salon. Is that OK with you?" Verity tapped her pen on the pad in front of her.

"That would be cool. I'd like to show it to you. See you then." The line went dead. Verity imagined her sister, looking perfect and with every single hair in place, scaring the bejesus out of every plumber in north London.

All afternoon, she spent her time speaking to

clients and negotiating divorce settlements. In the back of her head, she thought about her sister, and the keys she would collect, and why she needed to check. It rolled through her thoughts; she had no more control over them than the traffic that rolled past her office. She had spent the last two days trying to stop herself from sinking into the rising panic that swirled around her. Since she could remember, it had been her job to protect her sisters, to keep everyone safe. Her family was her responsibility, and her clients were an extension of that.

She climbed into her car. The car park no longer frightened her. She knew her mother and her sisters, inside out and backwards. She could step into any of their skins and think the way they would in any situation, she was sure of that. The four of them had lived so closely, they had breathed in the air as the others had breathed it out. There had been no money. There had sometimes only been pasta or rice with cheese, but they had been enough for each other, and they had laughed until they had to run to the toilet. They had sung and played and danced through the days. The rules had been clear: school, homework, dinner. Then be as loud, as crazy, as ridiculous as they wanted. They worked hard, and they played harder. Music was played loud in the evenings when she was growing up. All of them sang along, sometimes even with the right words. They danced, and they fought, shouting and screaming sometimes, rolling around, and pulling hair. But what they learned was that they were stronger together. They backed each other up. Her mother was a little unpredictable, but with three daughters and no money, maybe that was just a side effect.

The shop was at the better end of Camden. Trendy, but with style. The rent and the rates must have been eye-watering, but Verity knew Mim. Of all the people in the world, she trusted her sister's ability to make money. Inside, the flooring was down and dark, showing off the chrome and the gleaming mirrors. Verity pushed open the door, smiling. She was proud of her sister. This shop, which was the culmination of years of hard work. Of slogging through late nights and Saturdays, and working Sundays when she had to. Mim spent hours on her feet, always smiling, always making her clients feel special.

"Wow! Mim, this is fabulous." Her sister spun through the space, her hair in a perfect ponytail, her nails lacquered to a high shine. Verity held her arms wide, and Mim walked into the hug.

"What do you think?" If she smiled any wider, she would do permanent damage. "Oh, you have to see the towels. They arrived this morning." She took Verity by the hand and pulled her past the plumbers into the room at the back of the shop. A thick black towel with a white M embroidered on it lay across the back of a chair. "Aren't they wonderful? Of course, they won't last long, but they work with everything else." The smile that lit up her face was tinged with excitement. "I'm so pleased you came down to see it like this. It'll look different once it's full of clients. Are you going to tell me why you really need Mum's keys?"

Wrong-footed by the sharp turn in the conversation, Verity drew in a breath. "I told you I left my scarf there."

"No. Come on. Tell me what's going on." Mim sat down and crossed her legs.

"The thing is, I don't know. I might be completely wrong, but I want to check. Mum and Simon suddenly going on holiday, with no warning, it's not like her. Our father turning up at the same time, wanting to be daddy dearest, makes me wonder if the two things are linked. I just want to have a look around the house, to make sure that he hasn't somehow arranged the holiday to get them out of the house." Mim's eyes snapped wide open. "No, I might be wrong, but there's something strange. He asked someone to find out about me, to look into my life. It's made me feel uncomfortable."

"Why didn't you tell me before?" Mim wrapped her arms around her body.

"Because I don't know for sure. I want to check to put my mind at rest." Verity chewed her lower lip gently.

"OK. Here's the key." She pulled it from her overflowing handbag. "You'll tell me if you find anything, won't you?"

"I will." Mim raised an eyebrow. "I promise."

The plumber pushed his head around the edge of the door. "I think we have sorted it out. Did you want to have a look?" Mim nodded, and she was gone.

Verity wrapped her fingers around the keys and followed them back through the shop, waving to her sister on the way.

The house was twenty minutes away, thirty in the traffic. Outside, the trees were in full leaf, and the road was comfortingly familiar.

The street lights were on, and the pavements were wet from the rain earlier. It was all so exactly as it had been for her whole life.

The lights in the house were off, and the path to the door was in shadow. She took a breath and walked the familiar steps across the pavement. The gate creaked under her hand, just as it always had. The key turned easily in the lock. She stepped inside and turned on the light in the hallway.

She had no idea what she had been expecting to

find, but nothing was out of place. The house was exactly as it should be. She walked through every room. She had been worrying about nothing. In her old bedroom, she sat on the padded ottoman next to the window, where she had sat for hours as a little girl, hoping to see her daddy come home. She closed her eyes, leaning her head against the window frame. An hour later, stiff from sitting still so long, she let herself out of the house and locked the door carefully.

Further down the street, a man in a car, who had sat for as long as she had, watched her go.

21.

The notification from the court arrived on her desk. It was over. The decree was through. She dialled Jess, but it went to voicemail.

"Hi Jess, it's Verity, just to let you know that the decree nisi is through, so in six weeks, the divorce will be final. The court will send you the same paperwork. Speak to you soon. Bye."

The file for Jess's divorce could now move from her current pile to the next one, and once the last notification was given, it would move to the archive. She rested her hand on the folder. Each one represented the end of an era, people who had been unhappy, moving on, maybe the start of something much better. That was what she hoped was true for Jess.

She had sent Mim a text late the night before, to let her know that the house was fine and there was nothing to worry about.

The day ahead held had three meetings to get through, and she was ready, which would give her very little time for anything else.

After the first meeting, she came back to the

office to find a message on her desk from a police detective sergeant. She dialled the number, her brows pushed together and her lower lip trapped between her teeth.

"Hello. I have a message from Detective Sargent Benson to call back. I'm Verity Denton." She sat down and waited.

"Ah, Ms Denton, thank you for calling back. I understand you have been acting for Jessica Winborne in a divorce?" She could hear him checking the names, lifting papers, maybe to confirm that he had their names right.

"Yes. That's right." Verity waited for more information.

"I need to speak to you regarding your client. I understand you will be in meetings for much of the day, but I need to speak to you about this. May I call at your offices?" Verity took a breath, not knowing what the connection could be, but she could not reasonably refuse to see him.

"Of course. I am free for the next twenty minutes, then again at about one. Does that help?" She rested her head back on the chair and took a breath.

"I will be there at one. Thank you." He cut the call, and she shrugged to herself. Perhaps he had some information that would explain what was going on in her family. He might be useful. She tried Jess again, reaching her voicemail but hanging up without leaving a message.

The meeting was predictable, and she tried not to tap her fingers with frustration. They ran over slightly, so that it was just after one, when she showed her client to the door. Verity found a man, who she judged to be in his mid-forties, in a jacket which looked as though he had worn it too often, in reception waiting for her.

"Sorry for the delay. Please come through." She walked through to the office and watched him study everything they passed. He was sharp despite the scruffy edges, and she imagined that there was little he would miss.

She sat behind the desk and watched him sit opposite her. He raised a warrant card, level with his chin. Perhaps he imagined she would compare the picture with his face, or maybe it was a habit.

"You have been acting in a divorce between Mr and Mrs Winborne?" She nodded. "Mrs Winborne was found dead this morning, when her cleaner arrived as usual. Mr Winborne would be our immediate suspect, but he has an alibi. I need to know from you as much as you can tell me."

"Jess is dead?" Verity watched him. Her breathing hitched, her eyes searching his for any clue that this might not be true. "How? How did this happen? She has diabetes. Was it to do with that? I left her a message this morning. Oh. Maybe she was already gone?"

"I realise this is a shock. The post-mortem will tell us more, perhaps, but there were old injuries, as well as new ones. Did she ever tell you that her husband was violent to her?" His eyes were small and bright, entirely focused on her.

"No." He watched her think through the possible answers, raising an eyebrow to push her through the choices. "She did not ever tell me that her husband was violent. However, I saw bruises, she refused to tell me who gave them to her. She hid them." A tear ran down her cheek. "She was my aunt. My mum's sister. I will help you if I can."

"I'm sorry, I would be grateful. If you think of anything else, let me know. I will keep you in the loop. You should probably know that Mr Winborne gave Mrs Denton as his alibi. I am presuming a family member of yours?" She nodded.

"My mother. They are an item, and on holiday. I have been trying to work out what is going on in my family. Everything I hear lately makes me more confused." She shrugged. "If you find anything out, I would like to know." He stood up and held his hand out. She took it in hers and they shook.

"I'll tell you as much as I can. You know the rules." He raised an eyebrow and nodded. Passing her his card, he waved as he walked away. She sank back into the chair and watched him go, running her hands through her hair. Jess was dead, and perhaps Verity could have saved her. Perhaps she should have pushed for an answer, for a reason, before it was too late. She had allowed it to happen. Before she thought about it, she scrolled through the numbers in her phone, finding her cousin, and hitting dial. While the phone rang, she checked the card in her hand.

"Marcus? I am so sorry, I just heard." She heard her voice shake and gripped the armrest on her chair to settle herself.

"Verity, thank you. It means a lot that you called. I need to sort out Jem. He's in a bad way. Can I call you later?" His voice was catching on the words, as though they were rough in his throat. Her favourite cousin, and more than that, a good friend since they were children.

"Of course. Send Jem my love. Take care of you." The phone clicked, and she held hers against her chest, trying not to imagine the pain her cousins were dealing with.

22.

"Verity. Please, will you stop?" Mim poured a glass of wine for each of them. "If she wanted to tell you, she would have. She chose not to. Whatever was happening with Jess, she made a decision. It was not for you to force her to do things your way." Mim grabbed Verity's hands.

"OK. I'm sorry. I just wonder if everything is connected. Our Dad turning up, Mum and Simon, Jess and Simon divorcing, Jess dying. Is it all tied together?" She shrugged, pulling her cardigan closer.

"Could it be?" Mim sipped from her drink, tucking her legs underneath her on the sofa, her head tipped on one side.

"Jess was the only one who stayed in touch with our dad. We already agreed that he didn't come back to be with us; so, it begs the question, what did he come back for?" Verity sipped from her glass and rested back into the cushions on the chair. "Mum and Simon going on holiday out of the blue, too. Is it too convenient, a perfect alibi and all that? Or am I overthinking it?"

"Let's overthink it together. Mum doesn't even own the house, so he can't be back to get anything from her money wise. She had to sell the house, because she was broke. What about Simon? Could he have something our dad wants?" Mim sat up and put her glass on the table. "Do you think Jess was in a relationship with our dad?"

"I thought so, honestly, but now I'm not so sure." She ran her fingers into her hair and gripped her head. "The more I think about it, the less I know." She groaned, deep and low in her throat. "Mim, help me work this out. My brain is fizzing."

"Verity. We need to think this through. What could he be here for?" She pulled her sister's hands to make her pay attention. "You already said nothing had been touched at the house, so what is he here for? Why would he pay someone to find out about you, pretend this whole big family bullshit thing? Lola says he's living in a fantasy world, telling himself stories, but perhaps it's simpler than that. Perhaps he just wants to collect something he left behind."

"Mim, honestly, I think you might be right. He's still around, so he is still looking for whatever it is. Perhaps the man who grabbed me in the car park was trying to make me think Simon was the bad guy, when it was our father? Or perhaps they're as bad as each other. Either way, our mum and Jess were involved at some point, and I don't know if Mum's in danger." She ran her hand across her face. "I feel like there's something really obvious that I'm missing, but I can't see it, and I can't protect us if I don't."

"What the fuck? Somebody grabbed you in a car park? Why did you not tell me?" Mim sprang to her feet.

"It was two minutes. Nothing happened. He just told me to check who lent you the money. It's all sorted out now." She reached for Mim and wrapped her arms around her. "I didn't want to worry you."

"You were always there for us when we were growing up. But Verity, we're adults now. Stop trying to be our big sister. You're working way too hard at it all." Mim wrapped her arms around Verity and held on tight. "We love you, but you drive us nuts sometimes, you know?" They laughed together, and there were some tears too.

Verity pulled out a pad and a pen and started to make notes, detailing everything that she knew and everything that she remembered being told. Much of it could not be proved or might be only someone's opinion. Four pages later, head bent, and fingers wrapped tightly around her pen, she was too wrapped up in what she was doing to see that Mim had gone to find something for them to eat. When she finished, another three pages lay across the table. Mim looked over her shoulder, and together they read through the notes.

"OK, so I think we both agree that Mum going off on holiday with no notice is out of character. Do you remember how far ahead she used to plan when we were kids?" Mim's eyes widened.

"Yes, so maybe this holiday was Simon's idea. He was the one pushing to go so quickly? That's true. Right, so that's why you wanted to go and look at the house. You thought they had gone on holiday to get them out of the way? But perhaps it was nothing to do with that, perhaps it was to give Simon the perfect alibi. He was out of the country." Mim reached across the table and grabbed a handful of peanuts. "So why go through with the divorce? Why put himself through it if he was planning to kill her? That has to make him a suspect."

"This is what I mean. The more ways you look at it, the less sense it makes. I can't help thinking that Mum is either in danger or involved." She worried at the sleeve of her cardigan.

"Mum would never agree to Jess being killed. She's a bit strange, and she can be really annoying, but she has no mean part to her." Mim got up and topped up their glasses.

"OK, so back in the day, Simon and our dad were friends; or they worked together, or perhaps they were just married to two sisters, and put up with each other. We seem to have heard so many accounts of how it was. Did Jess and dad have an affair? Is the thing with Mum and Simon new, or has it been for years? I see what you mean about going in circles. Perhaps we should check the house again. Tomorrow, when the wine has worn off?"

23.

London's lights spread out below him. They twinkled in the darkness. This was what he had wanted. This had been the life he had been building since the day he walked out of the open prison where he had spent the last six months of his sentence. He had spent the time in prison wisely. He had planned and plotted, and so far, everything had worked. There had been setbacks, of course there had. He had imagined this night, when he was lying on the uncomfortable single bed, with the smell of the cheap washing powder making his nose itch.

The day he had spent had been one of the best of his life. Not being able to share his victory with anyone else did nothing to dim it. He lifted a heavy glass, swirling the brandy around, enjoying the warm aroma. He sipped from the glass, turning away from the view. The feeling of the warm brandy slipping down his throat brought a smile to his lips. He took the glass to his bed, and lay down on the soft, sweet smelling, freshly laundered Egyptian cotton covers. He took a breath, pulling in the night, and wallowed in his own success. Hard won, but he was going to enjoy every second.

The lawyer had been useful, but either Verity had seen through him or Basti had grown a conscience alongside his other skills. No interesting or useful information had been coming through from him for a few weeks. He had enjoyed hearing about how ferocious a negotiator she was. That she could be ruthless was no surprise. She was his daughter, more than the other two, who had no memories of him at all. Verity was his girl. She was the only one in that house who had missed him. She had been the only one who had wanted him to stay, and now she spent her professional life tearing families apart.

He closed his eyes, remembering her as a child. She was so honest, so earnest, her huge eyes watching everything, taking in what was going on around her. She had listened to what he said, nodding in the wisdom of childhood, agreeing with everything. How different she was now, sitting back from the table, watching him for clues and looking for lies, checking and double checking everything that he told her.

He had watched the other two look to her for guidance. She was more like their mother than their sister. Perhaps Serena had not been the greatest mum. She had always been a little woolly headed. Not as distracted as he had thought, though. She had surprised him, catching him unawares. He had believed that she had no knowledge of his life outside the house, or cared for that matter. She had known everything though, and he had known then, just as clearly as he knew on that night, that Simon had fed her information. Which was why he had found out too late, that what he had worked for all those years ago; his ticket out, his freedom, had all been stolen from him; by the only woman he had ever trusted. Serena was the only woman he had ever loved.

She had been so beautiful. His golden skinned girl, who had wrapped herself around him, almost from the first day they had met, and had never been away from him. She had whispered that she loved him, told him every day, in words, and in how she cared for him. It had been him who had walked away, safe in the knowledge that she would wait for him with their baby. She had been, until one day, she stopped waiting.

Clearly, it had been his behaviour that had pushed her away. The lies he had told her, the other women, the life he had, which had nothing to do with her. It made the fact that she had given up on them harder to accept, but he had learned to take responsibility. He had learned so many things during his time in prison.

Now that he knew she was out of the house, he would go and look, take his time, search every inch of the place, and find it. She knew it was important, she would have kept it safe because of that. Also, he knew Serena, and she struggled to throw anything away. The house would be full to the rafters, and searching would take time. He might need every minute of the time they were on holiday. Of course, he had delayed the start of the search, because Verity had arrived, just as he had been about to leave his car. He had watched her progress through the house with each light she had turned on and then seen her lean against the window in her old bedroom. He had felt a connection with her then. Both of them sitting through the night watch. He was unsure whether she suspected that he had other motives than he had told her about. Or perhaps she was taking a sentimental visit to the house where she had grown up. He had no way of knowing. He had watched her drive away, and decided to wait. To delay his search, even though his fingers itched to be inside the house, and to find what was his.

The new life that waited for him would be his soon. This night, looking over the city which had been his home, he had spent picking out landmarks across the London skyline. He knew his plan was taking shape, and that he was only a few steps from victory, was a taste of what was to come.

He closed his eyes again, and his breathing

deepened. The night closed in around him, and he drifted, his dreams filled with the little girl he had left behind and the huge eyes watching him from the top of the stairs. His daughter was a grownup, but she was still watching, her eyes just as perceptive. He would have to be very careful, and keep his distance from her, to keep his secrets.

24.

The phone buzzing on his bedside cabinet woke him. Bright sunshine spilled through the wide windows spreading the morning across the bed, and he opened his eyes slowly, against the glare.

The phone was still buzzing. He reached across the pillow for it. "Hello." He listened carefully. "Ten minutes." True to his word, he was ready to leave eight minutes later. Downstairs, Joel waited for him. The engine was running, and he slipped into the passenger seat.

"This meeting shouldn't take too long." Adam turned and watched Joel concentrate on the road. Joel was another useful thing he had found in prison. He paid Joel a percentage, enough to keep him happy and useful. A junior partner in their enterprise. Turning up to meetings with a man built like a small garage usually made things go his way. He hoped this morning would be no different. The truth was that his business was growing, he was making more money than he could spend, and Joel was good at what he did. Having Joel on the payroll meant that none of his customers had to deal with him directly.

As far as buffers went, Joel was the best. To the vast majority of the customers, Joel was the boss, Adam was the original invisible man. This meeting was different. It was going to be the one that paid his way out.

They parked in the street, in a trading estate out of town. The units were poorly maintained, and at least half of them were empty. Joel slung open the car door. Together, they walked to the building and hit the buzzer. The motor on the roller shutter whirred into life, and it began to lift away from the concrete.

Joel held an arm out and moved Adam to the side, away from the entrance. He was right, the people they were meeting were not to be taken lightly. He took the advice and stepped back. When the shutter was halfway up, a man in a pair of skinny jeans and a biker jacket bent double to duck under the roller.

"This door takes forever to open. I'm impatient by nature. It's good to meet you." He raised the cup of coffee he had in his hand in a toast. "You are hard to get a half hour with guys."

"We're busy. That's a good thing. It means that we are in demand. But I am sorry that you had to wait. I hate having customers waiting." Adam pointed at the coffee cup. "Do you have one of those for me?"

"Forgive me. My manners!" The man held out his

hand and led them into the warehouse. Inside there were motorbikes, and, on a table, three holdalls. The man poured a coffee from the pot and passed it over. "A coffee and your cash."

"Excellent coffee." Adam sipped. "Wonderful cash." He ran his fingers through the bundles of cash. They were used notes, just as he had stipulated.

Joel hefted the bag he was carrying onto the table and waited while they tested the product. Smiles ran around the warehouse as though they were catching. Joel grabbed the cash bags, and they were almost at the door when he spoke.

"Oh, by the way. I think you will want to repeat this deal in the future. If I'm right, then you will discuss nothing that happened today with anyone. If I'm wrong, then none of it matters. Should you want to do business again, call Joel." They left, climbing into the car, and driving away slowly.

"They'll sell a lot, I think, and be back for more." Joel's mouth curved into a smile. He nodded slowly to himself. "Another day in paradise."

"Perhaps. Thank you for today, Joel. Let's call into the drop. I have some things to do." Joel took three left turns, then three right turns. When he was sure that there was nobody following them, he drove to the place they called the drop. In a small suburban house, nothing out of the ordinary, the rear room on the ground floor had been made into a vault, complete with pressure sensors, temperature sensors, and triggers around the boundary that set off alarms on both their phones. They opened the door, eye scans, and fingerprints, before dropping off the money. It was not alone. The shelving against the walls was stacked with bags, each zipped and each containing cash.

Adam drove himself to the house where he had last seen Verity. The locks were simple; he slipped the picks into the mechanism and was inside as quickly as if he had a key.

He started in Serena's bedroom. It took time. running his hands through her clothes, checking pockets and drawers. He ran his fingers through her underwear and the cosmetics. Each inch and article was checked, he worked slowly and thoroughly. He searched the bedside cabinets and under the mattress. He crawled under the bed and pulled out the boxes and dusty shoes that were there. Nothing. He felt along the seams of the curtains and climbed up to look on top of the wardrobes. He felt underneath every drawer and shelf. Absolutely nothing.

Checking that he had left everything as he had found it, he moved on to Verity's old bedroom. It seemed that since he had left; it had changed a good deal. Slowly, and with tender care, he searched the room, leaving nothing to chance.

He questioned himself as to whether Serena would have hidden it in the kids' rooms, but he had already run the whole idea several hundred times. He had to search the entire house. No exceptions. His stomach reminded him he had not eaten since the day before. It was time for a break. He looked back from the door. It all looked exactly as he had found it. He let himself out and relocked the door. He would find something to eat, and maybe come back to search some more later. In the car, he stretched his shoulders and searched on his phone for somewhere he would like to eat. He almost missed the car parking two spaces in front of him, until Verity climbed out of the driver's door, and Mim from the passenger side. Slowly, not wanting to draw their attention, Adam slipped down in the seat, grateful that they had pulled up ahead of him and would not need to walk past his car.

25.

Verity slipped the key in, and together they stepped into their mother's house. It felt strange to be there without their mum shouting about something, no smell of dinner cooking, the washing machine not wobbling about. No kettle bubbling. The quiet was unnerving.

They walked through the living room and the dining room, into the kitchen. There was nothing that looked any different. Together, they climbed the stairs. The bathroom was the usual havoc of fragrances, towels, and bottles of bubble bath. Their mum's room looked as though a tornado had hit, but that was normal.

They stepped into the room they had shared as teenagers, where Verity had sat and fallen asleep only two evenings before.

"It all looks the same. I'm glad we came to check. I mean, we would have worried, wouldn't we?" Mim was already turning towards the door.

"No. That's different. These were the other way around when I was here last. The dolls. Remember, yours was called Marietta Pink, because she had the pink dress. Mine was called Molly Bolly Blue, because of the blue dress. They were the other way around on the shelf. I remember, because it made me smile that they were where we used to keep them, yours sitting closest you your bed, and mine too." Verity swallowed. "Someone has been in here since I was here." She reached out for the shelf to steady herself. "Could they have been here when I was here the other night?"

"No. You searched the place. Are you sure the dolls were the other way round?" Mim saw the panic cross her sister's face and stepped across the room to her. "I didn't mean that. Sorry. OK, so someone was in here. Let's check the rest of the house. If they are being so careful to search and put everything back, does that mean what they are looking for is small?"

"Yes, you're right! It must be small. They must have thought they had loads of time, too." Verity sat down on the window seat. "Do you think they're coming back? Maybe they found what they were looking for?"

"Maybe. Oh, you know what we should do?" Mim's face split with a smile.

"Lola-proof the place?" Verity returned the smile.

They spent the next ten minutes, as they used to when they were teenagers; wetting their fingers and sticking hairs across doors, drawer fronts, kitchen units. Lola had never known how they knew where she had been.

"OK, this will tell us that someone has been here, but it won't tell us who." Mim pushed her hair back out of her face. "I can get a camera, but I don't think we will be able to get it fitted today. I had some fitted in the shop. Just in case, by the till, so I can check back if money goes missing, and by the front door and the back door. I'll phone the guy and see if he can fit it for me? We only need one in the hall. That way, we can see who it is."

"Brilliant idea. Oh Mim, thank you. I've felt so much on my own with this." Verity crossed the hallway and wrapped her arms around her sister. "Thank you."

"Don't thank me. We're family, you idiot." Mim swept her handbag up onto her shoulder. "Come on, drop me to the salon on the way home and I'll phone the camera man."

"Mim, one thing. Don't tell Lola what we did." Verity picked up her jacket.

"Never! She'd kill us." Mim laughed, and they let themselves out of the house, locking the door behind them.

They climbed into the car and Verity checked the mirror before she pulled out. She saw nothing that worried her, and nobody she recognised, because he was already gone.

"Mim, what if it's our dad who is searching the house? Is it wrong that there's a part of me that wants it not to be?" She trapped her lower lip between her teeth. Her childhood dreams had become reality, but the possibility of her hero being the villain was shaking her belief system.

"No, not wrong at all. You remember him. I don't have that, so it means nothing to me that he's our dad. I just want to know." She reached across and held Verity's hand. The lights changed to green, and she had to let go so her sister could put the car into gear.

"I missed him so much when he went. You would have been very little, only two, and Lola was newly arrived. I was so lonely. Mum just sat and cried all the time. It was horrible. Jess stopped coming over for a little while. In the end, when she came back, it was such a relief. Mum was such a mess." The traffic was heavy, and they inched forward, following the car in front.

"That's when it started, you being in charge, looking after us all, wasn't it?" Mim swivelled in her seat. "I remember you checking my uniform was all laid out for school before we went to bed every night. You were such a control freak!" She tucked one leg under the other. "It was wrong though. Mum abdicated responsibility, and you took up the slack. We were never late, or unprepared, and that was down to you. I haven't ever said it. Maybe I should have, but thank you for looking after us."

"I suppose it was, but it really wasn't like that. She just wasn't doing it, and I helped. She's always been a little hopeless, but when dad was there, she was better, braver, I don't know, but she was different." Verity inched the car forward. "When he left, I was sitting at the top of the stairs. I watched him go."

"You never told me that." Mim tipped her head to one side.

"We've never really talked about it. He turned to look at me and winked." Mum was crying, and shouting, and a proper mess. "I sat there after the door closed and waited. I thought she would come and put me back in bed. It was cold, but she never came. In the end I went back and tucked myself in." A tear ran down her cheek and she swiped it away. "Stupid to cry about it. Too long ago."

"OK, Verity, I will call the camera guy and beg on bended knee to get him to the house today. We need to know, right?" Mim watched her sister pull herself together. "Right. If you turn left up here, it will take you back to your office. I know you're itching to be working. I can walk to the salon. It's only a little way up, but it will take ages in this traffic." Verity opened her mouth to argue. "No, don't try to look after me. I'm fine, and I will phone you once I have spoken to the guy about the cameras. Love you." She leaned over to kiss her sister and let herself out of the car.

Verity watched her go. She was something else, beautiful, stylish, and unaware that most of the men sitting in traffic were no longer paying attention to their driving.

26.

The Detective Sergeant she had spoken to before phoned before she made it back to her desk. He would like to talk to her again. She was fine with that. Anything that might find out who killed Jess, and why, was perfect for her. The guilt that dogged every moment of the day for her, and gave her no peace at all, worried at the edges of her mind. She had added in a question at the start of each divorce, along with why they wanted to separate, if there were any children, did they own the matrimonial home? She now routinely asked if there had been any violence, intimidation, or any other form or coercion or controlling behaviour.

Her phone buzzed. Mim had worked her magic, and they would fit the cameras that afternoon. She had even thought that someone might be watching the house, and had asked the fitter to leave his van at home, and go to the house in his car. It made her feel a little better, having Mim backing her up.

The police officer arrived. He was red around the eyes, his tie was on, but pulled sideways, and his shirt was crumpled. She would have bet her next cup of tea that he had slept very little in the last few days.

"Do you have any news?" She held out her hand to a chair. "Sorry, can I get you a coffee?" He shook his head and sat down.

"I need to ask you some questions. They might be difficult for you. The post mortem has confirmed some things that we believed, and changed some things that we previously believed, as is the way with these things." He shifted in his seat. "You told me that you saw the bruises, and that she told you that she was in a hurry to get the divorce through. Did she tell you she was under pressure from anyone, or that she needed the money for any particular reason?"

"She said she wanted it over as soon as possible. She showed me the bruises. I assumed that she wanted to get away from Simon, but to be honest, she didn't say that. Later I asked her who had hurt her, and she avoided the question." Verity squeezed her eyes together, wanting to be exact about what she was saying.

"She would have been a rich woman after the divorce?" He looked up from his poised pencil.

"She was already a rich woman. They were a rich couple. She would have been independently wealthy." She wrapped her fingers around her thumbs. "Sorry. I have spent years defending the fact that a woman is entitled to half of the wealth of the couple, because it's hers to start with."

His smile was wry. "My ex-wife agreed with you."

She held her hands up. "Fair enough." She shook her head. "What else did you need to ask?"

"I have to ask you about Adam Denton. Do you know him?" His eyes met hers.

"He's my father." She looked him straight in the eye. "He left when I was six and turned up a few weeks ago. I understand he was in prison. I have no contact details for him. He phones me now and then. I have met up with him twice." She cleared her throat. "I have a way I can leave messages for him. He chooses if he replies."

"Thank you. Can you try to contact him? I would like to speak to him." He tipped his head a little to the side.

"He might not be keen on that, but I will ask." She spread her hands on the desk. "Do you think he's involved?"

"I think he might well be. I just can't work out how." He ran his hand over his face. "He probably won't talk to me, but if you were to find out anything, perhaps you might tell me?"

"I will tell you anything I can." She held his gaze.

"I believe you." He shrugged. "That's unusual for me. I'm generally a very untrusting soul."

"I'm grateful for your confidence." She smiled for the first time since he had arrived. He pushed himself to his feet and was gone. He could have asked her the questions on the phone. It would have saved him time and a trip to her office. She had the impression that he liked to watch people tell him things, to calculate how much of the truth he was being told.

Her phone buzzed. The cameras were fitted and working. The email icon flashed up. She clicked on the link, and three pictures filled her screen. Her mother's hall, kitchen and the stairs.

There were instructions on how to record whatever happened. She followed the instructions and set the cameras to record.

"Mim?" She answered on the third ring. "The cameras are up and working. Well done."

"Thank you, big sister. We have to tell Lola. If we don't, she's going to go entirely ape." There was humour but also a little concern in Mim's voice.

"OK, I'll call her tonight and tell her what we did. She might be alright about it." Verity huffed a laugh.

"Yes, look out of the window. There are some piggies passing by. They're making lazy circles around the tops of the office blocks, along with pigeons and British Airways." Mim's sarcastic tone covered her laughter.

"Fine, I'll talk to her. I promise." She meant it, and she made the call. Lola was, predictably, angry that she had been told after the event. Being the youngest had hammered a wedge of anger and distrust into the cracking chip on her shoulder. It had rotted and festered and grown arms and legs until she could only see everything through that perspective. On this occasion, however, she had been entirely correct in reacting the way she did.

27.

He had watched the house for half an hour, and he was certain that there was nobody inside. The evening was drawing in; the days were ticking away; he needed to finish searching. The road was quiet, and he let himself in without incident. He had been right, there was nobody in the house. For a moment, he stood still in the hallway, listening carefully to the silent house around him. He needed to search the last bedroom upstairs, which took an hour, and the bathroom took longer. Inch by inch, he checked everything. He was starting to give up hope.

He checked the curtains in the upstairs hallway and ran his fingers under the edges of the carpeting down the stairs. Down into the hall again, and into the living room. He nearly jumped out of his own skin when the light went on.

"Hello. Do you want to tell us what you're looking for?" Verity, Mim and Lola sat on the sofa.

"Um. Hello." He had been caught. He knew it, and so did they.

"Hello. We knew the whole 'I want to be your dad' thing was bullshit, but breaking into our mum's house is a step beyond. You owe us some information." Mim's perfect ponytail swung against her shoulder as she spoke.

"I get it. Sorry. Look, you're right, I do want you to be your dad. However, that's not entirely the reason that I came back. There are other things. But among those other things, are you three." He held his hands out, somewhere between placatory and jazz hands.

"So, the other things would be?" Lola crossed her legs and waited.

"I left under a cloud. My relationship with your mum was rubbish. She had been unwell, as I'm sure you know, for a few years. The pills were making her either a zombie or totally distraught, sobbing and terribly depressed. I had no idea what to do. I know things are better now. Doctors understand more about these things, but, back then, they said it was the baby blues, and she should pull herself together. Then they gave her pills."

Verity checked with the others. They had no idea what he was talking about, either. She could tell from the frozen expressions on their faces.

"When did she start taking the pills?" Verity watched his eyes. He was checking the frozen faces, too.

"You have to know, Verity, that none of this was your fault." He lifted his mouth, as though it was a smile, but the whole room knew that this was not even close.

"In what way do you mean?" Mim sat forward.

"We, your mum and I, we were really, truly happy, then life just became more and more complicated. Verity, you were such an easy baby, so self-sufficient, so completely comfortable with life. We had no clue how hard being parents could be." His eyes glazed over, and he leaned against the door.

"So, back to the core question. What are you looking for?" Mim's ponytail slapped heavily against her shoulder.

"I left something behind. When I went away." He sat down on the only spare chair in the room. Strangely, he was surrounded by their mother's stuff, half completed knitting projects which would never be finished, and some random art materials. He perched on the edge of the chair. Verity almost felt sorry for him. Not quite.

"What was it? You have been searching the house for it, meticulously, but presumably without success, as you're still here." Lola rested her elbows on her knees.

"It's a key." He chewed his lip. Verity recognised the behaviour as one of her own.

"A key to what?" Verity waited. They all did.

"It belongs to me. I had to leave it here. You know I spent some time in prison. I had to leave it. If they took me into custody with it in my possession, I would have had to explain what it opened." He tipped his head on one side.

"Like a door key? Or a padlock, what is it?" Lola was up and pacing.

"It was like a door key, but a little smaller." He watched them closely. Mim and Verity looked at each other and then at Lola.

Mim jumped up. "Wait here." She ran from the room, and they listened to the pounding of her heels on the wooden floor in the hall.

"Does she know where it is?" He stood to follow her.

"Sit down. You have been away for a long time. You're a guest in this house, even if you broke in." Lola was pacing. She was between him and the door.

Mim pushed through from the hall. "Would you recognise it, in a pile of keys?" She raised an eyebrow.

"I think so. It had a keyring on it, with a pink pig on it." She held out a bowl filled with keys. His eyes lit up; how could he have been so stupid? Of course, Serena had put the key with her keys. She would not bother to hide it. He wanted to slap himself on the forehead for his own stupidity.

"Take a look." She pushed the bowl across the floor to him. Moving closer to him on her knees. His brows were furrowed in concentration.

His fingers ran through the keys. Picking up and discarding each bunch, checking house keys, the keys for the garage. The keys to a car their mother no longer owned. At the bottom of the bowl, he stopped. "This one, maybe? Yes, look, the little pig has faded, but it's still there. Can you see?" His face split with a smile and satisfaction. He had found the treasure he sought.

His three daughters watched him. "You can't leave with the key. You know that." Mim met his eyes with a glare.

28.

"It's mine." He spread his hands.

"We only have your word for that. Who knows, it might be mum's Auntie Harriet's front door key." Lola stared him down.

"Your mum doesn't have an Auntie Harriet." He smiled. "Look I get it. You're protecting your Mum. It's only right. But this is my key."

"You can have the key when mum gets back, and she can decide if you have it. Skulking in here when Mum's on holiday, sneaking about, it's just wrong. She'll be back in a week. We can discuss it all, like a proper family." Mim laughed, the idea that they were anything like a proper family was ridiculous. "Until then, I will be keeping this." She slipped the key into her pocket.

"I need it now." His voice was harsh, but he dialled it back. "Sorry, it's important to me. It's so that I can finish some things that I have started. I have been working towards this since they released me from prison. Please."

"What does the key open?" Verity had been quiet all the time everyone was talking, but he had watched her eyes, the sharp set of her mouth, and her silent concentration.

"It's a key to a cupboard. I left some things locked away, and I need to fetch them." He shifted in the seat, crossing his legs and arms.

"And now, please, can we have the truth?" She sat forward. "Don't imagine that we believe all the 'I want to be your dad' act. Clearly, you don't need a key to get into anything. I remember you, when I was little, but Mim and Lola have no memories of you. You're a stranger. So, if you want this key, either you had better tell the truth, or wait until mum comes home."

"I can see why you might feel that I'm being underhanded. Truly, I'm not." He met Verity's stare.

"Really? You? Underhanded? No, surely not. You broke into the house, and you have searched each room. You went through everything. It's beyond underhanded, it's creepy." Lola jumped up, unable to sit a moment longer. "Verity used to tell us stories about our daddy, who would come home and everything would be better. We believed it. Of course, we were children then. We are adults now, and we're no longer subject to the stories of childhood." The sarcasm dripped from her words. The breaths she took flared her nostrils, feeding the excess energy she had always had, and keeping her feet marching.

"I deserve that. I accept, I underestimated you three. Perhaps I should have known better. You have my blood." He dropped his eyes. It was a little too studied, too careful.

Verity cleared her throat. "You said mum was on pills, I'm guessing anti-depressants?"

"I think Prozac for a while, and then some other things added in." He studied his shoes. "None of it was your fault. She was always fragile."

"That's not the first time you have told me it was not my fault. Why are you so worried about it?" She wrapped her hands around each other.

"Not worried, but I know you. I recognise how you take responsibility, how you have taken care of your sisters. I know you have been sometimes the only responsible adult in the house, even when you were a child." His eyes locked with hers. "You always looked after her. Even when you were a little tot." He took a breath. "I used to watch you fussing around her. 'Let me help you, Mummy. I can get that for you. It will be OK, don't cry.' You took care of her. In a way, I was jealous of how you were with her. I couldn't do it. You just dived in. No matter what. I think it's what you have been doing ever since. This family is a heavy burden to carry for you." He watched the others turn to her for reassurance. "It was an unfair burden for us to allow you to carry. I am sorry."

"I remember her crying, on and on, but I thought that was when you left. I wasn't aware that she was unwell." Verity blinked her eyes. "Why did she not tell us? Not at the time, but later. She could have told us when we were older." Outrage at being excluded, sitting alongside sadness that her mother had been so ill.

"There must have been a social worker, health visitors, a team put in place to support her with this." Lola reached a hand across to grab Verity's arm. "This would be on your medical records, Etty. On all of ours, that we were at risk. If she was so out of it, then we were in danger." Her hand tightened around her sister's arm. "I know you have always felt you have to be responsible, looking after us. Maybe this is why."

"Right, well, maybe." Verity's breath was coming a little faster. "We're getting away from the point. The key remains with us. You can have it when Mum comes home and confirms that it's yours. I suspect that there is really not much to gain by continuing here. Time to go."

"Verity. You have to listen to me. I'm your dad. I only want the best for you. Please. Let me have the key, and I'll drop it back to you tomorrow." He lifted his mouth. There was something smarmy and untrustworthy about him.

"I'll think about it. Time to go." She crossed the room quickly. He started to push himself up. "No, not you. Nothing to search for, as we have what you're looking for. "Mim, Lola? Let's go." Her tone brooked no discussion. They were on their feet and moving before they had thought about it. She held the door open, and they moved fast. "You can let yourself out. Please lock up when you leave. I'll think about what you said, and leave a message for you with your lawyer, as you don't trust me with your number." She stepped through the door, then popped her head back in. "Night Dad."

He heard the clack of their heels on the floor, and the front door close behind them, and he slammed the palm of his hand onto the arm of the chair. He had been so close.

29.

Verity opened the door of her house and let them all in.

"Tell me how it works, Lola? This is your world." She double locked the door while Mim and Lola sat down. "Do you guys want coffee? Tea? Wine?" They both nodded. "Fine." She poured three glasses of an Italian red that was in the cupboard.

"The thing is, a GP can't just give out anti-depressants to a new mother, with children in the house at risk. Not without putting in place some back up; something to protect the kids. Do you remember there being a social worker?" Lola sipped her wine.

"No, but maybe they wouldn't have told me they were a social worker?" Verity sat on the edge of the sofa. "Would there be a record of it? You said something about it being on our medical records?"

"I'm not sure if that's true. I just wanted to worry him. It should be, theoretically, but medical records are sometimes a little better than others." Lola screwed up her mouth.

"I believed you." Mim's head snapped back to look at her younger sister as though she had never seen her before. "That's quite impressive."

"Patronising." Lola raised her eyebrows.

"Please. Not today." Verity slumped onto the sofa. "Right, I'll speak to the doctor on Monday and see if there is any record. In the meantime, I suggest you stay here tonight, so that we're all together. It's safer. He broke into Mum's house. Who knows? Let's just be a little careful?"

"Do you think he's dangerous?" Mim's head jerked back.

"I don't know what he is, that's the point. He's a stranger. I was maybe lulled into thinking I knew him, but none of us do. He has been out of our lives for such a long time, we have no clue who he is. Let's not forget that Jess is dead, and nobody knows who killed her. I'm just saying that we should be careful." She sipped her wine. It was rich and mellow.

"OK, you're right. Let's be careful. We need somewhere to hide the key in case he turns up. Or lets himself in." Mim pulled the key out of her pocket. "Any ideas?"

"He was really careful in the search at Mum's. He won't have that luxury if he comes here." Lola looked at the key. "He only recognises it because of the pig." Lola shrugged. "Take the pig off and add it to your house keys. He wouldn't know it from any other key."

"Oh my, you are a smarty-pants." Mim quirked a smile.

"Yes. I am. Don't forget it." Lola laughed. It was a joyful burst of sound. The giggle bubbled up through Mim, and fizzed through her, until they were laughing together.

"I won't. But you have to let me change this ridiculous hair you are walking around with." Mim laughed. "When the salon opens, I would like to make you and Etty and Mum, look very lovely, then we can have a party after closing time. What do you think?"

"I think we should definitely do that." Verity held her hand out to her sister. "I should say it more often, but I'm proud of you both. You're very talented people." She tipped her head back against the sofa. "It's time for bed now, though. Come on." She carried her glass to the kitchen worktop.

"Do you remember when Mum used to tuck us all into bed together?" Lola turned in the armchair and looked over the back of the seat.

"Yes. In her bed. I remember." Mim smiled at the memory.

"She didn't seem sad, or zombied. She seemed happy and normal, a bit anxious and worried, but not zoned out. Don't you think?" Lola rested her chin on her hand. "Something about his story stinks."

Verity pulled the bolts across the top and the bottom of the front door, then again at the back door. "Let's get some sleep."

"Let's share your bed." Lola held out her hand. "Like the old days." She smiled, and they climbed the stairs, bone weary from the stresses and strains of the day. "You remember Mum used to tuck the covers around Mim and me, but you were too grown up, far too independent." Lola nudged her with an elbow.

"I'll tell you something." Mim whispered in the darkness. "He doesn't need the key to open a door. He opened the locks at mum's without even trying." Verity pushed the covers away from her face. "It's OK Etty, I know you never liked the covers near your face."

Later, when the lights were out and the sisters slept, Adam sat in the car outside, wishing that he had found the right thing to say to make them understand. The house was so quiet and peaceful. Did they know? Or had Serena been so successful at teaching them the lie, they had no idea what the truth was? Tears ran slowly down his face. He had no right to ask them to plunge into the depths of despair, where he lived, alone except for the pain and guilt.

30.

Joel arrived in the morning with a bag of money and left to deliver more product. Even the huge sums of money he was amassing sparked no interest in him. They were a means to an end. A way of gaining the next foothold.

He dialled the number. "Verity. When does your mum get home from holiday?"

"Monday. Once she is back, we are going to talk to her about everything that has happened, including you breaking into her house and Jess being killed. After that, you can have a conversation with her. Agreed?" He listened to her pouring a coffee, imagined her adding milk.

"How will I know when you have spoken to her?" The urgency in his voice annoyed him. He was better than this. His whole life worked because he kept everything under control.

"Hard for me to tell you. I don't have your number." She took a breath and sipped her coffee. "Call me after seven in the evening and I should have more of an idea."

"Thank you, Verity. I could always count on you."

His voice chimed with something in her. He had always wanted her to be the responsible one, expected it.

"Don't thank me. I'm not doing this for you." She ended the call and carried her coffee to the sofa. A text pinged her phone, and she checked.

"Landing 6.30am Sunday will be home mid-morning. Do you want to come for lunch?" Of course, she had lied to him. She had bought them an extra day before he started hassling. She replied that she would love lunch, not so sure that her mum was going to love what they needed to discuss.

Saturday slipped away, and she spent the evening on the sofa with a book. She checked in with her sisters throughout the evening, but they assured her that all was fine. A growing sense that something terrible was about to happen had lodged under her rib cage, and no amount of self-reassurance would move it.

Sunday lunch was usually something that she dreaded, but on this Sunday, she was almost looking forward to it, hoping for a little clarity, perhaps.

Simon had decided to go and see Marcus and Jem, for which Verity was hugely grateful. The four of them sat around the table, and for once, Mim and Lola were happy to be quiet and let Verity spill out what has happened.

"I suppose my holiday pictures are going to have to wait then." Serena raised an eyebrow. "He was in my house? Going through things. Cheeky bastard." Mim laughed despite the seriousness of the situation. Their mum swore very rarely.

"He said you were on anti-depressants because of post-natal depression. Was that true?" Verity chewed her lower lip. "I wish you had told us you had been through that. We might have been able to help."

"I was on pills for a few weeks. Nothing major. I was just tired mostly. He's blown it up into something it wasn't." She reached for their hands. "I'll talk to him. We'll sort it out." She ran a finger under her eye. "I can't believe Jess is gone." She sniffed. "We fell out a while ago. Stupidness on my part, probably. Stubborn as a donkey, she could be. I loved her, though."

"That's the trouble with bloody sisters." Mim poked Lola.

"Language Jemima." They all hooted with laughter. "God, this is nice. I've missed this, just sitting around with you girls, laughing and chatting. It's been too long." A tear slipped from her eye and she wiped it. "Shall we order take-away, rather than cook?"

……………………..

Verity's phone rang at seven in the morning. "Hello?" She was trying to zip up her skirt at the same time.

"Verity. I need to see Serena."

"I said seven tonight."

"Yes, I know, but she came home yesterday. I don't want to just turn up. So, can you arrange it?" Verity had been caught in the lie. This was why she always told the truth.

"Fine. I'll arrange it. Does tonight suit you? Six o'clock?" He agreed that it would be fine.

She left work and went straight to her mother's house. He was already there. She let herself in and stood in the hallway. In the same way as she had as a child, she left her shoes at the foot of the stairs and moved four steps up. It was too familiar. Her parents talking in the kitchen, voices low, then raised. She sat, tuning into their patterns of speech. Her concentration focused on what they said, and more, how they said it.

"Serena, this is unfair. You kept this a secret. I know we had to, at the start, but they are grown up now." His voice was pleading.

"Easy for you to say. You walked away. I made a life for them. They're fine, they're better than fine. I did that. Not you." What were they keeping from her?

"It wasn't her fault, Serena. She was a child. She should never have been put in that position. That's on us." The silence stretched. "Look, Serena, I need that key. I won't interfere with what you tell her. You know what I think. Jess knew what I thought, too. I won't get in your way. I won't interfere, but I need that key." He was being sensible, sounding responsible.

"You won't interfere. You have a bloody cheek coming in here, after what you did. Don't tell me what to do with my daughters. You weren't here. You didn't do the work, and you don't get to choose what happens. The girls are all perfect, each one of them is successful, balanced, happy. That's what I did, out of the wreckage you left behind. If you want the key, then my instinct is to stop you from having it." The bitterness, the anger that swirled through her words, seeped under the kitchen door, just as she remembered from when she was a child. Verity listened. The gathering dusk wrapped around her in the hallway, while her parents argued on.

"Serena. Please, don't do this. It's on record, they will find it. She said she was going to contact her GP, she can request her medical records. Isn't it better if she finds out from us, rather than from a stranger?" She heard him pull out a chair, scraping it on the floor. "You know she's smart. She will understand why, but she's going to be hurt and upset, but we can at least explain it to her. We owe her that much."

"Adam, no!" It was a wail from an injured animal. "She might not find anything. It might be too long ago." She could hear the desperation in her mother, the fear. "It might just not be there anymore."

A tear escaped from Verity's eye. Slipping over her lower eyelid. She was unaware of it, or the reason for the heavy sadness that settled on her like a blanket.

"That's crazy. Serena, please talk sense. We had to do it. We both knew I was going down, and we also knew that one of us needed to be here for the girls. It was the only way out. Yes, I accept it was hard for you. We made the right decision, though. If she had been able to understand, she would have agreed. She was always so keen to help." Quiet sobs filled the silence.

"What did we do to our babies?" She sobbed. "Our poor little girls. It was us. Both of us."

"Serena. I'm sorry. I know you're hurting. Please see sense. We can explain. I'll tell her it was my decision. Make it clear. Perhaps it will be better for all of us. More honest."

Verity hugged her knees, frozen on the stairs. Her mind raced, pushing her to walk into the kitchen and demand the truth. Whatever that was, it clearly terrified her mother. She released her hands and ran her fingers across the stair carpet. It seemed a huge step to make herself stand up. She took a breath and crossed the hallway. Her hand on the door. It swung away from her, into the kitchen. Her parents both turned towards her. Frozen expressions, caught in the act of planning whether to keep on lying to her. Her breath roared in and out of her lungs, her brain fizzing. She felt a little light-headed and concentrated on breathing.

"You have something to tell me, I think." The whisper forced itself through her lips.

31.

"Verity." He stepped towards her.

"Love. Come in, nice to see you." Verity's mum pulled out a chair and steered her into it. She pushed two cups and a pile of laundry across the table, clearing the space in front of her. "Would you like a cup of tea?"

"No. I would like to know what the actual fuck is going on." Verity pushed her hands through her hair. Her breath was coming in gulps.

"Darling. I know you're upset. You heard me and your dad fighting. You've had a rubbish couple of weeks, with your dad and Jess and everything." Her hands fluttered to her throat, her fingers catching at the neck of her t-shirt.

"No. I sat on the bottom of the stairs and listened to you. I want to know, whatever it is." Verity gripped her hands together. Knuckles white and her teeth locked together.

"Nothing." A glare from Verity stopped the lie that was about to fall from his lips. "It all happened a long time ago. You were two, and we had a baby, a little girl. Her name was Molly.

Your mum was ill. They gave her pills. Like I told you, she was sleepy a lot of the time. It was a horrible time." They both turned at the sound, somewhere between a groan and a whoosh of air.

"Serena!" He reached her as she crumpled. "Come on." Between them, they helped her to a chair.

"Mum." Verity took her mum's hands in her own. "Just tell me. We can make it alright."

"I was so tired. Molly had been ill. I hadn't slept for days. You were both down for your nap. I crawled into bed and that was it. I was out for the count. You woke me up. I don't know how long I was asleep. You were telling me about it. I was still groggy." She dropped her head into her hands. "She was cold. Tiny little thing, in her cot, her skin was cold. I picked her up and cuddled her, trying to keep her warm, trying to get the heat back into her. She was such a pretty little girl. Beautiful. That was the last day I took the pills. It was my fault, my responsibility." Tears flooded her face. Dripped from her chin. Verity stilled, trying to take in what she had been told.

"I had a sister called Molly, and she died. Shit. Why don't I already know this?" She swiped her hands across her face.

"We couldn't tell you. We tried to block out the memories. It was for the best." Adam sat down heavily at the table.

"Why was it for the best?" Verity leaned to the

side so that she could see him.

Serena and Adam shared a look. There was enough energy rushing around the room to make Serena jump up from the chair. "Let's have a cup of tea, then we can all talk about it. Always better with a cup of tea." She had the kettle on before anyone else could move.

"Mum. No." Verity went to her and wrapped her in a hug. "No more. Just come and talk about it."

"Verity, we had no choice. Your dad was looking at a prison term. As it turned out, it was a short one. I was pregnant with Mim when he went in. She was born when he was still away. We both tried. When he came home, but the hurt was too much. Lola was a last hope for us, but she was only a tiny baby, and he had another prison sentence hanging over him, and we knew it would be a long one." Bitterness crept into her voice. "None of you knew by then I was the only one who remembered Molly. If I told you, it would damage you. What was the point?" She closed her eyes. "I did my best. On my own."

"But you kept it a secret from the start." Verity's eyebrows pushed together. "How could you do that?" She bit her lower lip. "How could you deny she existed?"

"You were a tiny child. I was hanging on by my fingernails. We got through the whole thing. Maybe not the right way, but we did it. We held it together. I did." She reached to run her finger down the side of Verity's face. "You and I sat together through the days and nights, and we grew stronger."

"I don't understand. How could you wipe her? How could you steal our sister from us?" Verity grabbed her bag from the table. "I'm going home. I need to think this through. Tomorrow, we will need to talk about this again. No arguments. You owe me the truth, and I will have questions."

32.

Verity checked her phone. The time was nearly three, and she was no closer to sleeping. She had trawled through her mind for memories. Anything that she might have stored. The only thing that nagged at the corners of her mind was a song. Singing a song, sitting on her mum's knee. Her mum was crying. Her hands were wet from trying to wipe the tears.

She closed her eyes, trying to hear the song in her memory. Nothing came. She steadied her breathing and listened to the silence around her. She drifted away and chased the thoughts through her dreams. Snatches of songs hovered at the far limits of her mind.

In the morning, she felt worse. The office was empty. Verity concentrated on working through the pile of folders on her desk and it took an hour. Every one of them was negotiated and the agreed settlements had been filed with the courts. She listed everything that she was waiting for and printed it out.

The senior partner was a good friend, as well as her employer. Her office door was open, but

Verity still knocked. "Hi Janice, do you have a minute?"

"Verity. Come on in. Are you OK?" She was standing behind her desk, sorting through some papers.

"Not really. I have some family stuff that has come up. Everything on my list is dealt with. Just waiting for decisions from the courts. I need to take some time off. I know it's short notice, and I'm sorry." A tear spilled over. "As you know, my aunt died. It's thrown up a few family issues." She watched Janice's face change.

"Verity. Of course. I am so sorry. I think you only took a week last year, so we owe you." She walked around the side of the desk. "Take the time you need. I will make sure your clients are taken care of while you're away. Go." She pointed at the door.

Backing out of the door, she held her hands up. "Thanks Janice. I'm grateful. See you soon."

The house was quiet. Since her life had been turned upside down, she felt less safe in her house, which had always felt like a bolt hole for her before. The ragged pieces of the song she was searching for ran around the edges of her brain. Coffee and more thinking time. Since she was a child, she had looked for time on her own, solitude to think through any problems which life had sent her. This one was bigger than any she had previously had to face. She pulled her shoes on and found her car keys. Imagining that her mum would be waiting for her. She was surprised to find the house empty.

She walked through the rooms, remembering her time in the house as a child, trying to find a single memory of the sister she had lost. She finished up in her old bedroom, with her old dolly, Molly Bolly Blue, on her knee. Her arms wrapped around the doll. Why did she name the doll after her dead sister? Surely her mum would have suggested a different name. "Molly is my dolly." She murmured under her breath. Her fingers wiped imaginary tears from the doll's face. "Don't cry." Her voice was hers, but also from somewhere else.

"Verity, darling? What are you doing here?" Her head snapped up.

"I'm trying to work out why you would let me call my doll after my dead sister." She watched her mother's face, there were flickers around her eyes.

"You were very determined. Nothing changes, I suppose." She laughed, but it was fake.

"I know that this is difficult for you to talk about. I get that it's painful. Please, just talk to me about it. Stop dancing around me." Verity reached out and took her mother's hand.

"Verity, it was a long time ago. Please, can we stop this? I lost my daughter. I told you, I had to put my grief to one side. To be honest, I really don't want to bring up all those feelings now." She sat down on the bed next to Verity. "I didn't want to lose you, and Mim and Lola, when I already lost Molly."

"If we can't tell each other the truth, then what is there to lose?" Verity swung her head so that she could look at her mother squarely in the eye.

"The truth is that I love you all. All four of you, Verity. Please stop this now. Just please, don't rake over all of it." She squeezed her eyes tight shut but not tight enough to stop the tears. Verity wrapped an arm around her and felt the weight of her mother's head on her shoulder. She felt the sobs. She felt the bones, the lack of substance.

A voice in her head whispered. "Don't cry Mummy." It was her voice, but not recently.

"Come on, let's have a cup of tea, and see if we can't sort this out, OK?" Her hands lay on her leg, and her mother's hand lay inside it. It was so familiar. Such a basic, simple way that they had always connected. It had been the other way around. When she was little, her hand was small inside her mother's hand. Now, her hand was the larger, the stronger of the two.

Downstairs, she poured the tea and pushed a cup across the table. "Drink this. You'll feel better." She sipped from her own cup. "I keep remembering things. I don't know if it's right or not, but there's a song. The more I try to remember it, the further away it moves. It's very frustrating." She reached across the table and smiled carefully. Verity took a slow breath in and out. She needed to be calm, If she wante to be at her appointment in less than an hour, and she wanted to leave the house knowing that her mum was calm and alright. Somewhere in her mind, she questioned why it was her responsibility that her mother was alright. However, just as she had several hundred times, she dismissed the thought.

"You were always such a good girl, so helpful, even as a tiny tot. You haven't changed. Nobody does, I suppose." The wistful tone in her voice was out of place, and it made Verity uncomfortable.

"Right, I've got to go. I'll see you soon once I know a little more." Verity pulled her handbag off the back of the chair.

33.

"Verity, please, whilst you are absolutely correct, you are entitled to see your medical records. It can be that seeing things in black and white makes it harder to deal with a death in the family, not easier." The doctor was only a few years older than her, but the patronising tone suggested a longer age gap. She recognised that she was irritating Verity and stopped.

"I know you're doing your job, but I need to know. There is something wrong in my family, and possibly, though not necessarily, it has something to do with why my aunt died. I understand what you have said, and I have taken it on board, but I need to know." Verity kept her voice steady, intent on not sounding emotional or angry.

"Very well. You should know, before I let you have this, that your early childhood notes were made by hand, and later transcribed onto the computer. Doctor's handwriting is proverbially difficult to decipher. We might need to double check anything that doesn't make any sense, OK?" Verity felt that she was being delayed, discouraged.

"May I see the notes, please?" She kept her tone and her gaze level. She watched the decision process move the doctor's eyes from one side to the other, and then to close her eyelids.

"Here you are. I printed off the notes which cover the time from when you were born until you were six. Please take your time. I would like to talk to you after you have read through them." She left the room and Verity opened the folder.

The first three pages were notes of her early life, her weight, a cold, a stomach bug. Nothing that stood out.

Then a chest infection when she was two, and another, a concern about bruises and a fall. Worries about her safety and her sister's. A description of her behaviour, an evaluation and report from a child psychologist. There was not enough information to be sure. Apparently, her ability to differentiate between reality and imaginative play was blurred. There were reports from social workers and health visitors. There was something called a 'family support plan' and later, the decision from the family support team, that following a weekly visit to the house, it was concluded that Molly had died as a result of an accident, over-medication of one parent had led to a lack of supervision.

She read the reports again. Nothing in there said

that they blamed Verity for Molly's death, but it screamed from the paper in her hand. She placed the pages face down on the desk, as though that could stop the information they held leaking out and seeping through her brain. It was clear. She had killed her sister. She was a murderer, a child killer, her baby sister. Her breathing was becoming a little ragged. How had they ever trusted her again? When Mim was born, and Lola?

The pages going forward showed that when Mim had been tiny, there had been additional support for the family, and frequent visits from social workers and health visitors. It was the same for Lola. The authorities had felt that her sisters needed protection from her. It had worked; they had survived her. A tear slid down her cheek, somewhere in her mind she had known. Babies had always frightened her. Too much responsibility, too vulnerable, too delicate. Far too easy to kill.

The doctor arrived back in the room with a cup of tea and a genuine look of concern.

"Verity. Here, drink this, don't think about it for a minute, let it sink in, and we can work out what you want to do next." She sat down and there was silence. Verity picked up the tea and realized that she would be sick if she drank it. It clattered onto the desk, slopping warm tea onto the wood. The tears fell in earnest then, fat, greasy tears which dripped from her chin and her nose. She made no attempt to wipe her face or to stem the flow. Her mouth opened in a silent scream, her breath coming in rasps, her throat dry as sandpaper and just as rough.

She felt a blanket around her, and gentle hands helping her to a couch. They clearly thought that she was having an episode and was dangerous. They were right about the second part.

She pulled the blanket tightly around her, the cold feeling making her shiver. Her teeth chattering. They would make a decision and lock her away if they saw how she was reacting. Every ounce of strength she had was needed to force her eyes to open. She scanned the room and pulled herself together. She needed to get out, into the fresh air, so that she could breathe. The room was too small. Her lungs felt too small to hold the oxygen she needed. Her head hurt as she stood up, gasping to pull in more air, her fingers raking against the neck of her t-shirt.

"It's fine. You're having a panic attack. Understandable. Look at me, Verity, look at me. Take a shallow breath, do it with me. Nothing bad will happen. You're fine. See, the breath is going in and out. In and out. That's it. You're doing fine." Together, they sat on the floor, just breathing, slow, careful breaths.

"I thought you were going to have me

committed." Verity choked and had to pull her concentration back to the breathing.

"You're not dangerous. I am not sure that you ever were. Certainly, at that age, you did not understand what was happening, or of the consequences. Your mum was unwell. The dosage she was given was too high. Her GP wasn't listening to her when she said she was sleepy all the time. It was a mistake. You and your sister were unsupervised. If you hadn't been, it would not have happened. The GP took early retirement, and it was all brushed under the carpet." Verity's eyes snapped to meet hers. "I am not saying I agree with what happened. Things have changed since then. But doctors are human beings too and flawed, tired, stupid. Not an excuse, but true." She took Verity's hands in hers. "Molly would have been safe. The system failed your family. Whatever you take from this, the important thing is that it was not your fault."

"You're not the first one to tell me that." Verity wiped her face and was surprised to find that it was dry. Her hands had stopped shaking, too. "I have to go. I need to deal with this stuff and talk to the rest of my family. Thank you for being so supportive." Verity was back. In control, pulling the pile of papers together. "I will speak to the family. They may want to see the records you hold on them. I have no idea how they will react." She ran her hands through her hair and pulled her bag over her shoulder. Holding it together, she measured her steps, kept them even, and left the doctor alone, hearing the door softly closing with a click behind her.

34.

Verity called her sisters as soon as she was home. She asked them please to come over. Straight away. Immediately. Now. They were there within twenty minutes, bringing hugs and chocolate.

"I've found out a load of stuff, and it's really bad. I need to tell you both about it. We need to talk it through. Then, once we have it straight, we need to talk to Mum about it." She took a steadying breath. They had to know, but telling them would break things inside them. It had broken things in her. "We had a sister. She was two years younger than me, and she died." She watched the two faces she loved most in the world crumple. "Mum was on anti-depressants. It seems likely that Molly died because either mum was out cold, or that I did something that caused her death when we were unsupervised."

She gave them the papers to read and waited in silence while they went through them. On the edge of her seat, watching their faces for any reaction, hardly daring to breathe in case the way they looked at her changed. She had spent her life looking after them, and she had let them down, before they were even born.

"Fuck." Mim crossed the gap between them and wrapped her in a hug. "Dad was telling the truth. She was off her head, totally zombied and she left you and Molly on your own. This is terrible. You must have felt terrible when you found out." Mim's tears wet Verity's t-shirt. "I can't believe we had a sister, and they never told us. I mean, really, what is that about?" Her chin wobbled with more tears on the way.

"Lola?" Verity was watching carefully. "Tell me."

"The lack of supervision of her dosage is one thing, unforgivable obviously, and she was, in a way, a victim of the way the system viewed post-natal depression. But our dad was still there. Why didn't he do anything? He could have looked after you, taken her to the doctor, demanded help. I don't know, leaving her there, alone with two tiny children, doped up to the eyeballs. That's seriously irresponsible." She breathed carefully. Measured, controlled. "You're right Mim, for once. Fuck."

"I thought you might be angry with me. We had a sister, I'm so sorry. I can't even remember her. I killed her, and I remember nothing. Except a song. It's strange, I am only getting little scraps of it just out of reach of my mind. I remember singing it, trying to stop mum crying. I expected it to make her happy, I think." She shook her head. "This makes no sense." She felt her forehead creasing with trying to catch the snatches of song.

"If there are fragments of memory, maybe you can get those back, I don't know, hypnosis or something?" Mim held Verity's hands.

"That's not as crazy as you might think, I mean, there's been loads of research on hypnosis, but there's good evidence that people are very suggestible in that state, and questions which are even a little biased or loaded can prompt answers which are unreliable." Lola stood up and went to the kitchen. She poured three large glasses of wine. "Drink this. If anyone ever needed a glass of wine, it's us."

"You're very calm about this, Lola." Verity tipped her head to one side.

"I'm not. I knew that there was something wrong. What Dad was saying when he wanted the key made no sense, or at least it only made sense if you know what happened behind what he was saying." She looked back at the papers in her hand. "We need to talk to Mum about this and find out the truth. She has lived with the lie for years, she might struggle to tell us the truth, she might have told the lies so often, she believes them herself." She sniffed. "Whatever the truth is, they stole our sister from us. They didn't even let us have the memory. There's a reason why.

People lie to cover things up, to protect others, maybe to be kind. Whatever the reason, it's a way of shutting other people out, and shutting themselves in." She took a breath. "We're going to struggle to get her to let us in to the secret."

"We can only try. I'm going to phone her now and ask her to come over. It will be easier here." Mim scrolled through her phone. She wiped her nose with a tissue in her other hand, her eyes still bright. "Mum. Hi, we need to talk to you. We're all at Verity's house. Just you, no Simon. OK?" There was a pause. Mim watched Verity curl up into a little ball against the sofa cushions, her knees tucked under her chin, and her arms wrapped tightly around them. "No, not tomorrow. We need to talk. Please, come now." She hung up the phone and collected the wine glasses. She put the kettle on. Wine was tempting, but tea would make for a more sensible conversation.

Lola was making notes on a notepad, that was her way of working through things. She made lists; she wrote it down; once she was finished, she checked her notes. Verity would normally have been right next to her, pointing out things she had missed and adding other points of view. Today, she was curled up into the corner of the sofa, as though she would like to disappear. The kettle boiled, and Mim made tea.

"Come on, please have a cup of tea. We need to decide what to say to Mum." Mim put a cup in front of each of them.

"I really don't think we need to say too much. Etty's in a bad way. Mum needs to see the consequences of her behaviour and confront them. We can help her do that, and on the way, find out what we need to know." Mim raised an eyebrow. "I'm not going to tie her to a chair and beat her up, Mim, for goodness' sake. I'm going to help her to come to terms with what has happened and we, as a family, are going to move on." She huffed a sigh. "Of course, that doesn't even start to deal with the issue with Dad and Simon, but one mountain at a time. I suppose." Mim stared at her baby sister, who was quite comfortable with all the madness of the day, and seemed entirely in control.

The doorbell rang, and she went to let their mother in.

35.

"Mim? You've frightened me half to death. Please don't do that, telling me to come here, and then hanging up. I was so worried driving here. Honestly, what were you thinking?" She bustled in, dropping her handbag and her coat on an armchair. She stopped when she saw Verity. Her hands reached out. "Verity? What happened, are you alright? Darling?" Mim stepped in between them.

"Mum. Please sit down. We need to talk this through. What's happened has hurt Verity. I need your help. We all do." Slowly and gently, Mim helped her to the armchair.

"OK, I am going to need you to focus on me, Mum." Lola looked up from her notepad. "We have some questions. There have been lies, we know that. From here on, we need the truth. I know that is going to be hard on you, after all these years. Some of the lies have become the truth for you, and that's fine, because it allowed you to give us all a life. We understand that, Mum. You gave us all a good start. Take a look at us. You did a good job." Lola waited, nodding to their mother, while she looked at Verity. Her eyes and her body closed against the world. "Let's be honest here. Lies have been told, and the fallout has caused damage. To repair the hurt, we need to tell each other the truth."

"I didn't mean to. None of it was on purpose. It just happened, and then, once it was out there, I couldn't take it back. You don't understand." A sob flipped through her. "Don't sit there judging me, Lola. I did what I did. Now I can see it was wrong. I accept that, but I did it to protect my family. I did my best." She wiped tears away.

"We aren't here to judge, just to put it right. Please Mum. Tell me the truth. Let us have what we need to heal. You used to tell us to care for each other, be a family, give each other what we need to be strong. I am asking you please to do that for us." Lola sat back and watched. The silence stretched, and the time ticked.

"Oh, for goodness' sake. What do you want to know?" Her fingers stretched, as though she could feel the truth, and pull it out of the lies.

"Maybe start by reading the paperwork that the doctor gave to Verity? I'm going to make some fresh tea. You read, then you will know what we are going to talk about. OK?" Lola went to the kitchen and left Mim with their mum. She focused on her breathing, filling the kettle, concentrated on being the therapist, not the client. Taking small steps and concentrating, to keep her hands from shaking, she carried the tea to the living room. "Here, drink this. You'll feel better." She rested her hand gently on her mum's shoulder. "Now tell me what happened."

"Verity was such a good baby. She slept through almost from the start. I thought another baby would be the same. Molly was full on, screaming through the night. She barely slept at all. She squalled like a rainstorm. Sometimes she was happy, and it was such a relief. I took her to the doctor. I thought there was something wrong with her. How could she be screaming like that without being in pain, or ill, or something? They gave me pills. Said I needed to calm down." She laughed. "I felt like I was walking on marshmallows. My head was made of cotton wool. I was on another planet. In desperation, I phoned the doctor, told them it was too much, but they said to keep on taking them. I was so tired all the time. I just wanted to sleep." Her eyes closed. "I haven't slept a night through since Molly died. I don't dare."

"It's OK, we just need to know what happened." Lola reached across the space between them, but their mother's eyes remained firmly closed.

"I can't tell you. It's too dreadful. Look at Verity, my darling helpful girl, she doesn't even know the worst of it, and she's already broken." She opened her eyes, focusing on the ceiling, the tears flowing unchecked.

Mim jumped out of the chair as though she had been scalded when the doorbell rang again. Half-way to the door, turning to see both her sisters and her mother watching her. She peered through the spyhole, and her eyes opened wider.

"Dad." She opened the door wider. He stepped inside. When she turned to look at everyone in the room, her eyes were as wide as the door.

"Wow, something happened here. I don't have to have psychic abilities to know that." He laughed a small, tight laugh.

"Adam? Why are you here?" Serena faced him. She pushed herself to her feet, which seemed to take an enormous effort, her hand reaching for the arm of the chair to push herself upright.

"I need that key. I have no idea what you are doing here. If you can just give me the key, I will be out of your hair." He shrugged, showing them his hands, as if they imagined he had something hidden up his sleeve.

"Nothing changes, does it, Adam?" Serena spat from the other side of the room. "You were a selfish bastard then, and nothing is new. It's all about you, isn't it?"

"Serena. Please don't let's rake over the coals again. We have moved on. Life is different now, we're different now." He stepped towards her.

"No!" Her body doubled with the scream. "Look at our daughter." She pointed at Verity. "This is what we did. We had a happy, gentle, caring child, and we hurt her. Our fault. Both of us, Adam."

"Serena, please. You could have told the girls the truth. I told you at the time that she would deal with it fine, if we just made it normal, and explained it. It was you who made a big deal out of it, your secret. I was gone. You decided I could have no contact with my daughters. You chose." He tipped his head on one side. "Now, give me the key." His voice harder, tighter.

"You might have been away, but they are still your girls." Their eyes locked.

"Oh, really?" He lifted his eyebrow.

"Fuck off, Adam." Mim and Lola drew sharp breaths. Swearing from their mother was a new experience.

"I did. Now I'm back. Give me the key and I'm happy to lose myself again." He shook his head. "Small enough price, surely?"

"She's right. You're behaving badly. Please, let's sit down and talk about this. We're a family, a little disjointed, surely, but a family nonetheless." Lola held out a hand, offering him the seat. "Truth is, Verity had your key, and she's not too talkative at the moment, on account of the ridiculous amount of trauma you two have introduced into her life. So, if you want your key, sit down. Help us fix this." She watched as he sat down. "Thank you." She sat down on the arm of Mim's chair. "Right, can you please tell us the truth? Tell us about Molly."

"Molly is my dolly." The voice that seeped from Verity, was not hers. It was childlike, sweet, a song that smelled of childhood. Both of her parents turned to look at her. Serena's face ran with tears.

"No, darling, please don't." She fell to her knees, her hands on Verity's face. "Come back to me, don't hide in there."

"Maybe you can tell us about the song, if you can't talk about Molly." Lola's eyes locked with his. They stared each other down over Serena's head.

"She used to follow Serena around, copying everything. She had a doll when Molly was born, she copied, taking care of the doll the same way. Little nappies, tiny clothes, rocking the doll in her arms, and singing songs like her mum did." His face twisted.

"No, Adam. Let me tell them. Let me do this my way. Please. You owe me that." Serena twisted on her knees.

"I don't care which of you tells us. Please, just tell us." Mim slid to the floor, taking Serena's hands.

"Verity was serious, watching, always. Molly was

like a ball of fire. She screamed and squalled. Verity stood watching her, telling her stories, asking her not to cry." She squeezed her eyes shut and shook her head. "I couldn't cope. Every night, she kept me awake. I couldn't think. I couldn't do anything. The doctors gave me pills. I grabbed them and forced them down my throat. They were hope and the chance to feel like myself again. I could barely keep my eyes open." She dragged a breath in. "I was desperate. I hadn't slept more than two hours at a time for nearly a year. These aren't excuses, they're just the truth. Before you remind me, I know loads of other people went through the same, and worse." She slid down against the sofa. "I had to sleep. Verity went down for a nap, but Molly just wouldn't lie down. She fought me. I had to sleep."

"So, what did you do?" Lola watched. Her face blank of any emotion. No judgement, just an empty space to tell the story to. Her mother shook her head, but she had gone too far. There was nothing to be gained or lost by holding in the last of the story.

"I put a pillow over her face. She slipped away. She was unconscious, I thought. The relief was so enormous. I never meant to hurt her, just I had to have some sleep. I turned around, and Verity was standing watching me, with her dolly cuddled against her." A sob pulled her breath in sharply. "Those huge eyes taking in everything.

I didn't even check Molly, I just sent Verity back to bed, climbed in to my bed, and I slept." She swiped her hand across her face. "It was dark when she woke me. Molly was exactly as I left her, but her face was blue. I killed my baby. I know I did. Not meaning to was no defence. I knew I had done it. I sat on the floor and cried and cried. Then I saw it. I saw Verity on the landing with her dolly. She was singing a song about Molly, putting a pillow over her face." The room was so quiet, the sound of their breathing was loud in the silence. "I couldn't remember clearly what happened. The pills had fuddled my brain. I wasn't thinking clearly." She stopped and wiped her face. Everyone in the room sat back, amazed by what they had heard, except Verity. She sat with her eyes focused somewhere far away. They all took time to soak up what had been said, and what it meant.

"What happened next?" Lola gently rubbed the back of her hands. "Get it out, you'll feel better."

"She climbed on my knee, wiping my face, singing her song, telling me not to cry. We sat on the floor for hours, with a dead baby in the cot beside us, and she sang her songs and told me it would be alright. It was. It was alright." Her voice rose in a cry. "We held everything together. Mim came along. Then you and we were a family. I always thought Molly was close by. I hoped she had forgiven me. Perhaps she had.

I have never been able to think of her clearly or remember what she looked like. She's always been surrounded with fog in my mind."

Mim sat back. The chair creaked with her weight.

"I have a question." They turned to look at her, and she took a breath, her jaw tight. "All this happened. You killed Molly. Slept, traumatised your other daughter, and sat for hours. Where was their father?" She swivelled to look at Adam. "Well? You saw the state she was in, and you left her with two babies. What happened?"

"It's a fair question." Lola turned towards their father.

"Not one I plan on answering." He raised his eyebrow.

"You don't want the key, then?" Mim matched his eyebrow raise with one of her own.

36.

"I have never forgiven myself, or forgotten Molly. The truth is, that I have to take responsibility for what happened. I know most of it was my fault. More so than your mum. I had no clue how to be a father. No idea. I had no memory of my own father. I messed it all up. Terrified by the responsibility, I ran, left my wife and daughters alone far too much. She was sad, angry. I felt trapped, and found places I needed to be, anywhere except where I should have been." He swallowed, rolling his lips over each other. Straightening himself in the chair, he focused his eyes on Lola.

"Molly was not my daughter. I knew it before she was born. The timing was wrong. When she squalled into our lives, she was angry and she had good cause to be. I looked at Verity, her dark wide eyes, so like mine, her thick dark hair. Molly had blonde curls and blue eyes. She was the opposite of my daughter." He dropped his head into his hands. "We argued, for months. It was horrible. We were horrible. In the end, I knew that I had driven her to the edges of madness. Molly knew, I know she did. The more we fought, the more she screamed. I wasn't there that day, because I had to go to court. There was a preliminary hearing. That's where I was." He met Mim's glare. "If you're looking for someone to blame. It's down to me. Your mum stayed and took care of you. You were born when I was in prison. Truthfully, though, I had been absent from the family for a long while before that." His voice shook a little, but he held it together.

"I don't want someone to blame. Is that what you think?" Mim paced the room. "I want to know the truth. We have been told lie after lie all our lives. We had a sister, and we had no idea. This is nuts. How is it you thought that was alright?" She turned on her heel.

"Right, so let's take a minute. We can all have what we want from this. But shouting doesn't help. We need to know the truth so that we can sort all this out." Lola spread her hands out in front of her. "I think we all need to take a little break. Verity needs to drink some water. It might not be a bad idea for all of us." She stood up and went to the kitchen. He followed her, his steps fast and urgent.

"Lola, sorry, but you are not in charge. I have answered your questions. Give me the key, and I'll go." Adam followed her to the kitchen.

"So, who is in charge? Tell me?" She swung

away from the sink, the water slopping over the edge of the glass onto her hand. "Are we going to wait for our mother, who killed her baby, or our father, who looked the other way while it happened? Verity isn't capable because she had to be told today by a doctor that she was suspected of killing her sister. Mim will give you a much harder time than I will. It's your choice. If you want to go, then go. You will leave without the key, though, unless you are prepared to be a father, for possibly the first time in your life." She carried the glass of water through to the sofa and held it while Verity sipped a little. Adam came back and sat down. "Good. Everyone is going to help to sort this out."

"Who was Molly's father?" Lola looked at each of them in turn. Neither of them answered. "Clearly it's important." She held her hands out to both of them. "How can you sit there and tell us that you killed your baby, but you can't tell us who her father was?" Her brows pushed together.

Verity sat up, abruptly. Her hand slapping across her mouth. She ran to the kitchen, Mim following close behind her. They sat and listened while she was sick.

"Mum?" Lola's voice held every bit of anger and frustration she was feeling. "Tell me, please."

"She was Simon's daughter." It was a whisper. "I was lonely, and he was there. Adam was out all hours, and then, when he was there, he was so angry, picking at me all the time. In some ways, Simon took advantage of the situation. He knows he behaved badly. He accepts that. I was worse in some ways, I suppose. I should have tried harder with Adam, but it's hard to try when someone is constantly telling you how stupid you are." The note of petulance was heavy in her voice.

"I was not saying that. I never said that you were stupid." His voice rose in volume and pitch. He threw up his hands and visibly reined in his temper. "I was a bit, I don't know, lost maybe?" He shook his head. "Look, all this belly button gazing is great, but it's not helping us move forward. Your mum had a thing with Simon, and Molly was the result. I should have behaved better, and so should she. We didn't, and a tiny child died. We carry that. It's the guilt that sits in my belly and makes me wish for the chance to put things right. But we can't. Sad as it is. We can't change it." He huffed a sigh. "It's why we tried again. Why we tried to be better, people, parents. We tried. We really did. Which is why Mim and you were born." He shrugged.

Mim walked slowly back to the sofa with Verity. "I have a question." She swished her hair. "If you killed Molly, and you watched and did nothing, why is it that the doctor's notes suggest that Verity killed her?"

37.

Verity watched them all. Their faces were a little out of focus. She was aware that all her family were in the room; and that Lola appeared to have morphed from the artistic flaky wonderful tornado that was her sister into a really sensible therapist. Mim was angry, she could tell from the swishing hair. There was something dangerous about it that reminded her of the noise a rattle snake makes before it sinks venomous fangs into something. It was a warning. Just the same. The thought made her pull her knees in tighter. The idea that something dangerous might slither past bright in her mind.

Lola's hands came into focus. She sat with them folded into each other. It was supposed to look calm, controlled, but Verity could see how much effort it was taking to keep herself in that position.

Her parents sat, mesmerised, like rabbits caught in the headlights of an oncoming car. Or maybe her idea about the snake was closer. They were cornered by something dangerous, and deadly. Shadows around the campfire, closer and closer on each circuit as the fire burns down. By the time the fire was down to embers, the predators would be too close. There was nowhere to run to.

Her stomach contracted, and she ran. Her hand across her mouth. She could feel a gentle hand on her back, smoothing her hair out of her face. Her stomach contracted over and over. Her breath rasping and her chest heaving. Each time she believed she was finished, and would be able to take a normal breath, her stomach contracted again. She had eaten nothing since that morning, so there was nothing to bring up, but her stomach kept on.

"Verity? It's ok. Just breathe, take your time. You had a shock, that's all it is. Nothing changed." She was so tired. She allowed herself to be steered back towards the sofa. All she wanted was to go to bed and sleep. Her eyes snapped open. Somebody had said there was something dangerous in the living room, she remembered that. It could hurt Mim and Lola. What was she thinking, leaving them in there with something like that? She walked slowly back to curl up on her cushions, her eyes searching for the danger, her mind racing, trying to find a way to keep them all safe.

Mim and Lola were taking turns to talk. Their voices seemed far away, and a little muffled. Verity pulled her knees in close. She wished the girls would come and sit on the sofa with her, where she would find it easier to protect them.

She turned her head to look at her mum. Serena looked strange. Her skin was grey. Perhaps she was coming down with a bug. So many of them around. So easy to catch something. Was that the danger? Lola was sitting too close. She could be infected. Her head ached. Panic rippled through her. Was she already carrying the germs? Was she the one putting them at risk? Her breathing hitched. She watched their reactions.

They were saying something, all of them. Saying something that should be kept quiet. "Molly is my dolly. Molly is my dolly." She whispered her song. A reminder. A way to explain something that she had forgotten.

"Not now, darling." Her Mum patted her hand gently.

Mim was shouting. Verity closed her eyes. If she decided against looking. If she chose to look the other way, made herself think about something else. Then it would be fine. They would be safe. A tear slipped down her cheek, because she knew that no matter how good she was at pretending, it was no good. They were all in trouble now. They had ignored the warnings and now the bad, dangerous thing would happen. She squeezed her eyes closed. A part of her brain trying hard to remember what the bad thing was, while the rest of her desperately tried to pretend that nothing was happening.

Lola's voice cut through the others. Hers was clear and strong, not shouting, but taking charge.

"If you won't tell us why Verity's records have her down as the one who killed Molly, then perhaps we need to talk to someone else?" The room took a breath, Verity felt it.

"I'll tell you." That was her dad. She would know his voice anywhere. Perhaps he would help them, maybe he would keep them all safe.

38.

"I came home and found them. Molly was long gone. I phoned the doctor, and they sent an ambulance, and the doctor came, and the police came. The whole house was full of people, asking what had happened." He ran his hand over his face. "It was horrible, all the pettiness, all the fighting, all my wounded pride. I felt like a complete monster. In the middle of it all, Verity was walking around with eyes as big as saucers, looking at all the strangers, freaked because her mum couldn't stop crying." He closed his eyes, as though that could block out the replay of the events in his head. "A policewoman made tea for everyone, and we all sat down. The emergency crew had done everything that they could, and we were left in the living room with our doctor, a social worker and a plain-clothes police officer. Verity was sitting on the floor with her doll. Nobody wanted to say anything. We just sat. Then Verity started singing one of her little songs. Her voice was so clear and innocent. She kept singing, 'Molly is my dolly' and we all watched her, putting the pillow over the doll's face. 'Go to sleep now. Mummy's so tired.' Her tiny hand was pressed hard down on the pillow. We all looked at each other. Nothing was said. The doctor hung his head. He knew he had, at the very least, contributed to what had happened. Serena had told him over and over that she couldn't cope, but he had dismissed her worries. Between them, they accepted it was a horrible accident. We did nothing to correct their decision. Perhaps we should have done." A tear slipped from his eye, and he swiped it with his sleeve.

"You allowed her to take the blame. You threw her under the bus for what you both did?" Mim's eyes opened wide, and her nostrils flared.

"I knew I would be most likely going to prison, and if your Mum was deemed unfit to look after Verity she would go into care. It was a rubbish thing to do. It was, I don't know, the least, worst solution." The sound of quiet sobbing took their attention away from him.

Lola cradled her mother's head while she cried. Her eyes met Mim's, and they both looked at Verity.

"I don't see how you could have done it. I think they also would have looked a little deeper." Her face watched him over the top of Serena's head. "They just accepted the actions of a tiny child? Those could have been taught, manipulated." Lola was outraged. She saw his face fall. "You taught her to do it, to sing the song, and pretend to suffocate the doll. Jesus, you are the worst possible humans." He shook his head to deny it. His mouth worked, but no words came out.

The silence hung between them. Lola was the first to move. She stood up, the speed of her movement taking everyone by surprise. "You need to tell us the rest. This is disgusting. I feel filthy just listening to you." The professional dignity and composure were gone. She was back to the Lola they all knew. "What was Simon's part in all of this, except that he was the father? Was everything that you have ever told us a lie?" Serena knelt up and reached for Lola's hand. "No. No more. Tell us the bloody truth."

Mim watched Verity climb slowly off the sofa and go upstairs. They could hear her rummaging about, and waited until she came downstairs. She handed over a small box to her father.

"What's this?" His head tipped to one side.

"I can't keep it anymore." She walked back to the sofa and curled up. They all watched as he opened the box. The small pendant on a chain glinted in the light.

"I gave this to you before I left." His eyes creased as he ran his finger along the chain. "You kept it safe all this time. Why don't you want it anymore?"

She gave him no answer, her eyes closed against

the intrusion of the room and the people around her.

"I am sorry Verity. Truly sorry." He looked at the pendant in the box, and slipped the lid back on, placing it carefully on the coffee table. "I should go."

39.

"I have to go away for a little while, darling." His heart broke watching her huge eyes. "I will come back. I brought you a very grown-up girl present. You can keep hold of it so that you know I will come back for you."

"Can you take me with you, Daddy?" She climbed onto his knee.

"No darling Verity, they won't let little girls go where I have to be. You look after Mummy and Mim and little Lola, and when I come back, we will have a lovely party together. You can wear your special necklace then." He wrapped his arm around her and swallowed the hurt that was threatening to make him cry. "It's a special necklace for very special girls."

"Girls who keep a secret?" His eyes closed against the dreadful thing he had done to the child he loved. He nodded, because he could not speak.

He knew why she had given it back. She could no longer keep the secret. The burden was too much.

The room watched the emotions from the

memory flit across his face. They were right, he was a monster. He had caused all of this because he had been too stupid and too frightened to behave properly.

"Where is Molly? I mean, where is she buried?" Mim's brows squeezed together.

"In Hendon." Their mother's voice was wistful. "It was bright sunshine the day we buried her. Even the weather was against us. I remember Verity skipping along the little roadway. After it was over, she asked why the box had to go in the ground, and we told her it was to remember Molly. I think she said Molly would like that, because she liked the park. Then we decided not to talk about Molly anymore. Now and then Verity asked about her, and I just shut her down. It was the only way I could cope. I was off the pills by then, and the full realisation of what I had done hit me. The grief, the loss, the guilt. All of it. I tucked it all away in the back of my mind. It was the only way to get through the days." She wiped her tears. "Lola darling, don't look like that. I know what I did was wrong. What I allowed people to think of Verity." She took a breath. "When Mim was born, the social workers and the health visitors came back, watching, reminding Verity to be very careful of her sister, not to hurt her. It was me they should have reminded. It was all me." Her shoulders slumped, defeated.

"Does she have a gravestone?" Mim ran her hands through her hair.

"A small cross." It has her name on and the dates.

"Right, so we have to go and see her tomorrow, I think." Mim paced the floor. "The other thing I need to know." She turned to her mother, waiting until their eyes met. "How many times had you done it before, because you had. You said you thought she was unconscious, so you had done it before, to knock her out. Maybe you just stopped her breathing a little too long that time?"

"Oh, Mim." Lola sank into a chair. "You're right. She did say that. Oh. For fuck's sake."

It was a heavy silence that sank between them. An acknowledgement of the terrible things that had been done. None of them could truly judge any of the others. They understood that the decisions had not been made in the clear light of day with a fully functioning brain. It was hard to imagine, none of them had been in that position. Yet it was such a dreadful act, that they could not compute the person that they knew and the act that they had been talking about. They could not knit them together.

"It wasn't the first time. You're right. I could have hurt her before that. It was only luck that I hadn't. She'd had a chest infection. Perhaps that contributed. Perhaps you're right, I might have held the pillow there too long. I don't know. I just don't know. If you think I have not asked myself these questions over and over, you're wrong. If you think you blame me, hate me, are angry with me, all of that, you can't be as angry as I am, or hate me as much as I do." She took a breath. "You're all grown up now. I can go to the Police and tell them what happened, get it all sorted out. I think that's the best thing."

"Hang on. Serena, how does that help?" He shook his head. "It won't bring back Molly. Look, do what you want to do. I'll get out of your hair. Please, can I just have my key?"

"Fuck off." Mim turned on him. "No. You selfish bastard. You should sit down and shut up." He folded into the chair.

"So why kill Jess?" Verity sat up and fixed her eyes on her father.

"No, no, no. You're not putting that on me. Nothing to do with me. I've done some stuff I'm not proud of, but I would never have hurt Jess. You have to believe me about that." He held his hands out in front of him.

"Clearly, we do not have to believe you. Perhaps we shouldn't." Verity was back. Mim and Lola breathed a little easier. She had always been the one they looked to for reassurance and strength. Seeing her retreat into shock was frightening. "Either way, whether or not you are telling the truth, we need to know why Jess was killed. I imagine the first thing you need to tell us is where Simon fits into all this." She watched his face and took the hand that Lola offered. Verity sat back and waited for his response.

40.

"Simon and Jess met at our wedding. Jess was a bridesmaid, and Simon was staying with some friends of Granny's so we said for him to come along. They danced all night and when the party was over, he took her home. He was obsessed with her. Before she had really thought it through, he had bulldozed her into engagement, and six months later they were married. He was successful, building his business. She was swept along with it all." Adam looked up and met four pairs of eyes. "He was aggressive, in business, and at home. What I told you was true. He was beating her up, to start with, he was sorry afterwards, but the more violent he became, the less sorry he was." He swallowed.

Serena straightened her shirt. "It was more than that. To start with, we were close. Jess and me. They used to come over, and we used to go to them. Then Simon started to make money. He was too focused, and she was lonely. They moved into a bigger place, and she rattled around in it. She made herself feel better by putting me down. I think, looking back now, that she was just unhappy." She looked at her daughters. "Verity was born, and Jess rushed out to buy little dresses. Marcus was born a year later. We had something in common again. Then one day I had a call from Simon, saying that he had caught Jess and your dad together. He was so angry. I came home, and we all argued. Blamed each other, I suppose." She shrugged. It was a half-hearted motion. "I don't know for sure what happened. I do know that I was so sad. Everyone went home, and I sat in the kitchen. I was so hurt. I just cried and cried. The next day I heard your dad had been arrested, and part of me was glad. Not a very nice part of me. Simon came over to see me. As you know, Molly was born, and it was very obvious that she was Simon's daughter. Jem was born not long after, and everyone could see that he was not Simon's. It was a mess." She pushed her hands through her hair. "We all behaved badly. I know that. Granny was furious. She came to see me and told me what she thought." Her face fell at the memory. "Jess and Simon came to an agreement to keep their family together, and I suppose we did too." She watched their faces for a moment. "We patched it up. We're family, after all, but it was never the same."

The room was heavy with exhaustion. This disjointed, broken family was doing its best, and failing. Verity watched her mother. She was drowning, and all of them were watching her.

She shook herself.

"Mum, stop. Just for a minute." Verity held her mother's hands. "It's not about blame. Please stop. OK?" She nodded until her mother nodded with her. "We need to go forward, find out how to fix where we are now. OK?" They kept nodding at each other.

They all took a breath, the whole family breathing in and breathing out. The day had been difficult, the time they had spent apart had pulled them in different directions, and coming back together made them spiky. Their father was a stranger, but their closest relation. He was clearly a criminal, back when they were small children, and perhaps now too. There was a shadowy part of him that was hidden from them. It being hidden made it no less visible. In some ways, the fact that he felt he had to hide things from them was more worrying than anything else. The feeling that there was more to come. The menace of it, hanging over them, was enormous, and filled the room, wrapping itself around them, like fog on an Autumn morning. He was unaffected by it. He was used to standing in the shadows, used to keeping everything hidden.

Their mother had surrounded herself in swirls of pink and happiness, pushing her pain and guilt down into the black hidden centre of her heart. She had looked after her daughters, never sleeping properly again, in case she might miss something. Never allowing herself to completely relax. The resulting anxiety, and the tension had stripped back her body, stealing her rounded curves, replacing them with sharp corners and angles.

Verity considered her parents, and those things that they had in common. They had been weak; behaved badly. The results had been horrific, and had caused catastrophic damage to their relationship with each other, and with their surviving children.

Verity's eyelids drooped. She had very little energy left and needed to focus. Letting her father leave, giving him the key that he wanted, would end the conversation, and it was so tempting. It would be a relief for it to be over. She knew it might mean that he was gone for good. The breath she took slowly could easily have been followed by another, and another, drifting into a deep dreamless sleep. Tempting, but not possible. She shook her head, trying to clear the cotton wool feeling that was dragging her down.

"I need coffee. Mim, help me make it. Lola, we all need to find some energy from somewhere. If this is going to carry on, or I will go to sleep. Come on. Sit at the table. The sofas are too comfortable." She pushed herself to her feet, and Mim joined her in the kitchen. They made strong coffee, and carried the cups back in. Lola and their parents had moved to the dining table, and Mim put a cup in front of each of them.

"OK. I know that somebody was hurting Jess. She showed me the bruises. She covered them with make-up, but it was bad. I should have told somebody." She sipped her coffee. "If it was anyone but Jess, I would have pressured her to leave the house, arranged a safe place for her, pushed her to report the assault, all of that, and more. I was too quick to accept her assurance that she was safe, that she was in control, which, as it transpires, she was not. My mistake." She sucked in a breath and placed her hands flat on the table. "I want to know everything that any of you know about who was hurting Jess."

"It's nearly half-past two, Verity. Perhaps we would be better to look at this tomorrow?" Adam reached across towards her.

"Really? Do you think? Maybe we should wait another twenty years until we get to all the shitty stuff this family has done to itself. I think we have done enough hiding and burying, don't you?" She spat the words at him, and he flinched, holding up his hands to ward off any further attack. "The least, the very fucking least, that you owe me, is the truth." The silence that met her words was, if not agreement, at least no argument.

41.

"I know that when Jem was born, Simon was beyond angry. He beat her through to the next week. Jem was nothing like Marcus. He knew, and worse, everyone else knew. The humiliation was what he couldn't get past. Jess turned up at the house with the kids a couple of times. She couldn't go to the police. He had too many fingers in too many pies. It would risk everything, and he would never forgive that level of betrayal." He shook his head. The memories were hard to think, harder to say out loud. "In the end, he agreed that she would move back in, and they would live separately. Outside the house, and in front of the kids, they were the perfect couple. They were like strangers, though." Adam shook his head. "Simon and I have that in common, I suppose, too proud, too stupid, to see the bigger picture."

"And lately? The divorce? That changed things. Maybe let loose some old feelings?" Verity sat forward.

"No, I think they both wanted it. They both wanted to be away from each other. He wanted to have control still. I know they argued over that, but he gave in, agreed to sell everything, split it down the middle. She hadn't gone after the business. She'd done as she had promised. Kept his secrets." He hung his head. "There's no love lost between me and Simon, but I don't believe he did it."

"I tried to speak to Marcus a few times, but he's not at work, and his phone goes to voicemail. Last time we talked, he said he was looking after Jem. Mum, has Simon spoken to either of them?" Verity held her mum's hands.

"Last week, I think. He got through to Marcus, but mostly it's voicemail, like you said." Serena's hand was worrying at the end of her sleeve.

"Who was Jem's Father?" Mim's fingers ran through the ends of her hair,

"I wasn't, if that's what you meant. I loved Jess as a friend. We had a brief thing, but it wasn't really us, and the timing was out by a long way." He closed his eyes.

"I need to sleep. Don't know about the rest of you. To be honest, I can barely keep my eyes open. I think Mim's right. We should all go together to see where Molly is tomorrow morning. I suggest we meet here and go as a family." She turned to catch her mother's eye. "OK?" Everyone was nodding. Whether it was agreement or exhaustion, she no longer cared.

"Once we have done that. We'll decide what to do next. Alright with everyone? Just to be clear, I won't give you the key until this is resolved, Dad." She pushed herself up from the table. "It's hidden. Nowhere here. So don't bother looking." She spread her hands wide. "Feel free to sleep here if you would like to." She climbed the stairs, each step a mammoth effort that she knew would be worthwhile when she could crawl between the sheets. Soft voices rolled up the stairs towards her, but they were far away.

She slid between the sheets, every muscle and joint aching and her mind screaming. She folded back the top cover carefully, as she had for as long as she could remember, before she lay down to sleep. Her hand rested on the soft cotton for a second, and she watched her hand while she breathed in and out again. While she thought through what she was seeing, from a new angle. She pushed her feet over the edge of the bed and pulled her dressing gown around herself.

She was at the top of the stairs before she had thought any more about it. Her mother was standing at the front door, with her hand on the lock, when she reached the bottom of the stairs.

"Why? I want to know why. Mum, every single night of my life, I want to know why I push the covers down, folding them away from me. I always have, for as long as I remember. My medical history said I had a few chest infections.

You said Molly did too." She tugged her dressing gown tighter around her body, then ran her hand through her hair. "You did it to me too, didn't you? You put a pillow over my face. It was only by chance that it was Molly, not me, who died." The room was silent. Verity and her mother were locked together, despite the distance. "Tell me I'm wrong." Her whisper was loud enough to be a shout.

She watched, they all did, as Serena slid down the wall, landing on the floor, her knees bent in front of her. Her sobs filled the silence.

"I'm right. I am, aren't I?" Verity slumped onto the stairs. "Fuck."

"I'm so sorry. I never meant to hurt anyone." Serena buried her face in her hands.

"Sorry, really doesn't cut it. Not anymore." Verity turned and pulled herself back upstairs. Whatever happened in her living room, she had no further energy to give. Her steps were slow, and she slipped and faltered a few times, but the sheets and covers were waiting for her. The sleep she slipped into was based on her exhaustion and filled with sad dreams about a tiny child sleeping too long.

42.

Mim and Lola had taken a sofa each. Verity needed tea. The kettle boiled, and she made three cups, weak for her, strong for Lola, middle ground for Mim. She carried them through.

"Tea." She announced. They woke slowly and reached for the cups before they were sitting up. Ordinarily, she might have reminded them not to spill, but not today.

They drank. The warmth filling them with a little hope and energy.

"Right. So last night was a bit mad." Verity placed her mug carefully on the table. "I suggest we have some breakfast and then we go to Hendon. If it's OK with you, I really don't want to see either of our parents today. I really can't get into that level of bollocks again." They both nodded and sipped. The previous day had been exhausting. They all needed a break from it, and though visiting their dead sister's grave could hardly be thought of as a fun day out, it offered the possibility of some closure. Verity threw bread into the toaster and they nibbled the edges. "We also need to push harder to get hold of Marcus. Something is going on there, otherwise why wouldn't he take our calls? Perhaps he knows more than we do." Mim raised an eyebrow, but said nothing.

Once they were in the car, it only took half an hour to reach the cemetery and then to find the office. The lady behind the desk was quiet and helpful, and quickly found Molly's grave, providing them with a reference number and a map to help them locate it.

They were quiet. Calm and peaceful, walking through the graves, lined up. Hundreds of people, who's lives had been happy or sad, or maybe just boring, but who were now all allocated a reference and a mark on the map, just like their sister. They linked arms, supporting each other through the sadness. The pain of what they had discovered and the loss of the sister who had slipped through life, leaving no memories, settled heavily on them.

"It's near here, I think." Mim pointed to the map. "Maybe in that section there?" She pointed away from the path. They would have to walk between the graves to reach it. The grass was longer, it was a little wilder than the manicured area they had walked through before. "This one? No, the next one." Mim leaned down and pushed some wildflowers out of the way so that she could see the small cross. It had slipped a little to one side, but the name was clear: Molly Denton.

"I think the wildflowers are nicer than all that tidy, clipped grass and arrangements." Verity's voice caught on the words, as though they carried spikes. "I'm sorry Molly. So sorry." Her whisper brought Mim and Lola to her side.

"You have nothing to apologise for, Verity." Lola slipped her hand into her big sister's.

"I should have at least remembered her. Not let her drift away, as though she never existed. I will always feel bad about that. I know, I know, I didn't kill her, couldn't have stopped Mum, couldn't have made Dad pay attention, but I could have remembered her." Mim wrapped an arm around her and pulled Lola in with her other arm. She hugged them tightly.

"I know we fight and argue, and sometimes I can be a bit prickly, but I promise I will try to be a better sister." Mim kissed them both on the cheek. "Oh shit. We have company."

They all turned to find their parents standing on the path, watching them.

"Time to go." Verity turned away from the grave and walked past both of them.

"Verity? Please, can we talk to you?" Her mother's plaintive tone stopped her progress.

"You had the chance to do that last night, I think. Do you have anything further to tell us?" Verity's tone was cold and hard as an ice cube in her mouth. "Tell us now if there is anything more."

"I wanted to tell you how sorry I am. How dreadful I feel. That I know it was wrong, all of it. I get that now." She reached out a hand to her daughters.

"I meant anything about Aunt Jess, why she died." Verity's eyes stung with tears. She swallowed hard to keep everything together.

"No. I don't think so. Of course, I should have told you before. I was just trying to protect you. Last night I had no sleep at all. I think we all feel dreadful. Why don't we sit down and talk about it?" She smiled, hopeful that she knew her daughters well enough to resolve the problem.

"I am too angry and hurt to deal with your problems at the moment. You will, for the first time ever, have to deal with them yourself. Oh, and incidentally, blaming me for a murder you committed is not protecting me. I think you'll find." She turned away. Her eyes were still stinging, and the tears were coming thick and fast.

"It was not murder. I did not...." Whatever else her mother had to say, Verity heard none of it, because she was too far away, and getting further away with every stride she took. Mim and Lola followed behind her and they reached Verity's car together.

"Sorry. You don't have to come with me. If

you want to talk to them, it's fine. Right now, I'm going to find Marcus. I know he's hiding something, and we are his cousins, so he can stop bloody giving us the brush off, and speak to us." Verity dug in her pocket for a tissue, and wiped her eyes.

"Can I come too? I want to see Marcus." Lola said, her hand on the car door.

"Absolutely." Mim nodded. "Me too."

Verity took a breath and opened the car. They left before their parents were back at the car park.

43.

"Marcus! Please open the door. We need to talk to you." Verity banged on the shiny black paint. The house was in the middle of a terrace in west London. "Marcus. Please open the door. I need your help." She pulled her phone out of her pocket and dialled his mobile. They could hear it ringing inside. "For goodness' sake, I can hear your phone. I know you're there. Don't make me phone the police and tell them I am worried for your safety."

The door opened a crack. Verity was eye to eye with her cousin. Usually witty, urbane, and beautifully dressed, she was shocked to find him unshaven and unkept.

"Marcus? Can we come in, please? We need to talk to you." He shook his head and kept his body against the door.

"Please go away. Jem's not coping. I am trying my best to sort everything out and grieve for my mother. I know you mean well, but I really need to be left alone with my brother to come to terms with what has happened. Please stop phoning. It's not helping." He moved the door a little closer to the frame.

"Marcus. I know this is a really rubbish time for you. I just want to help. We always helped each other when we were kids. We were always there for each other. Please. Please, let me help you." Verity rested her hand on the frame. He took a breath and gave in, stepping back from the door.

"Is Jem here?" Mim put her arm around Marcus, her face tilted up to his.

"He's asleep. He's been in a terrible state. I couldn't bear to lose him, too." He ran his hands through his hair.

"You need to sleep. We'll sit with Jem, take turns with you, that way we all come out of it in one piece. OK?" Verity saw he was about to argue. "You would be doing me a huge favour. I'm trying to avoid my parents at the moment." She reached across and held his hand. "We can do it together." Whether he gave in because he was so exhausted or because he genuinely thought it was a good idea, none of them knew, but he did. He agreed to go and sleep once he had extracted a promise that one of them would sit in the spare bedroom with Jem while he slept.

Every hour they swapped places, keeping their promise, and at the same time giving each other a rest. Marcus slept through the rest of the day and into the late night, when he woke, bleary and grateful. Lola slipped into his bed and slept, leaving the others to keep watch.

"He tried to take pills. I caught him, but I think he swallowed a couple. It's probably why he's slept so long." He sipped from the coffee Verity put in front of him. "I should warn you that he's pretty angry at you for acting in the divorce. That makes no sense, I know." He held his hands up. "He was angry with Mum and Dad, too. The last time he spoke to her, they had a fight. He can't forgive himself. He said some terrible things." They sat together. The silence was comfortable, and he looked a little less grey.

Mim arrived back from the shops with bags full of bread, eggs, cans of soup and beans. It was comfort food, and it would keep them going. She made toast and put it in front of Marcus. "Eat. You need to have something in your stomach except coffee." He nodded and took a slice. After an hour, he was struggling to keep his eyes open. He lay down on the sofa and Verity covered him with a throw and watched him sleep.

Jem wandered into the kitchen, a little before three thirty. It surprised him to find his cousins in the living room, but they were expecting that.

"Hi Jem. I was just about to make some tea and toast. Will you join me?" Mim wrapped a hug around him, and Verity watched as his head drooped onto her shoulder, and she held him while he cried. Mim had always been better than she had at this sort of thing, the gentle, supportive, hugging sort of thing. Together, they stood in the kitchen. Jem had always been a little fragile. They had learned to take care of him, to protect him from the harshest things in the world.

Verity put a plate of toast on the table and watched him eat it. She made drinks for everyone, and they all sat down together at the breakfast bar. Marcus was snoring loudly on the sofa.

"I don't deserve all this. Marcus has been so kind to me, and you. I did something dreadful. I said horrible things to my mum and my dad. Truthfully, I've been a complete brat." He shrugged. "Nothing new there, right?"

"We all have arguments. Auntie Jess was always the first one to say that everyone makes mistakes, loses their temper. She would have forgiven you. Just as you would have forgiven her, if there had been time." Verity covered his hand gently. "We're here because we're family. We love you Jem." He nodded, and sipped his hot chocolate.

Verity checked her phone just before she fell into bed at a little after nine in the morning. Mim was already breathing slow, deep breaths. There were messages from her mum and dad. She read a couple. Apologies from her mum and requests for the key from her dad. Her eyes stung with lack of sleep, and she was glad to slip herself into the bed next to Mim.

She closed her eyes and thought her way through the conversations she had held with her cousin while they sat together in the kitchen. His face pulled tight with grief, his eyes red rimmed, and his hands tight with anxiety. She had rested her arm around his shoulders, as he went over and over the last conversation he had with his mother. His guilt eating away at his conscience. She had convinced him to take his pills after a long discussion, and he had been able to relax enough to sleep. Marcus had agreed with Verity that the only way forward was for him to speak to the doctor to see if there was anything that could be done to help his brother.

They had all watched, helpless to slow Jem's spiral downwards, fuelled by anxiety and his guilt. Nothing they said or did made any difference. It seemed he could not hear their kindness or their pleas.

"The medication makes less difference every day. I had hoped we would be able to calm him enough, help him through it, but I need to get the doctor involved." Marcus ran his hand through his hair. "Verity, I am so far out of my depth, I have no clue whether I am helping him or making it worse." She had wrapped him in a hug, feeling his fear for his brother, and for all of them. Verity had told him nothing about what they had discovered from her parents. He had enough to deal with.

They sat together and waited for the doctor to arrive. The receptionist had promised the doctor would attend within the hour. It had taken three, and although he was apologetic when he arrived, he was clearly distracted and overloaded.

He spoke to Jem for ten minutes, and Verity had to admit, despite her instant dislike of the man, that he had reached Jem as none of them ever had.

He had given Jem different pills, and they hoped they would work. For the moment, he was asleep. Lola and Marcus had offered to stay up so that Verity and Mim could sleep a little. When her alarm rang, her eyes were glued together with too little sleep, but she pushed her feet out of the bed and told Mim it was time to get up.

Lola's eyes were drooping. They had all been running on hardly any sleep, and Jem's anxiety was infectious.

"Go to sleep Lola, I'll check on Jem." Verity smiled, watching Lola's eyes close.

44.

The curtains were closed, and the room was in darkness. Even given the gloom, as she peered into the bedroom, it was clear to see that Jem was missing. She turned on the light and checked the rest of the room, then the bathrooms. He was gone.

"Marcus! Lola! Mim! Jem's gone." She made her way back to the lounge, checking each room. Marcus met her in the doorway. "Where would he go?"

"All he has talked about was the fight with Mum. He might go to her house. Or he might just walk around. Sometimes he does that when he's upset. I thought the new pills would help." He sank against the wall, his arms over his head.

"Mim, maybe you and Lola drive round and see if you can see him walking and I'll go to Jess's place, see if he's there. Marcus, wait here, he might come back. OK?" Verity threw open the door and ran to the car, scanning up and down the street. Mim pressed the fob on Marcus's keyring, running towards the flashing lights.

Verity pulled up outside Jess's house, throwing the car door open. "Jem? Jem, are you there?"

The side gate was open a little, to the path that led down the side of the house into the garden. Verity pushed the gate further open and stepped into the shadow of the house. "Jem?"

The patio furniture was lying sideways, chairs and tables tipped over and scattered. Verity's brows furrowed.

The broad lawn was neatly trimmed and the flower beds were weed free. The whole place was manicured, barely a blade of grass out of place. Jem was sitting on the grass. She pulled her phone out and dialled Mim. "Jem's at the house. Can you come?" She hung up once she knew they were on the way. "Jem?" She stepped towards him, careful to move slowly, unwilling to frighten him. "Can I sit with you?" Jem made no comment, and gave no reaction to her being present. She sat on the patio, a few feet away from him. "Hi Jem." She edged closer. The grass was springy and warm. "Can we talk? I was worried when I couldn't find you. Glad that we are together now." There was no sign that he had heard her. "I always liked this house." She turned towards him, and back to look down the garden. "We used to roll all the way to the end of the grass, with our hands stretched out over our heads. Over and over, until we were giddy and giggling. Do you remember?" She reached her hand out to her cousin, her fingers spreading, blades of grass springing between them.

"No. I don't remember. I can't find the memories in my head." He turned to look at her. His eyes met hers, but they were unfocused. "It's like everything is locked away in my head, and I don't have the key." She held his hand.

"I don't really understand it. None of us have all the answers. We love you. All of us. When you're ready to find a key, we will all be waiting for you." She moved a little closer.

"I had a fight with my mum. I can't remember what I said, but I remember her face, how it looked. She was shocked. I must have said something terrible." He shook his head, as though he could dislodge the memories. "I don't know what I said." He shook his head as though it would clear his fuddled brain. "I had hurt her, over and over."

"Sometimes the more you try, the harder it is to remember." She squeezed his hand.

"I don't like the pills. Verity, can you tell them that I don't want to take them anymore?" He turned to face her. "Marcus says I need them, but they make me feel fuzzy." His eyelids drooped. She watched him lift his head backwards to try to keep them open.

"Do you want to come back to Marcus's house? I can take you in the car if you're tired?" She turned towards him again.

"No. I think I want to stay here." His eyelids closed, and he lay down, turning onto his side, away from her, and tucked his hands under his chin. His breathing was deep and regular.

"That's fine. When you wake up, we will all be waiting for you. It's all going to be fine, Jem." She ran her fingers through her hair. Watching him sleep, she wanted him to be alright, to really laugh and sing and be himself again. They had all taken some damage. Verity rested her head in her hands. She listened to his breathing. She slipped her jacket off and laid it over her cousin.

Mim arrived with Marcus and Lola. They all sat and watched Jem sleep, and it was calm and quiet in the garden. Lola leaned against Verity, her eyes closing. Tears leaked from her closed eyelids. Verity held her a little closer and swallowed hard. They had all been through some bad days together, and there would be more to come, she imagined.

They were all looking down the garden, which was why they only saw Simon arrive once he was a few feet away.

"What the fuck are you doing here? What is this, some sort of hippy commune?" Marcus jumped to his feet, scalded into action by his father's words and tone.

"Dad. Jem's been unwell. He's asleep now. The

doctor changed his pills." He stepped towards Simon. "I have been trying to reach you for days. I needed your help."

"Not my job Marcus. You know I'm rubbish with all that stuff. He's sleeping, nothing to do here." He dropped his voice to a whisper. "Send your cousins home, and you take Jem to yours. I'll pop over later. I've someone coming to have a look at the house." Marcus stepped away.

"Your son, my brother, is ill. I needed your help. My cousins stepped up when you didn't. I don't care who is coming to see the house. Jem is more important." He kept his voice steady.

"Don't tell me what is and is not important. You jumped up, little shit. You take your posh school voice and go stick it. Take your brother with you. Go on, all of you. Fuck off." His face was red, his neck straining at the collar of his shirt.

"Uncle Simon?" Verity stood up, holding Lola's hands. "Since you're now with my mum, and we have found out a great deal about what went on between our parents and you; I suggest you stop behaving like the arsehole we all know you to be. Just for once, it would be nice if one person in your generation of this family surprised us by being a normal fucking human." She knelt on the grass. "Jem, love, your dad's being an idiot. We'd best leave him to it. Can you come with me? You can sleep when you get home. OK? Great, thanks

Jem." She glared over her shoulder at Simon.

Mim slipped under Jem's other arm, and they slowly walked him to Verity's car, sliding him into the back seat with Lola. Marcus stormed from the garden with a face like thunder. "Come to mine Marcus. Let us look after you both for a while." He stopped and stared. Finally, nodding his agreement.

Half way home, her phone started ringing. She answered without thinking on the hands free.

"Verity? It's Basti. I know I was an idiot, but I need to talk to you. Not on the phone." His voice was as far from his usual self-assured, confident tone as it was possible to be.

"Basti, life is a little fraught at the moment, to say the least. Can it wait?" She indicated to turn right.

"It's about to get a whole lot more than fraught. Please Verity, I need five minutes and then I'm going to find a convenient stone and crawl under it, until everything has blown over." She looked across at Mim in the passenger seat, who was listening intently.

"OK, I'll be home in about half an hour. Come by after that." She ended the call and caught Mim's raised eyebrow. "I was seeing him for a while. Not anymore. He was Uncle Simon's divorce lawyer." She pulled up outside her house, and between them they helped Jem inside.

"Why did you say half an hour?" Lola steadied her cousin against the door frame while Verity unlocked the door.

"I want Jem inside and safe, and I hope Marcus will be here by then, so he can hear whatever Basti has to say." Verity took some of Jem's weight, and they helped him upstairs and into the spare room. He was asleep before they took his shoes off.

45.

Marcus brought Jem's pills and the shopping Mim had picked up earlier. When Basti arrived, he faced a whole room full of people.

"Can I talk to you on your own, Verity?" He chewed his lip.

"These are my sisters, Mim and Lola, and this is my cousin Marcus. I am happy for you to say anything in front of them. If you tell me on my own, I will repeat every word to them." Verity pushed her hair back out of her eyes.

"OK. Right, so first of all; sorry. I know I said it before, but just to be clear, I was an idiot." He shrugged. "We clearly agree on that point." He rubbed his thumb over his fingers. "Right. I have no idea how much you know about your father. Your dad's a fairly dangerous human being. He also employs some people who are dangerous. I had a call from him and he was furious. He thinks I might be able to intercede on his behalf." Her raised eyebrows brought his hands out in front of him, a defence against her disapproval. "I am here to do that, with very little hope that you would listen to me. I am extremely fond of my kneecaps, and will put myself in excruciatingly embarrassing situations to keep them where they currently are."

"You're saying my father threatened you?" Verity's brows bunched together.

"Look Verity. Believe me, or don't, totally your choice. He's a scary person, and he has a limited amount of patience. I'm just the messenger. I know you have no reason to trust me, but please be careful." He reached for her hand, but she made no move towards him. "OK. I'll see myself out." He turned away, with his shoulders slumped.

"Basti?" He turned back towards her. "Thanks for the warning. I'm sorry you're caught up in this." She leaned her hands on the back of the sofa and watched him leave, hearing the click of the lock as he pulled the door closed behind him.

"Marcus, we have some family issues going on with my parents." She sat down at the table. "There have been some explosive revelations. It all goes back to when we were kids. It could be tied into what happened to your mum."

"I think Jem was there. I think he saw something or heard something. He's been pretty much off his head since it happened. He had a fight with mum. You know Jem as well as I do. He's angry for two seconds, then he's back and apologising, and wanting to hug and make up." They all nodded. Jem had a short fuse, but he blew his temper out almost before it was lost. "He would have rushed back in to make up with mum."

"You think he walked in on whoever killed your mum? That's dreadful." Lola closed her eyes.

"I think if they had seen him, they would have killed him too. I guess they didn't know he was there." Marcus accepted a cup of coffee. "Thanks Verity."

"What did he tell you about it?" Mim nodded to Verity and took the cup.

"He's not making too much sense. It's like he's telling me about a dream or something. He says it was his fault. He says that over and over. I know he could just be feeling bad about the argument. I might be wrong, but he won't be talked round on that one. He said he was hurting her for a long time. I don't know what he meant." He sipped from his cup. "Sorry about my dad earlier."

"The days of apologising for our parents are over, Marcus. Trust me, we used up all our apologies in the last few days." Mim squeezed his hand.

"You know who would know what happened back in the day?" The blank stares told Lola that nobody did. "Granny Hetty. She would have known what her daughters were up to."

"Even Mum said that she came round and told her off, so she did know. Whether she will tell us is another thing." Mim sat up straighter. "Only way to find out is to visit. Lola, let's you and me go together. You were always her favourite. If she tells anyone, it will be you." She snatched Verity's keys from the table. "I'm borrowing your car, OK?" Lola had to run to keep up. The door closed behind them, leaving Marcus and Verity in silence.

"What do you think Jem meant when he said he was hurting your mum for a long time?" Verity sipped her coffee.

"We all knew that Jem was not my dad's son. They thought it was a big secret, but I don't remember not knowing. People said things. Jem always felt bad about it, that dad used Jem to hurt her. Could be that?" He shrugged.

"Why didn't we know?" Verity smiled. "It's one of many things I have found out recently." She rested her hand on her cousin's arm.

"What's the deal with Basti?" He nudged her with his elbow.

"I was seeing him for a while, until he told me that he was working for my dad, paid to find out about me, and report back." She dropped her head into her hands. "I hope he didn't tell my dad everything!" She groaned at the embarrassment, then snapped back to sitting up straight. "Least of my worries at the moment. Get some sleep Marcus, I'll listen for Jem. Let's hope Granny

Hetty remembers what happened." She patted him gently on the arm, her head tilted at an angle. He nodded and went upstairs. He had stayed over before, but usually after too many glasses of wine, not after the implosion of his family.

46.

"Granny Hetty?" Lola knocked on the back door and pushed it open.

"Hello?" Granny Hetty had never understood subtlety. Her hot pink top was tight across her ample chest, and the turquoise cropped trousers stretched across her hips and thighs. "Hello my loves! Wonderful to see you both. Come on in. I was just about to have a cup of tea. Great timing, girls." She bustled through the kitchen and popped the kettle on. "I picked up some lovely Bakewell tarts earlier. We can have a good catch up." She poured the tea and arranged the treats on a plate. "Lola, carry these please. Mim darling, bring these." Their Granny led the way into the cramped living room, where ornaments and furniture competed for space. She settled herself into her favourite armchair and waited to hear what had brought her granddaughters to her door.

"I know you love me girls, but something must have happened to bring you to me, so drink your tea, take a deep breath, and tell me all about it." She ran her tongue across the front of her teeth and smiled.

"We've found out some things in the last few days. About Molly, and what happened when she died. What our mum and dad did, and how they let Verity take the blame. Our father has come back. Jess is gone, and Jem is having a huge meltdown. We are taking turns to watch him in case he tries to kill himself. We need to know what happened. You were there. Please, tell us the truth." Lola watched her granny's face.

"Yes. Well. Right. I knew someday this would come home to roost. My girls were a little wild. Your mum once told me 'Adam's an idiot.' I laughed at that. All men are bloody idiots. What did she think she was going to get as a replacement?" She laughed, but halfway through it became a sob. "My daughter is dead. We can't even bury her until her body is released by the police. Somebody killed my baby. My other baby killed her daughter." She fished a tissue from her sleeve and wiped her tears.

"What we need to know is, well, everything. We are trying to work out why anyone would want to kill Jess. It seems likely that what happened to her is tied in with everything else. Can you tell us anything that we don't already know?" Lola reached across to her granny. "I'm sorry to ask."

"You know all about Molly and how they blamed poor little Verity. She was such a sweetie. Molly was so pretty, but she was very angry. What your mother did was unforgivable. I told her so at the time. Your dad was as bad." She chewed her bottom lip and ran a finger under her eye. "It hurt Jess when everyone found out that Simon was Molly's dad. Of course, it did, but that was mostly pride. I think they had grown apart long before that. Marcus was so like Simon, and Jem wasn't. She had taken her revenge, and it was brutal. My daughters, I love them both, but they were hard and vicious human beings." She worried at the tissue in her hands.

"The thing is, Granny, Jem had an argument with Jess just before she died. He's tying himself in knots with guilt over it all. We need to find a way to help him." Mim tipped her head to one side.

"You know your dad is a villain. Back in the day, him and Simon they worked together. I know they had a falling out. Sleeping with each other's wives that was a symptom, not the cause. It was revenge. Whatever they fell out over, it rumbled on for years, ended up with your dad going to prison. He killed the guy, but I know Simon was there, and nothing was mentioned in court over it. A deal was done, is what I'm saying. Jess knew about it." Their Granny dabbed her eyes with her tissue. "She came here, and she was furious. She told me Simon had set Adam up. He had been arrested." She shook her head slowly.

"So why now? What has changed to bring all this

to a head?" Lola leaned forwards in her seat.

"You dad left something. I don't know where, but I know it was evidence against Simon. He could have used it back then, but he didn't. Jess told me that Simon would pay for what he had done when Adam came home. I suppose that's what's happened. She was bitter. The years were hard on her. Simon provided for her and the boys financially, but she had no love, except from her kids." She shrugged. "I always thought that she kept Jem too much of a baby, but he was all she had. Jess was a hard cow sometimes, but she didn't deserve this." She took a deep breath. "As far as your mum is concerned, what she did to Molly, and blaming Verity, I was so ashamed. To be honest, I've been so sad about how my girls turned out. They were lovely as kids. I must have made mistakes with them. I don't understand what I did wrong."

"I know. We can't understand it either. Verity wouldn't speak to our parents earlier. She's too messed up still. I mean, it could have been both of them. Molly wasn't the only one." Mim was looking at her hands, almost talking to herself.

"She did the same to Verity?" Granny Hetty sat bolt upright.

"Yes, Verity still can't sleep with the covers near her face. Never has." Lola watched her granny's face.

"Oh, my God. Did she tell you that it was her? Your mum? Did she say that she did that to Verity?" She crossed the space between them and grabbed Lola's hands.

Lola thought back to the conversation. "No, not in so many words. She was crying and saying she was sorry, I think." She looked at Mim who was nodding her agreement.

"I don't see why your mum would do that. Verity was such a good little one, all you had to do was put her to bed, and she slept." She was shaking her head. "I'll talk to her and see what I can find out. Maybe she'll tell me what really happened." She pushed a hand through her thick hair. "Drink your tea, girls. You haven't had a sip."

47.

Verity put together some food for them all. She heard the front door close and assumed Mim and Lola were back. She walked through to check it wasn't Jem letting himself out, and found her father sitting on the sofa.

"Hello." His smile seemed the same. Maybe everything about him had changed. Certainly, her perception of him had.

"Why don't you come in and make yourself at home?" She was still angry, and a little frightened.

"Verity. I need to explain some things to you. Without the others shouting and crying. You and I have always been the grown-ups in this family." He patted the sofa next to him. She shook her head but sat on the other sofa. "OK. Whatever works for you." He rested his elbows on his knees. "I need you to give me the key. It is what will stop all this havoc. Once I have it, I will disappear. Life will go back to normal." He spread his hands, the solution to the problem.

"This key means that you will leave? You came

back for the key. You had no intention of reconnecting with us. All you wanted was your key back." She smiled, but there was no humour there. "If you aren't staying, then you can tell me who killed Jess. Least you can give me in return for the key you want so badly."

"You have always been an excellent negotiator, even as a little child. Basti told me about your reputation, how tough you are. I meant what I said. I am proud of you. Surely you can see how it is. I can't stay around." He smiled the winning Dad smile she remembered. "Once I'm settled, I'll let you know where I am, and perhaps you can come and visit. I'll probably go to Thailand. Look, I know that Basti told you who I am, what I am capable of. I don't want to have any violence. You three are my daughters, after all."

"What are you saying? Are you threatening us? You're our father." Her breath came in gasps. Her thoughts were full of Lola and Mim and whether he meant that he would hurt them.

"Your mother is a complete wreck. I have to get on with what needs to be done. I think that the key I need from you is on your key ring. Hidden in plain sight, so to speak." Her eyes snapped wider at his correct guess. "I thought so. Very clever." He smiled, the one she remembered. "Help me keep them safe, Verity. Just like you always have."

The front door opened and Mim and Lola walked in. They stared at their father sitting on the sofa.

"Hello girls." He smiled widely at them. "Verity and I are just going to pop out for a while. She'll be back with you in no time, but we need to use her car. Give her the keys, Mim."

"Where are you going? Verity?" Lola's eyes snapped wide.

"I'm going to take him to wherever he wants to go, and he is going to keep us safe. Take over from me here. OK?" Mim dropped the keys into Verity's hand.

She felt his hand in the small of her back and shrank away from his touch. "Come now. We don't want to be late, do we?"

She slid into the driver's seat of her car and checked the keys in her hand. Car, front door, back door, desk, office, and one other. The one that used to be attached to a pig. The one he wanted. Also, the one that would keep her sisters safe.

"Where to?" She looked at him.

"Drive." He looked straight ahead. "I'll tell you when to turn."

She pulled away from the pavement. He watched the road ahead of them, and she drove, turning left and right as he directed. They drove up through Hendon, through to Mill Hill, and out to Edgware. He directed her through the shops, and down through a side street, and she parked as directed. He held out his hand for the key. She opened her door. "I'll be coming with you."

A light drizzle was falling. The spring sun had finally broken, and the air felt cleaner. "I am a far too indulgent father." He laughed.

"I want to see what all this bloody fuss has been about." She walked a little faster to keep pace with him. The building on the corner was non-descript, discrete. He raised an eyebrow at her and pushed the highly polished bar that moved the silent door against the plush carpet. It took them into the North London Safe Deposit. Even the air smelled expensive. Certainly, the receptionist did. He showed his identification, and an account number, and she smiled a smile which was practiced. She picked up the phone, and a man appeared who took them through gates and impressive looking vault doors. The wall of numbered boxes covered the back wall. The man turned to them.

"Number please?" The man almost stood to attention.

"27-4." Her birthday. He raised an eyebrow at her. The breath she was taking stalled somewhere in between her lung and her throat. The man inserted his key, and her dad held out his hand for her keys. Verity sorted through them.

Front door, back door, office, desk. One other. She held it out to him. He inserted it into the other keyhole. Together they turned, and the door popped open with an expensive sounding thump. The man pulled out a box from inside and they followed him to a windowless room, where they could open the box in private.

She stood back. This was, after all, his box. He lifted the metal flap. Inside was a bulging notebook, which he slipped into a pocket inside his jacket. He tipped the box up and emptied the rest of the contents onto the desk. A tiny dress, and a small blue soft toy rabbit.

"These were Molly's. I put them in here because I couldn't bear to part with them." He shrugged. "Guilt, I suppose." He turned to her. "I don't suppose you remember Rabid Rabbit, do you?" He smiled at her. The tiny cotton dress in his hand was fragile in his grip.

"No. I don't even remember Molly." She shrugged. Her eyes burned with tears that she was determined to keep under control.

"Would you like her rabbit? A keepsake, perhaps?" He held it out to her.

"Thank you." She took the toy. "What is in the book?"

"Evidence, proof. Why we came here." He smiled and passed the keys back to her. "I won't be needing the keys anymore."

"Does this mean you're leaving?" She ran her fingers over the soft fur of the toy in her hand.

"I have to collect some money and pack, but yes, I will be." His brows pushed together. "Will you miss me?"

"I don't know. My life has been turned upside down since you came home. But I have waited since I was six for you." She shrugged. "A small dilemma."

"If you need me, leave a message with Basti. He will be able to contact me. OK?" He folded the dress, slipped it into his pocket, and pulled open the door, nodding her through.

48.

"Right, let's get going. I want to get this book to Basti. He will be handling it all for me. I know you're angry with him, and me, for sending him to find out about you, but he's a nice man, good, all the way to the soles of his shoes. He's not like me, and I will tell you the truth about this one. He's argued and fought with me almost as much as you have. You'd make a good couple." He held up his hands at her expression. "None of my business, you're right."

Upstairs, their silent footsteps on the thick carpet took them to the front door. She zapped the car, and they slipped into the seats. She pulled away from the curb and indicated to turn left. He watched in the side mirrors and then swivelled in his seat to watch behind them.

"Are you confident to drive fairly fast, Verity?" He asked, his voice quiet, but close to her ear.

"I don't usually. Why?" She looked across at him.

"Please trust me on this one. Swap seats with me?" His eyes met hers. "Bad things might happen. I want to get us both away, and I need to drive fast. You need to warn your sisters and cousins to get out of the way of what might be on the way to your house right now." She believed him. Against any sensible ideas in her mind, she believed what he was saying to be the truth. She pulled up the handbrake, and pushed open the door, pulling the back door open and throwing herself into the back seats. He lifted himself into the driver's seat. While she clambered through the gap between the front seats, into the passenger side, he pulled out. The car lurched into a gap she would not have taken, leaving horns blaring in their wake.

He turned right, left and right again, taking them through the back streets, driving faster than she would have dared. She held tight to the seat and closed her eyes when they passed parked cars with no gap to speak of.

"Nice car, Verity." He was concentrating hard. She could see it.

"This is insane. Fuck! That was a little too close." She closed her eyes again.

"No, it's fine. There aren't any scratches." He took another corner, and they were back on the main road, cutting across the traffic and into another side road. He drove, and she held on. "Phone and tell them to get out. Not to any of their houses. Tell them to go to a hotel or something. Not to book ahead." He slammed his foot on the brake and took another corner.

She dialled. "Mim? There's been a problem this end. Can you get them all out? Not to your house, or any of yours. Go to a hotel. Don't book ahead. Just walk in. Try the one near me. They always have vacancies." She listened to her sister for a second, then cut across her. "Bad things are coming, Mim. Please, I'm trying to keep you safe. Now. Please Mim." There was more talking, but she could hear that there was understanding too. "Thanks Mim. Love you." She ended the call.

"Now call your mum. Tell her dad says '53 go', she'll understand." He cut through an industrial estate and came out onto the Finchley Road. She dialled.

"Mum? Dad says to tell you 53 go." In a surprise move, her mother thanked her and hung up. Clearly, this was a side of her parents she had never known existed. "Now what?"

"Now phone Basti. Tell him to be waiting outside his flat in three minutes." He cut across a black cab, and was rewarded with a blast of the car behind's horn and some shouted abuse.

"Hello, Basti?" There was an awkward pause. Nothing she could do but grasp the moment. "Dad says be outside your flat in three minutes." He agreed, with the same swift understanding her mother had given, he hung up. She looked sideways at her father. This was different, certainly not what she had expected. Basti and her mother; although neither of them liked him had jumped to do his bidding. Certainly, in Basti's case, there was a fair amount of fear in the relationship. They both accepted his instructions. They had taken his directions with calm and understanding. He took another corner, throwing her sideways into the door, followed by a hard left and right.

He swung the car in to the pavement and Basti moved fast, throwing himself into the back seats of the car. "Verity, hello."

"Smooth. Good grief, you two are hopeless. Hold tight." He pushed the car around a corner, through back streets and back onto Finchley Road. "You ready Basti? You know what to do?"

"Absolutely. No worries. How long until we get there?" He was thrown sideways as they took another turning.

"We'll be there in a minute." His voice faltered as he fought with the steering wheel to keep the car stable as he took another turn, going back in the other direction.

"OK. This might be my last chance, and believe me, these are not the circumstances under which I would wish to have this conversation." He cleared his throat, and they sped through a junction as the lights changed. "I have been an idiot. Not expecting any argument about that.

But I am asking for another chance, once all this is over. Don't decide now. Once all this is sorted out, I will be able to talk to you about it. Then perhaps you might agree to me calling you."

"For fuck's sake, Basti. Are you some sort of period drama character? I'll talk to my daughter about it. Just please do as I've asked." He slammed on the brakes and Verity looked up to see that they were outside the Golders Green Police Station. "Go! Run Basti." He passed the notebook through between the front seats. Basti grabbed it, and exploded from the back door of the car, and into the police station. "He's not a bad bloke. I trust him." She listened to the wheels screeching around corners and wondered if her father's approval was a point in Basti's favour or a mark against him.

"Verity. Call and check the girls are safe. Get a room number." She nodded.

"Mim? Are you all in?" She nodded to herself. "OK, room number? Right. Stay safe." She hung up.

"Right, Verity. I am going to drop you at the station. I want you to catch a train. Watch for anyone behind you. Get a cab from the station to the hotel and sit tight. I will be there in an hour or two. Stay out of sight. OK?" He pulled up outside the underground station. "Got money for the train?" She nodded. "OK. Go." She pushed the door open and walked through the bus station and into the underground. Inside, she bought a ticket, and checked behind her.

Had she fallen for his lies again? The train pulled in, and there were only three people who boarded, including her.

Two stations later, she jumped in a cab, and ten minutes later, she was inside the hotel and looking for the room.

"Mim?" She knocked. The door flew open, and she was wrapped in a hug. "Oh, my God. I don't know what just happened, but it was the most scared I have ever been in my car."

Jem was sitting on the bed. "Verity. Thank goodness we have been so worried." She sat next to him.

"We have been worried about you too, Jem." She held his hand. "Glad to have you back."

49.

Verity was expecting a telephone call from her dad, but when her phone rang, it was an unsaved number. "Hello?"

"Hello, this is Detective Sargent Benson. We spoke previously regarding your aunt." He took a breath. "I have now had back the full results from the postmortem, and I can tell you that you were right. Her diabetes caused her death, a massive heart attack. It seems that she had not been taking her medication. Apparently, that is a risk for type one diabetics."

"That can't be right. She was so careful, she ate healthy food, she avoided sugar, she lived on lettuce, for goodness' sake." Verity sat down on the bed. She could hear him flipping through pages. "She had an infection last year, something to do with the injections, so they put her on tablets. I know she would have taken them religiously."

"No. No medication in her system. Not a trace. It seemed, however, that she had been taking large quantities of amphetamines. Which would have contributed to the heart attack, in the opinion of the forensic pathologist." She heard the slap of the papers on a table.

"She would never do that. I know she wouldn't. She'd been diabetic for years, and she never missed her meds. Please, you have to believe me. She would never have put her system under additional load." She caught Marcus's eye across the room. "Hang on. I need to check something. I'll put you on loud speaker, ok?"

"Yup, that's fine." She could hear the confusion in his voice.

"OK, in the room with me, I have Marcus, and Jem, Mim and Lola. Of all the people in the world who knew Jess, her two sons and her three nieces knew her better than most." The others in the room turned to face her. "This is Detective Sargent Benson on the phone. He has the results of the post-mortem. He says there was no trace of her meds in her system. No insulin. But that she had large amounts of amphetamines in her body. Is that likely?"

"Never. Mum was so careful. She had pills in the kitchen, in her handbag, in her bedroom, everywhere. She never forgot to take them. There is no way she would take any illegal drugs." Marcus turned to the others and found they were all nodding, agreeing with him.

"Can you check the pills that were in her bag, in the house, make sure the pharmacy didn't make a mistake?" Verity held her hand out to Marcus. He took her hand and pulled her closer.

"I can do that. We have her handbag. If you are all adamant that this would be out of character." All of them shouted at the phone. "Ok, I get it. I'll check and come back to you." He hung up.

"He says there was no trace of her medication in her body. There should have been." Verity leaned into Marcus.

"I saw her take her pill that morning. Before we argued. I saw it. She took it out of the little box in the kitchen cupboard. I watched her take it, and drink water to wash it down." Jem sat forward. "They must have made a mistake."

"Had she been alright? I know the divorce was stressful, but physically, had she been well?" Verity reached for Jem's hand to gain his attention. "What do you think, Jem?"

"She wasn't sleeping well, and she was worried. I saw some bruises on her neck once, when she came out of the shower." Jem pushed himself off his chair. "She said she had bumped herself getting out of the car. I believed her."

"I saw bruises too. She asked me to hurry up and push the divorce through. I tried to talk her into moving out of the house. She was not interested, and she refused to tell me where the bruises came from. I wish I had pushed her harder." Verity held out a hand to Jem.

"I'm sorry Verity. I wish I had tried harder. Oh my God, I wish that I hadn't argued. Most of all, I wish I could go back and be there when she needed me. None of us can." He pulled her in for a hug. "I know you loved her too." He rested his head on her shoulder. It was such a gentle gesture. It brought tears to her eyes.

"It's been such a fucking hard week, hasn't it?" She tucked herself into her cousin. "Thank you, Jem."

Marcus's phone rang, and he picked it up. "Dad?" He listened for a little while. "Hang on, I'll ask." He turned to Verity. "It's Dad, he is trying to find your Mum. Do you know where she is?"

"No. I spoke to her this morning, but she didn't say where she was going." Marcus relayed the information back.

"Any idea where your dad went?" Marcus chewed his lower lip.

"No clue. Sorry." She crossed to the other bed and put her arm around Mim.

"We had a call from the police. They said that mum had no medication in her system, that makes no sense, does it?" Marcus turned away from them. "I will. OK." He ended the call.

Verity slipped her feet out of her shoes and flexed her toes. Her phone rang, and she grabbed it. "Hello? Thanks for letting me know. Right.

Yes, I will." She ended the call. "That makes no sense. They had already analysed the pills in your mum's handbag. They were Ritalin. That's almost pure amphetamines. Could the pharmacy have made a mistake, or could someone have switched them?"

"Who would know where she kept them all? She had those little pill boxes all over the place. I'm not sure I would know where all of them were." Marcus shrugged. "We're going round in circles."

"No, Verity's right, I would have known where most of the boxes were, and if I wanted to find out, I could have looked for them. So could you, Marcus, and dad. Auntie Serena, she had been coming round a fair bit recently, and we all had keys." Jem shrugged.

"Why did my mum have keys?" Lola sat up straighter. "I would have thought they would have avoided each other, after what's happened."

"I think she mostly came round to fight." Jem shrugged. "I know she had keys though, because she came to collect some of dad's stuff."

"Ok. So, if you agree that she wouldn't do it on purpose, then we have to think that someone switched the pills. Someone who knew her that well would know that it would kill her. " Verity sat down on the edge of the bed. "We know that you wouldn't do it, Jem, or you, Marcus. I have to say, I'm not sure I could say the same about your dad or my mum." Verity felt Lola's hand in hers, and it helped. It gave her the strength to carry on. "You should know that my mum killed our sister, and could have easily killed me. I have no clue about what your dad did, but frankly, my dad is a complete nightmare, and I feel that yours is no different." Verity ran her finger under her eye and was surprised to find it was dry. Perhaps there were no more tears left, or the fact that her sister had died had been assimilated into her normal life. Which was scarier? She had no frame of reference.

"Verity. I need to ask you about the lawyer who worked for my dad during the divorce. Basti, who came to your house. I get that you were seeing him." He ran his hand through his hair. "No problem with that. From what he said and your response, I'm guessing he worked for your dad, too."

"Yes." Verity felt her hand grip the covers of the bed.

"Do you know what your dad hired him to do?" Marcus leaned forward, his wrists on his thighs.

"Initially, to find out what he could about me. Later, to do whatever my dad wanted, I think. Most recently, to take a notebook filled, I believe, with evidence against your dad to the police." Verity wrapped her arms around her body, hugging the worry she was fighting to hold steady. She ran through her feelings in her head. She was worried about Basti. Was he in danger? She was worried about her dad. He was absolutely in trouble. Her sisters, the danger they were in, made her feel sick. "I don't have all the answers, but I know bad things happened when we were all kids, and it's coming home to roost."

"If it was my dad, or your mum, I want to know. Are you OK with that?" Marcus glared across the room at her.

"Who are you being now, Marcus? Is this your gangster persona?" Verity laughed. "I love you Marcus. You are smart, and a really good lawyer. Leave the mob boss bullshit to our dads, OK?"

"Sorry, OK." He had the grace to laugh too.

"Help me to work out what happened to your mum. I can't do it on my own. We all bring something different to this. If we work together, maybe we can work it out." Verity felt Mim's hand on her shoulder.

Marcus smiled across the room. Jem was leaning gently against his brother, his eyes focused on something far away.

50.

"Verity? I'm out of the police station. Just wanted to let you know I've spoken to your dad, and he's safe. They have held me in the station for the last four hours while they decided if I was being helpful, or if I was taking the piss." His voice sounded tired. "Your dad asked me to thank you for earlier, and to tell you that you are safe to go home. He will phone you in the next half hour or so to let you know more about what has happened." She heard his feet on the pavement and thought about what he had done for her father. Would she have done that for a client? She had put herself at risk for clients with violent husbands; to bring them and their children to safety, but none of them had been, so far as she was aware, career criminals. He had been brave.

"Did you see what was in the book?" She heard him breathe out, slowly.

"I did not. However, if they fail to act on the allegations, I assured them that your dad made copies and will send them to the newspapers. I promised they will run the story if only to shame the police." His chuckle warmed her heart. He had lied for her dad too. She was starting to remember why she liked him.

"Right. Well, thanks for letting me know. I'll give you a call once everything is a little clearer." She cleared her throat.

"Take care Verity. I'll wait for your call." He hung up.

"Basti says it's safe for us to go home. I think we should hold on for an hour, just to be on the safe side. Is that OK with everyone? I'll order pizza and pick it up from reception, so I can have a look and see if there's anyone around." Everyone seemed happy with that. She dialled and ordered. The relief that the whole thing might be over with was immense. After hours of stress and waiting, they were hungry. The company promised delivery in thirty minutes and she wandered down to reception after twenty. Her phone rang while she was sitting on an uncomfortable chair next to a plastic flower arrangement.

"Hello? Verity?" He sounded pleased with himself.

"Dad?" She sat up straighter.

"Did Basti call you? He did a great job. Nice guy, did I mention that?" He chuckled. "I wanted to let you know I'm alright, and to thank you for earlier. The family will be a mess for a while. I hear that Simon has been arrested. He will be busy for some time. I'm leaving in the morning. I'll send you postcards." He took a breath and let it go. "We always seem to be saying goodbye, don't we? Once I'm settled, maybe come and see me. Who knows, you might be able to bring Basti with you?"

"What about Mum?" Verity chewed her lower lip. "Will they arrest her with Simon?"

"Oh, God. We can't have this conversation right now. Just trust me. I'll explain everything. Your mum's not a bad person. The things she admitted to the other evening, most of them weren't her. She was ill. We had to. Well, you'll see when it all comes out. Shit. I'm going to run out of time on this visit." She could hear his fingers tapping on the phone. "Verity. I'm leaving you loads of unanswered questions again. I'm sorry. Just please, can you suspend judgement until I can explain it all to you?"

"I'm going to keep on looking for answers, whether you're here or not. I have to know who killed Jess. The rest of our family bullshit is on the back burner for the moment." She thought about it for a moment. "Take care of yourself, dad. Safe journey."

"Thanks, love. I'll be back. I promise. You'll always be my girl." He sniffed. She struggled with the tears that threatened. "You should be safe to go home when you're ready. Make a good life Verity."

He hung up the phone.

She held the phone close to her chest and closed her eyes. Each time she thought she had moved forward; he pulled her back. She would miss him. Not the drama and the worry, but yes, he was still her dad.

The pizza delivery arrived, and she carried the boxes upstairs. They shared them and ate the soft dough and stretchy cheese together. It was time to go.

Her house was closest, so they went there first. She opened the door with the spare key that Mim gave her; and found an envelope on the mat. Her car keys were inside. Her car was parked in the street. She shook her head. He had been around the corner from the hotel.

Marcus answered his phone when it rang. He took notes and nodded, confirming he understood. Finally, he ended the call and sank into the sofa. "Jem, dad's been arrested. They listed all the charges. It's bad. Apparently, they have very good evidence. His lawyer says he will argue for bail, but it will take time, if it happens at all. He's looking at thirty years or more." He swiped his hand over his face. "Verity, is this the result of whatever your dad had delivered to the police station?"

"I imagine so. I don't know what there was in the book, but, yes, probably." She watched his reaction. "I'm sorry." Tears were running down her face. She was in no position to stop them. Marcus crossed the distance between them.

"No, no. Verity, stop. Our parents lived their lives, and my dad sailed close to the wind too often. If he did what they accuse him of, then he will need to pay for that. Not your fault. Never your fault." He wrapped his arms around her. "Fuck. Our parents are beyond the pale." He started to laugh. There was a touch of hysteria about it. "Don't take responsibility for our parents. Love you cuz." She nodded into his chest. Not able to speak, or put together a sentence. "Jem and me are going to mine. We need to chill out and do boy things." He laughed. She felt the vibration of his chuckle through his chest, and it made her cry more. "Be brave Verity. No crying." He pushed her hair out of her face.

"Ok." She sniffed. "Love you cuz."

"Call Basti. I liked him." He smiled down at her.

"Fuck off, Marcus." She smiled, even though it was wobbly.

"Fair enough." He turned. "Jem? You ready to go?" His brother nodded. "Mim, Lola, thank you for rescuing us. Our wonderful cousins are, as always, our saving grace."

He waved. They all did. Then it was only the three girls left.

"Dad said he was going in the morning. He has to be taking money with him, cash. He won't be able to put it through banks. How would he go? How could he take it all with him?" Verity demanded an answer from her sisters. They looked blank. "He can't carry it on a plane. What about driving it?"

"Cars are searched going on the ferry." Lola stood up. "Private plane?"

"Maybe he'd still have to go through customs, though, wouldn't he?" Mim shrugged.

"Boat? Does he know how to drive a boat?" Verity looked from one sister to the other.

"Do you drive a boat?" Lola raised an eyebrow.

"Not the time for semantics, Lola." Verity shrugged. "If he had a boat, it could be anywhere."

"Maybe we're asking the wrong question. You said he told you to tell mum a code." Mim pointed at Verity.

"Go53, or 53go. Yes, he did. She just accepted it." Verity confirmed, nodding her agreement.

"Can we ask Basti if he knows what that means?" Mim slumped down into the sofa. "Or if he knows where the boat is?"

"We can try. I'll phone him." Verity picked up her phone and scrolled through the numbers. Her finger hesitated over his number. Shaking her head at her own reaction, she pushed her finger onto the screen and listened to the ringing. "Hello, Basti?" The girls watched her across the room. "Sorry to bother you. I just had a couple of questions." She closed her eyes. It was so hard to ask for his help. "Basti, do you know what go53 or 53go means? Hang on, I want to put you on speaker so my sisters can hear too, OK?" She laid her phone on the table and pressed the button.

"OK. I know it was a code for your mum. We talked about it all before I met you. Setting up things that would help in an emergency. 53 go, means that she should leave the house immediately, and go to a safe place." He cleared his throat.

"Right, thanks. Do you know where she would go?" Verity's fist tightened on the arm of the sofa.

"Yes, well, I know where your dad expected her to go. That may not be the same thing. She may have chosen to go somewhere else." He huffed a breath.

"Do you know where my dad keeps his boat?" Lola's eyebrows shot upwards towards her hairline.

"I do. Or, at least I did. I imagine he might be on the move." He paused. "Are you thinking of trying to find him? Verity, that might be a really bad idea."

"I need to know where he is. It's really important.

My Aunt is dead, and I think I know how it happened, but I need to talk to my parents. Basti, please help me. I just need to have a conversation with them." Verity stood up and moved closer to the phone. "Please."

"Verity. Please understand what you're asking. It's not just betraying a client's confidence. It's also crossing someone who can do me a huge amount of physical damage." He was all lawyer now, his suit was back on, and he had buttoned the jacket.

"Don't pull that bullshit with me. I know the game you're playing. Basti, this is me. You know how hard it is for me to ask. I'm begging." She knelt on the floor and leaned on the table.

"Last I knew, he was in St Katherine Dock. The moorings are numbered. He was at number 53." Basti paused. "I'll meet you there." The line went dead.

"Looks like mum and dad are back together." Lola closed her eyes. "Is it just me, or do you think they have been telling us a load of rubbish to stall everything until they could run? What was all that with Simon?"

51.

St Katherine's dock was new to the three of them: restaurants, bars, loads of people around. The marina was separate from the main area, and gated, presumably to protect the enormous yachts that were moored there. Verity might not have been a seasoned sailor, or any kind of sailor for that matter, but even she recognised that the floating gin palaces were millions of pounds worth of toys for exceptionally wealthy people to play with. When they sailed from there, they would be straight out onto the Thames, all the way through the middle of the most exciting city in the world, and down to the sea. His audacity took her breath away.

Basti was leaning on the gate. "Hello." He pushed himself away from the railing.

"Do you have the code for the gate?" Verity looked beyond him to the boats.

"I do. Please, can you tell him you worked it out yourself? That I refused point blank to tell you where he was?" His top button was open, he was looking casual and cool, and she wished there was time for looking that good.

"Come with us. You can tell him yourself." She shook her head at her own silliness. He shrugged and punched in the code. The gate swung open, and they walked through, one at a time. They listened to the clank as it closed behind them. "Where is fifty-three?"

They checked for numbers, and counted down from 135, which was next to the gate; walking along the wooden planked pontoon. A corner took them past seventy and through the sixties. They took a wrong turn, which brought them through to the forties, and they had to double back.

Fifty-three, when they found it, was a ring on the pontoon, just like all the others. The boat that was tied to it was beautiful, sleek, and powerful. Understated, not like some of the others which were hugely ostentatious. This was built for speed. It was beautiful. It took Verity's breath away.

"Nice. Very nice." Lola's whispered comment was what all of them were thinking. "I have a question." They all turned towards her. "How do we get on it?" She turned to Verity. "Will it be wobbly?" Her voice was unsteady.

"No, I think that's more in little boats. Don't worry." Verity reached for her hand with a reassuring smile. Lola was trying hard to hide her fear.

"Shall I phone him and see if he will come out to us?" Basti pulled his phone out of his jacket pocket.

"Yes. Thank you." Lola's relief was clear, and her voice steadier.

Basti pulled his phone out and held it to his ear. "Hello?" Surprise chased confusion across his face. "Serena, is Adam there, please?"

Verity turned to look at her sisters. Had their mum come to the boat when she ran away from the house?

"Please, can you put him on?" He raised an eyebrow at Verity.

She kicked off her shoes on the pontoon and reached out to pull the rail on the side of the boat towards her. The end of the rail had a small flat step where she pushed herself up onto the boat. "Hello? Dad?" She walked to the back of the boat, where the walkway, which was narrow and seemed very close to the edge. The walkway dropped down into a wider area, with seating around the edges and a door into the cabin. Slowly, being careful not to slip off the narrow steps, she climbed down into the wider area, turning when she heard the door open. She kept her hand on the rail and turned towards the sound.

"Mum?" Her mum closed the door behind her and smiled widely.

"Verity? Lovely to see you, as always, but why are you here?" Her voice was higher than usual, her smile filled with teeth, but no eyes.

"I wanted to find out a little more about the last time you saw Jess?" Verity sat down on the cushions at the back of the boat and patted the cushion next to her.

"Well, it was a while ago, before I went on holiday, I called by the house to pick up some of Simon's stuff. He needed some more clothes, so I called in. Jess was fine with it. We chatted, not for long, but it was nice to see her." She shrugged. "I didn't stay for long. Of course, if I had known that it would be the last time I would see her, I would have stayed longer."

"Why did you have a key to her house?" Verity watched her mother's eyes. A tiny movement confirmed that she had hit a nerve.

"I don't, Simon does, obviously." She patted Verity's leg. "Nice to chat, darling, but I need to get on." Serena stood up and held out her hand, showing Verity the way off the boat.

"When I called you the other day, and gave you the code, that meant to run here, right?" Verity stayed exactly where she was. "So, dad and you, are you back together?" Serena's hand fluttered to her throat.

"It's early days. We are just trying to see where it might go." She pushed her hair away from her face.

"Taking the book to the police station, Simon being arrested, all of that. Is that all part of the plan?" Verity peered around her mother to look through the glass door. "Where is dad?"

"He should be back soon. Let's walk down to the gate to meet him. Perhaps we could all go out for some lunch together." She started to collect her bag and shoes together.

"Why would he leave his phone when he went out?" Verity sat on the cushions, determined not to be moved.

"He has his phone. Don't be silly." Serena's voice shook a little.

"No, you answered it when Basti called him. So, his phone is here. Where is dad?" She leaned back against the cushions. "Maybe I should phone back the police and ask them to investigate. They might be able to find him for us. What do you think?"

"I think you have forgotten who you are speaking to. I am your mother, and I am, frankly, tired of your insolent way of speaking to me." She dragged in a breath. "I know I've made mistakes. Verity, I never said I was perfect, but I was there. I brought you and your sisters up. I looked after you."

"Although, not so much with Molly." Verity met

her mother's stare and watched every breath in and out.

The expression on Serena's face ripped through surprise all the way to fury and back again.

Mim's perfect ponytail swung over her shoulder as she tiptoed towards them, in time for her to hear the end of the conversation.

"Mommie dearest. How nice. Where's father of the year?" Mim sat down next to Verity. "Your hair looks really bad. You aren't using the products I gave you."

"That's harsh Mim. She's been a little busy." Verity wrinkled her nose. "What is that smell?"

"Lies?" Mim raised her eyebrow.

52.

Simon sat in the small cell. It smelled bad. The metal toilet in the corner had no seat and looked as though he had been a good deal younger when it was last cleaned.

The same two officers who had brought him in had been questioning him about ancient history for most of the day. He knew the only people who had known what he was up to in those days were Adam and Serena. Adam had written notes, promising that they would be insurance. He had taken the fall for both of them. The bastard that had fathered Jem had been shooting his mouth off. Despite everything with Serena, and Molly, and the souring of their own relationship, their loyalty to each other was guaranteed, by each of them knowing too much about each other's past misdeeds, to betray the other.

That night, they had gone looking for Gerry Mulhern. They had to go to three pubs and two working men's clubs to find him, but in the end, they had run him to ground. He had been telling the world that he had fathered the bastard that Simon Wimborne was raising as his own.

The insult was beyond bearing. Simon would, naturally, be the first person to be questioned. Of the two, he was the better earner, and he promised to take care of Serena and the girls. It was decided.

Between them, they had beaten the loud-mouthed idiot until he stopped breathing in and out. Simon left the scene, arriving with Serena as arranged before eleven, having a bath, while she took his clothes away and disposed of them.

Adam took the body out to Epping Forest, where he dug a shallow grave and disposed of the idiot who had fathered Jem, then been foolish enough to talk about it.

Jess opened the door just before the sun rose, and took his clothes, disposing of them. He soaked in the bath in her ensuite bathroom and pulled the plug; before washing himself clean, scrubbing his fingernails and clipping them short and washing every part of him again, then the bath, the floor, everything. Finally, he showered, dressed in the clothes he had left there earlier, and left Jess alone with her children.

Simon knew all this because they had planned it together. Jess had told him later that she had cried while he was in the bath. She knew that she was saying goodbye to her best friend. Whatever else he thought about their relationship, he knew Adam had been a friend to her.

He sat down on the flat foam cushion, which they laughingly called a bed.

He had prided himself, over the years, on his planning. Tiny details had been his obsession. Perhaps, though, pride came before a fall. He had believed his own legend. He had trusted his own abilities, and that had been his downfall.

If they had evidence to back up the accusations they were making, and he had very good reasons to believe that they did, then he was going to be spending a substantial part of what was left of his life in prison. It was payback, and if he was completely honest with himself, he deserved it.

He had been to see Jess. He didn't want the boys to have to do it. She had looked like a stranger. There had been bruises on her face, which had surprised him. Even putting those to one side, she looked like someone else. Not his Jess. Even when she was alive, she had stopped being his Jess a long time ago.

He ran his hands through his hair. Life had been heading in the right direction, before the turn that he had failed to predict.

He knew that Adam had made the move against him. Nobody else would have had the balls. In a strange way, it felt right. They had started out together, two skinny kids, stealing cars and motorbikes. Graduating to selling whatever they could turn a profit on. Adam had been his best friend, and he was talented. He could pick locks and move through a building so quietly it was as though he was holding his breath. They were good times. The best. Two young guys, full of promise and living life to the full. They had been golden.

When Adam married Serena, he had sent invitations to a few friends, but not to Simon. He had kept her a secret. Simon had managed to finagle an invitation, anyway. He had known the moment he saw her arrive at the church. He had turned along with the rest of the church, and watched her walk up the aisle.

Her hair bounced on her shoulders, her dress was sleek, skimming her curves. It was sexy. There was nothing innocent or virginal about her. Simon watched the ceremony, and he knew why Adam had kept her quiet.

Her sister had the same vibe. Jess had been hot, in a dangerous, burn your fingers way. He had thrown himself into her and tried to ignore his thoughts and fantasies about Serena.

He knew he should sleep. They would be back for him soon, and rested he would be in better shape to deal with the questions that were coming his way, but his mind was too busy turning over everything he knew, searching for what had happened to turn his life inside out. He had thought he finally had everything he wanted in his hands. Serena was finally his. Adam was leaving the country, Verity, Mim and Lola were angry with their father, and their mother, but they would come round, they would accept him. Marcus and Jem had been looking after each other. They were angry too, but they would be alright, they were grieving. Jem had always been a little fragile. It would pass. He had even avoided having to give Jess her half. Life had been his, like a prize, at the end of a long race.

Yet, he was in a smelly cell, and they had enough evidence to hold him. His lawyer had been told that they would apply to hold him longer, pending further investigation, and fully expected to be granted additional time.

Serena might have been arrested, too. He closed his eyes as a groan escaped his lips. She was the best thing in his life. If he had dragged her into whatever this was, he would never forgive himself.

The door of his cell clanged open, and the officer from earlier called him out. They had another set of questions to ask. He trudged through the grey corridors, the smell of industrial cleaning fluid, a pleasure after the odours of his cell.

53.

Lola pulled her phone out of her bag. The screen said Marcus was phoning. "Hello?"

"Lola. I had a call from my dad's solicitor. They're applying for an extension. They are holding him on very serious charges. He hinted at murder. Shit, Lola, can today get any worse?" There was a wobble in his voice.

"Yes, I think it can. Verity and Mim are on the boat I can hear them talking to mum. I can't go on there. You know I can't go on a boat. I feel sick just standing next to it. We don't know where our dad is. I am standing here on my own. Basti said he had to go before dad found out he had told us where to look. I am on my own here. Boats are not my thing." She watched the boat move on the rope moorings, her stomach heaving along with it.

"I can come down there. Jem will come with me, if it will help." She couldn't answer him. If she opened her mouth, she would be sick. "Fuck. How did our families get so messed up?"

She turned away from the swaying boat and

tried to ignore the gaps between the planking of the pontoon and the water below. "Our families are messed up because of our parents. They were horrible human beings, and we grew up in the slime they created. We don't have to be like them. We can choose." She swiped away the tears. "Maybe we can be better." She took a deep breath and turned back to the boat. "Don't worry about coming down. Take care. I'm going to sort this out." She hung up and walked back towards the boat. Her sandals landed with a slap on the wooden planking. She took a deep breath, steadying her breathing, slipping her bag to hang across her body. Her hand was slick on the chrome rail. She concentrated on her breathing, lifted her left leg, and pulled as hard as she could, pulling the boat towards her, and her right leg up to join her other one. Her toes gripped, her eyes closed, and the boat wobbled back to right itself, taking her stomach with it. She breathed through the nausea, but would get beyond it. One breath at a time, she kept her eyes shut until the boat steadied.

Her grip was tight around the rail, she inched forwards. She could see Mim and Verity, looking towards her, and the back of her mum's head.

They were talking. She couldn't hear exactly what was being said, but none of it sounded friendly. She concentrated all her energy on stepping and not slipping. Slowly dropping to sit down and slide down to the step below, she allowed herself to listen, now that she could share her concentration.

"Verity." Their mother held her hand out to her side. "Don't be childish. I would have thought that you would be happy that your parents are back together, trying to make it work." She raised her hand to flutter at her throat. Lola knew it was what she did when she was lying.

"Mum? Can you tell me where dad is? I don't believe that he went out for a walk. Please, can you tell me?" Verity leaned forward, watching her sisters' faces. Their frowns and furrowed brows told her loud and clear that neither of them believed their mother, either.

Serena slumped into a seat. "Why are you being so difficult? Verity, what are you trying to make it all into such a big deal for?" She ran her hand up her neck and into her hair. "I am waiting for your father to come back just as much as you are. Honestly, you seem to think that everything has a sinister meaning. You are being so suspicious."

"Good grief, I wonder why! In the last week, we have found out so many things, and here we are." Nobody moved. "You have told us so many versions of what happened when we were kids. But you still haven't told us about Jess. She's dead, and I am absolutely certain that you know more than you have told us."

The silence was thick, and Lola sat still, watching her sisters and her mother. She watched her mother's hands, shaking a little, and she knew that Verity was right about Jess. Whatever had happened between the two sisters, Serena knew more about it than she had told anyone.

"Jess and I argued. You argue with your sisters, Verity. Good grief! When you were teenagers, I thought you would pull each other's heads off. All sisters argue. It's what families do." The loose flowery skirt she was wearing was pleated between her fingers. She slumped into the seating area opposite her daughters. Her fingers still worrying at the fabric of her skirt. "I loved my sister, just like you love yours. I would have done nothing to hurt her."

"You were living with her husband." Mim's voice was quiet. "You had a baby with her husband." She stood up and took a step towards her mother. "You did a great deal to hurt her." She closed her eyes. "Did you do more than that? We have to know."

"Mim will you stop? You're as bad as the prosecution over here." She waved her hand at Verity.

"This is what you always did. You set us against each other when we asked difficult questions. It's been something that you use for such a long time, I really never noticed, until now." They spun around to see Lola sitting on the edge of the seating area.

"You're on the boat. Way to go Lola!" Verity stood up. "You're right though. Mum has always used the divide-and-conquer method of parenting."

"Fine, let's all go together and see if we can find your father. As a family, united, and pulling in the same direction." Sarcasm dripped from Serena's words.

Serena held out her hand, pointing to the pontoon, knowing that Lola would be only too pleased to leave the boat.

They watched Lola slither down to the wooden planking, keeping a tight hold on the railing until her feet hit the warm wood. Her relief was enormous. Verity waited until her mother was on the wood, and Mim had jumped down before she followed them.

"He said he wanted to go for a beer. My guess is he's at the bar up on the marina." After the bright sunlight, the inside of the bar was dark, and their eyes took a little while to adjust. Long enough to lose track of their mother.

54.

Her neck snapping from one side to the other, Verity looked at her sisters. She pulled in three deep breaths.

"She has to be heading back to the boat. She just wanted to ditch us." Mim shouted over the noise of the bar.

The three of them turned and left the bar, just in time to see the flowery skirt they had all been looking at just minutes before travelling fast down the marina towards the gate. Her legs pounding down the distance.

The girls ran, closing the distance, but the head start their mother had given herself was more than they could gain back. Each stride took her closer to the gate. Verity pulled her phone out of her pocket and dialled Basti.

"Code. Please give me the code to the gate." Her breath came in rasps, dragged through her lungs and huffed in and out of her mouth.

They heard the gate clang closed, Mim and Lola slowed. "Keep running. I have the code." She passed them, reaching the gate and punching in the numbers.

They reached the boat. The engine roared into life and slowly pulled away from the pontoon. Verity's lungs burned, but she reached for the rail, and pulled as hard as she could, Mim joined her. Lola came to the front of the boat and grabbed a rail. She could see the rope, and she might even be able to reach it, but she would have to let go of the rail. She closed her eyes and took a breath. Holding with one hand on the rail, she pushed the other hand as far as she could, and felt the fibrous structure of the rope between her fingers. A small yelp escaped from her lips. She pulled it as hard as she could and stepped back. The ring on the pontoon was next to her foot, and she looped the rope through it. Pulling and heaving against the force of the engines.

Verity and Mim came to help her, and they tied the rope off. The engine noise died, and Serena came to the side of the boat.

"Good job Lola. I know you're frightened of the water, but you still grabbed for the rope. Proud of you." Verity's voice came in between breaths.

"Untie the boat." Serena's voice was quiet.

"No." Mim met her mother's stare.

"Adam. Tell your daughters to untie the boat." Their father stepped out of the door and stood looking down at his daughters.

"Sorry, I wanted to tell you properly, not like this. We're back together. The thing is, Simon is going to be really upset with me. Right now, he can't do much about it, but that won't last long. We need to get away." Adam leaned over the rail. "I'll be in touch as soon as we're settled."

"Tell us what happened with Jess." Verity met his stare. "I'll untie you, if you tell us."

"It was Simon. He swapped the pills. He couldn't bear the idea of giving Jess all that money, so he swapped her pills for Ritalin. It was the end for your mum and him. She lost her sister. I lost my friend, but your mum came back to me. We realized, after we left Verity's that we'd missed out, we'd been missing each other for years." He held out his hand and Serena took it. "She agreed to give me another chance. Simon won't accept that, not without looking for revenge. That's another reason we need to go."

Verity looked at her two sisters. They shook their heads. They clearly believed none of it either. "But what you told us about Molly? That was true?"

"Yes, it was. To my shame." His eyes dropped. "I should tell you all something else." Verity felt Mim and Lola move closer to her. He held up his hands. "No, nothing bad. Just that I'm proud of you. All of you. I know your mum is too, but she's been here looking out for you. I haven't." He shrugged.

"Why not just talk to us earlier? Why hide?" Lola's breathing still had a little way to go, to reach normal.

"Your mum thought it would be too much for you to take on board, after all the other revelations, that we are back together." His hands held the rail, but his grip was loose and confident. "Also, it's safer if I'm out of sight with everything going on with Simon."

Verity checked with her sisters, and they all nodded. In a way, they were glad to untie the rope and wave goodbye. Their parents were havoc. Both of them had ripped through their children's lives like a wrecking ball. It was over, and that was enough. They walked back to the car in silence, and Verity slumped with her hand on the steering wheel.

"So tired." She muttered.

"Absolutely." Mim rested her hand on Verity's knee.

"I can't believe I actually climbed on a bloody boat." Lola watched people walking into the marina. "A boat." There was true amazement in her voice.

55.

The engines puttered. He kept his hand on the throttle, carefully passing the other boats moored in the marina.

Serena sat next to him and watched his careful movements. "Thanks."

"What did I do?" He risked a sideways look and smiled.

"Lied to the girls. It was kind." She looked down at her hands.

"I didn't lie to them. Simon is going to be really annoyed." He chuckled. "You only did what you did because of Simon. I know that."

They passed out of the marina and into the main waterway of the Thames, passing two boats filled with tourists and keeping the engine slow and steady. They were holding their breath, knowing that Simon would, as soon as he was able, be sending vengeance spinning towards them. There was no standing their own ground. The only option was to run.

"How long before we get out into the sea? I won't feel safe until then." Serena wrapped her arms around herself.

"Simon will still be at the police station. He won't be able to contact anyone. Not yet. Keep it together, love." Adam pulled her towards him. "I'm starving. Any chance of a sandwich?" She shook her head at him, but pushed herself down the steps into the small galley and put a sandwich together. Her handbag was in the way, and she moved it to the floor. She made a plate of sandwiches and two coffees,

They were making progress. The sandwiches lasted almost an hour, and the river was widening. They were coming to the open sea. Adam eased the throttle back a little, and the engines responded with a roar. The boat sprang forward, cutting through the waves and dancing through the afternoon sunshine.

"Now, we need to be on the lookout for ferries and cargo ships. They are slow to turn. We will have to avoid them. I'll need your help." She nodded and looked out across the water. "I'm setting a heading, like we talked about. See the gps? It will beep if we go off course. It's like a sat nav but for boats." His eyes twinkled at her. "I'm glad you decided to come with me." She leaned her head on his shoulder.

"Me too. Is that a ferry?" She pointed, and he took a look.

"I think so. Nicely done. I'll have to promote you

to first mate." He laughed.

"I don't think so, mate. I'm the bloody captain." She left her hand on his thigh and watched the open water all around them. The waves were higher, and the wind was picking up, lifting her hair from her face. They dodged around the ferries and two enormous cargo ships. They saw fishing boats and took a wide route around them in case they were pulling nets behind them which could wrap around their propellers.

Each detour made the array of instruments beep. Serena watched carefully. "Look at the map. Here, we're here, and this is where we're going. We'll be in Dieppe before it's fully dark, I hope." He watched the seas around them. The land behind them was long gone. "Oh, I meant to tell you, I got you a present." He pulled an envelope out of his pocket and passed it over. Her brows pushed together, but she opened the envelope. Inside were two passports. She opened one. "Is that you or me?"

"My picture, but a new name"? She ran her finger over the picture. "They look real."

"They are. You are now, Mrs Sandra Wyatt. I'm Tom Wyatt. We'll disappear, eat good food, drink good wine, and spend some time together. OK?" He ran his finger down her forearm.

"Sounds good to me, Tom!" She giggled. "Seems like you thought of everything."

"Look. See over there? I think that's the French coast. We're still an hour, maybe a bit more out, but we can see where we're going." He risked a look across at her.

"OK, tell me when we're about fifteen minutes out, I've a surprise for you." She looked away, studying the water, checking for any other boats. Now that they were closer to the French coast, there was always the possibility of running into the customs boats that patrolled the coastal waters. In the distance, she could see the ferries crossing to Calais, but they were on a ferry route too, and this was no time to be complacent.

An hour later, the lights were brighter and more defined. "That's the marina, see over there? That's where we're going. I booked ahead, so the harbour is expecting us." He slowed the engines. He had been right. It was late afternoon, and they were nearly there.

Serena slipped down the stairs again and came back up with two glasses. "You won't be driving for too much longer." She swirled the brandy around the glasses. "Let's drink a toast. To us!" She clinked her glass with his and watched him tip it down his throat. "You always drink as though you're taking medicine!" She shook her head in mock disapproval.

She watched him run his finger around his collar. His breathing hitched.

"Are you ok?" Her hand rested on his shoulder.

"No. I......" His eyes searched left and right.

"You just took a massive amount of insulin. Your body is trying to deal with it. It's not nice, but don't worry." He slipped from the seat, each breath a struggle, a fight to keep going. His body struggling with the process. "You'll feel light-headed, and a little confused. Then you'll go into what's called hypoglycemic shock. It's OK. I'll look after you. You might feel a little tingly around your mouth and lips. It's all OK."

Carefully, she helped him to the seating area. His body bent double against the wracking pains, and worse, the fear that gripped him. "Why would you do this? What did I do to deserve this?" He spluttered, spitting and coughing.

"Do you know what would make you feel better?" She ran her hand over his hair. "A swim. You'll feel better for a nice swim." His eyes opened wide. She knew he was afraid, but it really made no difference. Holding his feet, she pushed them up over the edge. He was still gasping and choking. Heaving against the weight of his body, she pushed him up to the edge and pulled in some deep breaths. He was heavier than she had imagined. Steadying herself, standing with her feet apart to balance, she pushed with everything she had, and he toppled, with a satisfying splash, into the water. She turned back to the controls, without looking back, and steered the boat carefully into the marina, finding a mooring place. He had booked ahead, and they were expecting her.

....

Adam floated on his back. She had been right, the cold water had helped. Not enough, of course. His hands and feet were doing nothing to help him stay afloat, and soon, he was sure he would slip under the water and not come back up. It was peaceful, lying there, drifting along with no better place to be. That was, he told himself, the best option. Better than meeting a ferry, he imagined. The water was colder than he had imagined, and little by little he drifted, looking up at the skies and remembering his time with Serena, with their kids. He sank a little deeper, and the water welcomed him with open arms.

....

She tied the boat up and unloaded the luggage. Her handbag, the new passports, and the suitcases full of money that Adam had stowed so carefully in the boat, ready to leave.

Joel was waiting for her. He had his own luggage. He put his arms around her. "I thought you would be here earlier. Good to see you, baby." She leaned into his chest and watched while he loaded her bags into the car. He was cute, but her patience was limited. She would have to think about how long she could put up with his bullshit.

56.

"Granny Hetty?" Verity opened the door a little wider. "Come on in."

"Sorry Verity. I needed to talk to you girls. Mim and Lola came to see me. I should have told them everything. Of course, I didn't. Too many years of keeping secrets. It's become a habit." She bustled her way to the sofa, accepting the offer of tea, and slumping into the soft cushions. "I need to tell you. I have to tell someone. Verity, you're so clever, always were, even as a little tot. You can tell me what I should do about it."

"Granny Hetty. Here. Have a cup of tea, and take your time. Tell me what it is that's worrying you." Verity put down the cup and waited.

Hetty pushed her jacket off and eased her feet out of her shoes. "Now I'm here, I don't know where to start." She took a sip from the cup.

"My daughters. I make no excuses for them, but I should have told you before now. You should know what happened. Why they are, the way they are." She sipped, and Verity noticed that the cup rattled into the saucer.

"I was married young. I had no clue what I was doing. I thought he was the bee's knees. To be truthful, I thought I knew everything there was to know. It turned out I knew nothing. My parents warned me, but I was determined. We married on a Saturday, and I was floating on air. When we got home, I thought it would be romantic. I expected wine and roses." She huffed out a laugh. "He beat me sideways, threw me around the flat like a rag doll. When I woke up in the morning, I was on the bathroom floor, my face was swelled up like a balloon, and my body was black and blue."

"Granny Hetty! I'm so sorry." Verity moved to the sofa and wrapped her arms around her granny.

"No. That's not what happened. Please let me tell you. If I stop now, I might not be able to start again." She took a deep breath. "It was the violence that turned him on. Some men like stockings and suspenders, some like big boobs. He liked violence." She shrugged. "It was bad. It got worse. In the end, we found out I was pregnant, and he stopped hurting me. Serena was born. I thought it was going to be better, but after a few months, he started again. He was more careful. Bruises that were kept out of sight. He stopped when I got pregnant again. Once Jess was born, it started all over again." She wiped her finger under her eye. "My brother took him out for a drink and told him to never lay a hand on me again. Her came home stomping and spitting. He told me what had happened, and he was furious."

She put her face into her hands. "He stayed away from me, but he was stewing. I knew it. He came home one night with a friend from the pub. He told me I had a choice. I could sleep with his friend, or he would beat the girls." She sniffed back the tears. "I did what I had to. I had to protect my girls."

"He did that to you? What a bastard." Verity held her hands. "I see how they grew up confused, growing up in that environment."

"No, you don't understand. It was worse. He loved it when they fought. Kids fight, but he encouraged them. Rewarding the winner. A smack for the loser. I tried to step between them. That made it worse. The girls were wild, vicious. I spent half my time up at the school. They were always in trouble." She shook her head. "By the time Serena hit her teens, they were rolling drunks. They would be waiting outside the pub until their dad pointed out the ones to attack. He took what they stole. I was in a mess. He never touched me again, but he didn't have to. He brought home paying clients to do that. Sometimes he charged them less if they would hit me, especially if he could watch. The whole thing was a mess." She sniffed. "The day it all happened, they overheard what he was saying.

He thought they weren't back yet. He was telling some bloke to beat me up. I was crying, asking him please not to do it. He gave me the choice again: Do as I was told, or he would let his friend have the girls. I gave in, as I always had. They waited until I went into the bedroom with the man, and they called him out into the alley behind the house. They beat him with a lump of wood, or something. He died. It was a horrible thing. What they did, it was terrible, but he was worse. He was a monster. I found out afterwards that he had been telling them, if they didn't fight, or whatever he wanted, he would hurt me." She pulled a tissue out of her sleeve and wiped her eyes.

"I pulled it together. We told the police we had no idea what had happened. I was able to get a job. We were doing alright. The girls did better in school. We were happy, or happier, without him." She squeezed Verity's hands. "Then Adam came along. He saw the wildness in Serena, and I know he wanted to hold it, taste it. He was obsessed with her. They were married less than six months later. Simon wanted her. I could see it at the wedding. He settled for Jess. It was more subtle, but those girls were still fighting. When Molly was born, I knew they were out of control again."

Verity rocked. Her arms were wrapped tightly around her waist. "They were both really troubled people. That doesn't mean what happened to Molly was OK." She sat back.

"No, you don't understand. I know who killed Jess. If I'm truthful, I knew, as soon as I heard she was dead. I had always known what would happen, but I'd closed my eyes, and pretended." She pushed her hands through her hair. "Serena phoned me the next day, asked me if I heard about Jess. She was trying to keep a lid on it, but she was excited. I could hear it. She was on holiday, but I knew it was her." Her fingers stretched and flexed. "They had been fighting each other. Jess was covered with bruises. Serena had been beating her up, but that hadn't been enough. That was Serena's way, poke, poke, punch, punch."

"My dad told me that Simon killed Jess. He didn't want to give her the money for the divorce." Verity's brows pushed together.

Hetty patted Verity's hands. "Your dad is a fool. Your mum was right about that. He believes that Serena will stay with him. She has moved on. She's back to the wild." Hetty breathed deeply. "Their father told me once that living with us was like owning three tigers. He never knew when the attack would come, but he was certain it would. Serena and Jess killed their father. Calmly and without any guilt. They enjoyed it. She's out there now, wild and dangerous. I tried to talk to her, but she's beyond anything I can say.

It would surprise me if your dad's still alive."

"Perhaps you're wrong about it. Maybe they're genuinely trying to make a fresh start. My dad said Simon is in big trouble with the police. I thought that was about Jess, too." Verity nipped her lower lip with her teeth.

"You're a good girl, Verity, considering who your parents are. You are an amazing human being. Your sisters too. I'm proud of you, and Marcus and Jem. My daughters made some huge mistakes, but they brought some wonderful kids into the world." She smiled, unsure and fragile. "For that, I'm grateful."

"I have a question." Verity rested her hand on Hetty's arm. Hetty nodded. "Why did you stay when he beat you, forced you to have sex with other men, all that stuff?"

"I believed him when he said it was my fault, or worse, when he blamed my family. I left him once. Serena was three, maybe a little more. Jess was a baby." Hetty swallowed. "I packed up and went to my auntie's house. She lived in the country. I had two weeks there. It was bliss, so safe. The kids played in the garden, and we were happy. She was on her own, and she was glad of the company." She shook her head. "He turned up, one morning, and it was like the sun went behind a cloud. He grabbed my arm and told me to get in the car. I held back, and he gave me the choice of getting in the car or he would hurt my auntie." Tears fell then, and she wiped her face. "I packed the kids up and we went home. After that, there was no going back. He would have gone after everyone I loved, including my girls. When they killed him, I was free, but they were still carrying all his mad ideas."

"Granny Hetty, what do you think will happen? You know her better than anyone. What will she do?" Verity's raised eyebrows were met with her granny's sad eyes.

"I always knew that someday it would bubble to the surface, that one of them would kill the other. Whatever I did, it was there, between them. Now, she's off the grid." Her hands twisted the tissue between her fingers. "If Adam is still alive, he's in very grave danger."

57.

The sun shone down on the French countryside. The air coming in through the windows smelled warm, and it felt good. Serena parked the car in the village square and walked to the shops, picking out tomatoes that smelled ripe and wonderful. The cheese was soft and lovely. The bread was too good to resist. Paying, she smiled and thanked the woman behind the counter, feeling content with the day. She drove out of the town, and the fields opened out on either side of the road. She could smell flowers on the breeze.

There was something very different about the way she felt here. In fact, she had felt better since she had called in to see Jess the morning before they went on holiday. They had argued; they had fought, not for the first time over recent weeks. Jess had been angry, banging crockery and glasses around in the kitchen. Serena had poked. Small bruises. Her fingers leaving their mark. Jess had taken some laundry up the stairs, still muttering to herself. Serena had smiled to herself. Jess was too angry. She had never seen things clearly once she lost her temper.

Serena's hand was in the handbag on the counter before Jess made it halfway up the stairs. She tipped the pills from the box into the bag she had brought with her and poured the Ritalin tablets into the box. In the kitchen cupboard were boxes and boxes of insulin, most of which went slipping into Serena's bag. It was easy to calm Jess down. Serena had apologised, explained that she was under stress, that everyone seemed to be upset with her. Jess just wanted her to leave and allowed her upstairs to collect some of Simon's clothes. It was easy to switch the pills in the bedroom, and then back down, to load the bag of shorts and shirts into the car, ready for their holiday. It was enough. Three days later, she was sitting on a beach sipping a cocktail when Jess's insulin levels dropped too far, her symptoms masked by the amphetamines, and her body, tired from years of controlled diabetes, rewarded her with a massive heart attack. Serena had never in her life been more excited.

The early years training from her father had finally kicked in. She was the winner, riding high. She had finally beaten her sister, and there would be no return match. No slap from her father. Never second best. No festering resentment. She was absolutely and completely the winner.

The aftermath was brutal. She cried, raged, drank until she was incapable of lucid thought, and woke knowing that she had killed her sister, the only person in the world who understood her. The only person who had been through everything she had. She had waded out into the sea and kept walking. Simon had been on the phone to Marcus, and then Jem. She had kept going. There was no reason to stop. Not even to slow down. Her feet had caught on the rocks, and she had stumbled, sending her head under the water, tasting the salt on her lips. Her eyes had stung from the tears she had been crying as much as the sea water.

Her sister had been her competition, her enemy, but also her cell mate, her only friend, her partner in crime. She remembered her sister's face, fresh with blood spatters the day their dad had died. When she caught her with an unexpected punch, then watching her face, filled with glee when she had caught Serena. She had killed her sister. The guilt ripped through her and she sank to her knees, letting the waves wash over her head, coming up spluttering and choking.

The sand had been warm, and she had sat and watched the horizon. Hot tears ran down her face and dried in the sun.

When Simon emerged from the lengthy phone calls, she was back in control. They had a quiet dinner, and he drank a little too much, and fell asleep with his mouth open. His snores sent her out of the villa, collecting a glass of wine on the way. She sat on the balcony and listened to the noise from a bar down the road. The music was loud and people were dancing in the street. She was jealous. How wonderful to be able to dance, throw your hands in the air, and be wild and free. No dead sister to keep you sitting still. Where was Adam when she needed him? Simon's snores reminded her of the choices she had made.

Pulling the car into the side of the road, she wiped her tears and pushed open the door, slamming it closed and leaning against the side of the car. The sun was warm on her face. She had been through it all, and was making sense of it. One step at a time.

She opened the boot, checking that the road was empty first, as far as she could see in both directions, which was a long way. There was nothing. No cars. No bikes. Not even a cat.

Joel was starting to smell, and it was time to leave him behind. She grabbed his feet and pulled until they were dangling over the bumper. She grabbed his shirt and pulled. This was not the first body she had moved. She knew he would be heavy, and she was right. He had been enormous, and it took everything she had to pull and lever him out. Slowly, she tipped his body over, and watched him fall onto the dusty ground, leaving her panting. He had not required the finesse of insulin. She had used a hammer. It had been sufficient for the job.

"Sorry Joel." She pushed him with her foot, so that he rolled away from the road. A little luck would see him found in a week or more. The wound on his side had stained his shirt, but it was dark now. The red had gone. She could see that the side of his head was dented. The hammer had done the work. The stab wound in his side had made sure. She wrinkled her nose at the smell of him.

She climbed back into the car. Joel had been a nice guy, and he had added to the pile of cash which Adam had brought to her.

Adam. She missed him. He had been good to have around. She should have held back. Not given him the pills she had stolen from her sister. The pills her sister needed to stay alive. She slammed the flat of her hand onto the steering wheel.

She was alone. That was how it had always been. She had always had to make her own way.

Her phone rang. She closed her eyes and took a deep breath. Verity. Her wonderful, smart, amazing daughter. Why would Verity be calling her?

"Hello?" She thought about driving away, but it would make no difference.

"Mum?" Smart girl, so clever, so strong.

"Verity, darling. What's happening?" She closed

her eyes and tried to imagine a world where she had not just dumped a body.

"I have to ask. Is Dad OK?" Her voice shook a little.

"What do you mean?" Her fingers curled around the steering wheel.

"I know you killed Jess and I'm worried you killed dad too. I know about what happened with your dad and I'm so sorry. So, so sorry." Verity was trying to keep her voice steady.

"Clearly you have been speaking to my mother. She's a very strange and deluded person. You know she used to sleep with men for money?" Serena clapped her hand over her mouth. She had to stop her dad's voice from coming out like that.

"I heard a whole lot of things today, none of which were comfortable to hear, but I understand a lot more about how your life became what it is today. Please, can you tell me if dad is OK?" Verity was begging. Serena could hear it.

"Your dad is fine. We decided to go our separate ways through Europe. I dropped him off near Dieppe. I'm sorry I did now. To be honest, I wish he was here." Serena hit the button for the loudspeaker. She turned the ignition key and checked in the mirror before she pulled out onto the empty road.

"I've phoned him, but there's no answer." Verity's voice broke over the words like a wave.

"He's probably just taking a few days to himself. I'll meet up with him in a few days, and I'll tell him to call you. Stop worrying. Everything is going to be fine." Serena kept her eyes on the road.

"OK. Let me know when you meet up with him. Oh, and mum?" Serena hummed an answer. "I miss you. We all love you. Please come home safe."

"OK, my love. Take care. Speak soon." Serena ended the call. She drove, not even nudging the speed limited. Tears ran down her face, blurring the road. It was hard to hear that Verity missed her. Harder to know that she had maybe too many lines to find her way back.

The beach car park was nearly empty. The last time she had been at a beach had been the day Jess died. There were spaces everywhere, but she drove around, looking for the right one.

In the end, she found a space in the corner, next to a fence. She had a choice to make, and it seemed right to make it there. Part of her thought it was time to go. She could swim out into the sea. Perhaps she might meet Adam out there in the waves. Her girls would find out. They would know what she had done. The days of pretending would be over. She pictured Verity,

Mim and Lola. What if she never saw them again?

Time ticked by, slow as treacle. It was hot in the car. Sweat trickled down her back, and she made her decision.

She started the engine and opened the windows. A little breeze would be more comfortable. Tears came again, and she wiped them away.

Foot on the pedal, she drove away, and kept on driving. Sometimes she stayed in a town for a few days, sometimes only for a night. Each day gave her a little more distance from the things that she had done.

On the morning that she pulled into Marseille, she knew this was somewhere that she could stay for a little while. A vibrant fishing port, bars, restaurants. Not too clean and shiny. Perfect. She ate lunch at a restaurant near to the sea. The fish was perfectly pan fried, and the salad crisp and light. She savoured every mouthful and left a generous tip.

The sunlight glinted on the water, and for the first time in what seemed like forever, she felt that she was taking steps towards being the person who she wanted to be.

When the shadows lengthened and the sun dipped towards the sea. Serena found a small hotel. She was glad that they had a vacancy, and took a shower, finding a thin dress, to go out for a walk through the evening. The bars and restaurants spilled their lights out onto the streets, and the music played from each building. She turned down the offers for dinner at several restaurants from the staff standing outside. The need to walk a little further before she sat down to eat again felt important.

She saw him down the street, half in shadow, half lit by the bulbs under the awning. He was looking straight at her. She took a breath, knowing that this was what she had been waiting for. She had known that he would come. Since the first day she had met him, she had known that he was hers. She had loved Adam. He had understood her, but he had never entirely belonged to her. Not in the way Simon had. Perhaps that was why she found Adam so attractive. He had been a challenge.

"Serena." He stood in her path, waiting for her to come to him. There was something different about him.

"Simon. Are you out on bail?" His eyes sparkled. There was something harder about them.

"There'll be a trial, and I'll be spending a long time in prison. Adam made sure of that." The bitterness in his voice chopped the words short. "How far did he last with you? I knew you would have to kill him. Once I realized that you had killed Jess. I hear his flunkey's body was found a few days ago. You've been busy, my love." He leaned into her and kissed her cheek.

"He almost made it to Dieppe." She dipped her head to lean against his chest.

"Could you not have just stayed with me?" He closed his eyes and leaned into her.

"I was being kinder by leaving. You know that. I don't mean to be cruel, but I know I am." He turned away from her, so that they could walk together, his arm still around her shoulders.

They stopped outside a small bar, and he signalled the waiter, and then ordered two glasses of wine. They sat and sipped. There was quiet and peace between them. "I miss you, Simon. I know why you're here." She signalled the waiter, and then shook her head. "I'll go to the bar, or we'll die of thirst before he gets here." She returned with the two shot glasses and put them on the table. "Here we are. I settled the bill. Sambuca, your favourite." She smiled across the table and raised her glass in a toast. "To being completely messed up, but having a good time anyway!" He clinked his glass against hers, and they drank, swallowing the whole glass in one mouthful.

"Walk with me a little way." They left the shops behind them, and with them, the twinkling lights,

"How did you know where to find me?" She

turned her face towards his.

"My guys have been following you all the way across France." He huffed out a sigh. "You know that I can't leave you here, right?"

"I know. But you will be in prison. There is nowhere for me to be there, either. Whoever takes over from you will want me gone." She rested her hand over his on her hip.

"So, you understand my dilemma?" She nodded; her eyes wet with tears when they met his. The pain was not so bad as she had imagined. Sharp and deep in her belly. Her knees buckled, and she slumped to the pavement. Carefully, his hand beneath her head, he cradled her, allowing her to rest back against a wall. "I've always loved you, Serena." Tears spilled from his eyes.

"Don't cry." She raised her hand to touch his face, but it stopped midway. It was a journey too far. "I'll be fine." Her voice was a whisper, the last breath that escaped her.

He watched for a minute or two, then laid her head down and walked up the road. His feet felt numb, and his stomach burned. There was no choice but to stop. He leaned against a wall, his fingers spread wide, his heart pounding. When he slipped down towards the ground, he was smiling to himself. He had been so sure that he was in control, but she had been two steps ahead of him, as she had been since he had first met her.

No matter how fast he ran, he would never catch her. She had put something in his drink. Not for the first time, he imagined. The pavement was still warm, even though the sun had set a while before. His body struggled against the huge dose of insulin and the amphetamines in his system, and the thick layer of fat around his mid-section. His heart was the first thing to give out.

58.

Verity straightened her dress and opened the cubicle door. The main door was a little open, and the hum of conversation filtered through. She checked in the mirror; her make-up was fine, and her hair looked good. The news that she had received from the French police fifteen minutes before, though it had been ridiculously broken down by their poor English and her rubbish French, she had understood, that her mother had been found dead, and that a knife had been involved.

Verity had been sharing a table with Basti and Marcus. They had all been invited to the Law Society annual event and had decided to go together. She had told them both, or had started to, when Marcus had received a phone call, and the process had begun again. She had excused herself from the table and retreated to the toilets. Her mother and Simon were both dead, and she had no idea how to feel about any of that. Perhaps it was shock, and the normal emotional responses would arrive soon.

She phoned Mim and told her the news. She was

quiet, but not emotional. Lola was surprised, but accepting. There was nothing left to do but go back to the party.

The only question that remained to be answered was whether her dad was responsible for both of their deaths. Or was he also dead in France. The questions which had hung over her mother and Simon were beyond answers. Perhaps she would never have learned the truth, even if they had survived. Each layer of lies had only been covering another. What point was there in uncovering more lies and more deception? She nodded at her reflection in the mirror. Time to draw a line under the whole thing, and move on. The eyes that looked back at her reminded her of her father. Was this what he had done when he left them behind? Was she any different at all from her parents? She ran her finger under her eye and checked, but there were no tears.

There were no tears at all.

....

His eyes struggled to open, they felt as though they were glued together. The sunlight streamed through the window, and pushed his eyes closed again.

The nurse took his blood pressure and temperature. He watched, but he was only half awake.

The rest of the day drifted past, his mind slipping easily from awake to asleep and back again. The bed was comfortable. The sheets were cool, and he was happy. It seemed to him that it was a long time since he had been.

When the nurse came back, he opened his mouth to ask some questions. The sounds seemed hard to find. She smiled and patted him gently on the back of the hand.

Another night, and he slept better than he could remember. Perhaps they had given him drugs, he wondered vaguely, and drifted off again.

In the morning, a different nurse brought a drink, and he sipped. It was the most delicious thing he had ever tasted. He whispered, the question, what is this? The reply made him chuckle. Water. Who could imagine how wonderful it could be?

He felt stronger. His arms and legs wanted to move. In the afternoon, the small ward was deeply quiet. He slipped his legs over the side of the bed, testing his strength, and opened the small cupboard. Inside there was a grey tracksuit. He had no clue who it belonged to, but, slipping it over his head and pulling it slowly up his legs, it seemed to fit.

There was nobody to ask him where he was going. He struggled a little with his balance to start with, but holding the edge of the bed for a while steadied him. By the time he reached the door of the ward, he was walking well. Outside the building, he turned back and checked the sign. Hospital Dieppe. If the boat was still in the harbour, he was close.

He walked slowly and carefully through the hot afternoon sun. The town was closed for lunch, which suited his purposes. There was no rush. He knocked on the door of the harbourmaster's office.

"Bonjour." He leaned against the door frame, tired from his walk in the afternoon sun.

"Monsieur?" The man raised his eyebrows.

"My French is dreadful. I hope your English is better." He threw a smile across the room and received one back.

"Of course. How can I help?"

"My wife brought my boat in for me. I wonder, can you tell me where she abandoned it? I'm Adam Denton." He smiled the lazy lopsided smile that he knew worked with his face.

"Of course you booked ahead." The man checked his records. "Bay sixty-two."

"Merci." He sketched a small salute.

He climbed up onto the boat. It was harder than he expected. After he had taken a few deep breaths, he retrieved the spare key from under the step into the cabin. Inside, he found that she had taken the money that was obvious. He had taken the precaution of hiding the rest where she would not imagine there were cupboards. The panelling inside the boat slid to reveal spaces which were filled with cash. He smiled to himself, and pulled out the maps, looking for a destination.

The small shop which served the marina sold him wonderful bread, cheeses, ham and tomatoes, olives, and bottles of wine and brandy. He was ready. The darkness wrapped itself around his boat, and he slept. His body was recovered from the drugs his wife had given him, and his brush with death. He remembered the shocked faces of the fishermen who had pulled his body from the sea, but little else.

When the sun came up, he drank good coffee, and ate wonderful bread. It was time to go.

The rope slipped from the ring and he chugged out of the harbour. The fishing boats were already on their way out into open water, but otherwise he was alone with the sea and the wide sky.

He thought about contacting Verity to let her know he was alright, but that would bring up questions about where Serena was, and he had no answers for his very focused daughter, or indeed, for himself.

For the moment, perhaps it was enough to enjoy the early morning sun glinting on the water, and the fact that he was breathing in and out, when he so easily could have been under the water.

....

Her mother's ashes, along with her aunt's had been interred. It had rained the whole day, and she had stood with her two sisters and said goodbye. There had been no tears. In the months that followed, she worked hard, dealt with clients, visited the refuge, just as normal, but she felt nothing.

On a Saturday morning, in an attempt to raise her own interest, she walked up to the market, browsing the stalls and looking in the shops. She saw him cross the road towards her, dressed in his off-duty lawyer uniform. Tidy but informal.

"Verity." His smile took her by surprise. She had forgotten how much she liked it,

"Basti." He fell into step with her, pointing to a café, and raising an eyebrow in question. She nodded, and they found a table.

"I came looking for you. I have something I need to pass on." He dipped his hand into the inside pocket of his jacket and pushed an envelope across the table to her. She checked the back. It was still sealed. "It came to me in a package with some other things."

He ordered coffee for them both while she held the envelope in her hands. The waitress brought them their drinks, and the silence between them stretched.

"Thank you. For bringing it, I mean." She stared at the writing, recognising it. He nodded. He sipped his coffee and watched her. Finally, coming to the conclusion that she would only open the letter when she was alone, he shrugged, and took a last sip.

"Take care of yourself." He covered her hand with his, just for a moment, and paid for the coffees on the way out.

59.

Dear Verity

I am taking some time out, travelling around and seeing the sights. Sorry to say, it didn't work out with me and your mum. We separated in Dieppe. I have no clue where she is now, but I suppose she will be in touch.

I have things I need to tell you, tons of things, but they can wait. Some can't. I want to apologise for being a rubbish dad and not being around.

When I paid Basti to tell me about you, it was wrong of me. He's a decent guy, and I pushed him. I'm not a decent guy. All I'm saying is if you like him, don't blame him for my actions.

Send my love to Mim and Lola. Or say hello, whatever you think is right.

I'll be in touch, once I find somewhere to stop for more than a couple of days at a time.

This necklace is yours. No strings attached. No secrets to be kept.

Love

Dad

....

She fastened the necklace around her neck and picked up her coffee. It was cold, and she pulled a face.

A fresh one appeared on the table in front of her.

"I didn't order..." She expected to find the waitress by her side.

"I walked to the end of the road and wondered if you might like a fresh cup of coffee." Basti smiled down at her. "And some company?" He watched her take a breath and think about it. She smiled back, and he took that as an invitation. "Brilliant." He sat down opposite her. "I thought we might try Icelandic food, if I can find a place." He raised an eyebrow.

"OK. Let's see if we can find that." She smiled across the table, tucking the letter back into the envelope.

"Nice necklace. Is it new?" He tipped his head sideways.

"No. It has always been mine." Her smile felt more comfortable on her face than it had done. "Thanks, Basti."

Printed in Great Britain
by Amazon